A
GENERATION
RISING

FIRE AND STEEL

VOLUME ONE

A

GENERATION RISING

GERALD N. LUND

DESERET
BOOK

SALT LAKE CITY, UTAH

© 2014 GNL Enterprises, LP

Library of Congress Cataloging-in-Publication Data

(CIP data on file)

ISBN 978-1-60907-992-5

Printed in the United States of America

Publishers Printing, Salt Lake City, UT

10   9   8   7   6   5   4   3   2   1

IN MEMORIAM

Lynn S. Lund
1942–2014

She caught my eye when I was twenty;
She held me transfixed for over fifty years.

She had the gift of music placed within her in the premortal life;
She shared it joyously with her family and the world for nearly
seventy years.

At thirteen, she feared that, like her mother, she might go years
without having children;
At her passing, sixty-four of her immediate family members came
to say farewell.

She was a paid teacher of children for nine months; she taught
and mentored children, grandchildren, young women, auxiliary
leaders, missionaries, members, and her husband for over five
decades.

She had a sensitivity to the Spirit that was often quite astonishing,
often proclaiming how things would be with individual family
members long before they came to pass.

She was my first reader, my most loyal supporter, my most astute,
most honest, and therefore my most valued critic; though rarely
credited to her, her input and insights permeate the books I have
written and the things I have taught.

She was the love and light of my life, the joy and exultation of my
soul.

I cherish the countless memories we made together; I see her
stamp and her mark and her influence all around me.

I look forward to the day when I shall step through that golden
door that provides entry into the eternities and find her waiting
there to greet me.

"BEHOLD, I HAVE REFINED THEE,
BUT NOT WITH SILVER;
I HAVE CHOSEN THEE
IN THE FURNACE OF AFFLICTION."

—ISAIAH 48:10

"BEHOLD, I HAVE CREATED THE SMITH
THAT BLOWETH THE COALS IN THE FIRE,
AND THAT BRINGETH FORTH
AN INSTRUMENT FOR HIS WORK."

—ISAIAH 54:16

PREFACE

A Generation Rising is the first volume in my new historical fiction series, Fire and Steel. This multigenerational series will span about seventy years. In this series, I will introduce two new fictional families: one a simple farm family from Bavaria in southern Germany, whom you will meet in this volume, and the other a ranching family from rural Utah. However, in volume one, I introduce only the family from Germany. The Utah family will be introduced in volume two.

These two families will experience some of the most turbulent times in the history of the world, including

- An explosion of technology that will profoundly alter people's lives—electricity, the telephone, the automobile, household appliances, radio, movies, television, and the atomic bomb.
- The "War to End All Wars," later called World War I.
- The October Revolution in Russia and the rise of communism as a dominant world order.

- The Spanish flu epidemic, which cost the lives of about 100 million people worldwide.
- A catastrophic global financial collapse.
- A Great Depression that lasted nearly a decade.
- World War II, which dwarfed the first global war in scope and ferocity and which, for the first time in modern warfare, saw major attacks from both sides against civilian populations.
- The deliberate and systematic annihilation of six million people deemed to be inferior and undesirable.

These events created profound crises in the lives of individuals on a scale most of us today can scarcely imagine.

Both families are fictional, but the events they will experience are not. And how they choose to respond to the unbelievable financial, social, political, and emotional upheaval in their lives will be representative of how real people on both sides reacted to these powerful forces swirling around them.

The Individual in Crisis

Understanding how individuals react in times of great—even catastrophic—crisis has long been a great interest of mine. In my late teens, I became fascinated by how various people responded when their lives were turned completely upside down. I first studied individuals in war—not just soldiers who faced combat, but also civilians who saw war roll across their own lands.

Soon, my interest expanded to any situation in which individuals were placed in crisis, such as being caught in a major natural disaster or living under oppressive, totalitarian regimes. It seems to me that such crushing circumstances reveal the best and the worst of the human spirit. I have read of incredible acts of selflessness, courage, endurance, and faith. I have also read of cowardice, cruelty, exploitation, greed, and a loss of all common sense.

Fire and Steel

Iron is the fourth most abundant element in the earth's crust. In its cold state, iron is not very malleable. But someone discovered centuries ago that when iron is heated until it is red-hot, it becomes highly malleable and can be hammered into a new shape. When cooled again, the iron holds the new shape permanently. However, iron is "soft" enough that when it is shaped into a cutting edge, such as in a sword, knife, or axe, it quickly dulls.

As more centuries came and went, blacksmiths made three history-changing discoveries:

First, when they accelerated the cooling process by plunging the red-hot iron into a tub of cold water, the metal was strengthened considerably. This process, which is called "drawing out the temper," produced tempered iron.

Next, blacksmiths discovered that the hammering of red-hot iron not only shaped the metal but also strengthened it. One might expect the violent and prolonged blows to weaken the metal, but the opposite was true.

Finally, and perhaps most significant, someone discovered that if you add a small percentage of carbon to molten iron, the metal is strengthened even more dramatically. This carbon alloy of iron is called steel, which is even stronger and harder than tempered iron.

Thus, through the art of the blacksmith, man learned that strong, tempered steel is the end product of three dynamic forces:

- The fire of the forge.
- The hammer and the anvil.
- Sudden, drastic change of environment from the red-hot coals to cold water.

"Pure Steel"

Many years ago in a class at Brigham Young University, we were discussing the pioneer period of LDS Church history. The professor was making the point that these people, for the most part, were not frontiersmen or explorers or even rugged individualists like the mountain men of earlier times. They were city people, factory workers, simple farmers, and tradesmen. Some came from elegant homes and relative luxury and comfort. Many, especially those from Europe, were from the poorest classes.

Then they received the call to come to Zion. In faith, they answered the call. They crossed the plains in wagons, by handcart, or on foot. Upon their arrival, often with only a few days' rest, they were sent out to establish new settlements.

As we were discussing all of this, one student raised his hand. "That is really quite amazing," he noted. "How were they able to do so much?"

Without hesitation, the professor responded: "Oh, that's easy to explain. By the time they had crossed the plains, most of the physically weak had died, and most of the spiritually weak had dropped out. So what Brigham Young had left when they arrived in the Valley was pure steel."

God Himself used the imagery of the blacksmith's forge to describe how He strengthens His people:

"Behold, I have refined thee, but not with silver; I have chosen thee in the furnace of affliction" (Isaiah 48:10).

"Behold, I have created the smith that bloweth the coals

in the fire, and that bringeth forth an instrument for his work" (Isaiah 54:16).

When we talk of those early "tempered Saints," we are astonished at their faith, their courage, their endurance, and their tolerance for suffering. We share their stories from generation to generation because they inspire us to be greater.

But you don't have to read very far in the journals and histories to find examples of those who broke under the pressure, who threw up their hands and cursed either God or the prophet, who either stopped in place or turned around and went back. I have come to call them the "dropout pioneers." These were the ones who couldn't endure the heat of the fire, or the blows of the hammer, or the sudden and drastic alteration of their lives.

This is the theme of Fire and Steel—how life itself provides the needed conditions to temper and strengthen individuals. The two families in the story will face the fires of tribulation, feel the hammering blows of adversity, and see everything they hold dear totally upended. They will be violently ripped away from their comfortable lives and plunged into circumstances that will try them to the very depths of their souls. *A Generation Rising* begins our story.

GERMANIA

Germania and the Holy Roman Empire

By the time of Christ and the Christian era, the Roman Empire, with its insatiable quest for land, riches, slaves, and power, had swallowed up much of the European continent. One could leave the Roman capital and travel in a northwesterly direction on well-maintained Roman roads for 1,200 miles.

But if one traveled due north, up the long boot of Italia and across the Alps, one quickly reached the northern border of the empire. In the vast lands to the north of the Danube River and to the east of the Rhine lived a collection of tribes so fierce, so warlike, and so incapable of being civilized that eventually the Roman legions fortified the southern border of those lands and left the people alone. Caesar called that unconquerable north land with all of its dozens of tribes *Germania*.

The *Germani* were not farmers other than having small garden plots cultivated by individual families. They were hunters and warriors. No one owned land as permanent property. Each year the tribal chiefs would assign land to the clans, who then parceled it out to their people. But the next year, everyone was impelled to move to a new place so that the people didn't become focused on the land and lose their zeal for war. This also kept them from building permanent shelters against the cold and the heat. Too much comfort weakened the character, they thought.

The men generally each had one wife, and adultery was rare. The opinions of women were respected to the point that they often accompanied the men into battle to give them counsel and encouragement. Robbery among their own people was not tolerated, but it was encouraged when it involved outsiders. Often, senior chieftains would lead plundering expeditions to give the young men experience in battle and help them avoid idleness. To the *Germani* peoples, the highest glory was to lay waste to lands bordering their territory, thus making them uninhabitable. They saw this as proof of their valor. It also kept their borders secure from invasion.

The *Germani* did not keep written records, so not much is known about them from the ensuing centuries. They must have consolidated the tribes to some degree, because when the French King Charlemagne was appointed to be the first ruler of what came to be known as the Holy Roman Empire, the Kingdom of Germany was largest group within it. In the minds of Germans ever after, the Holy Roman Empire came to be known as the First German Reich.

The Protestant Reformation and the Thirty Years' War

After Charlemagne's death, the empire limped along for centuries, almost dissolving due to the weak leadership of Charlemagne's successors. Then in AD 962, Otto I, Duke of Saxony and king of Germany, was crowned emperor by the pope.

The former rights held by the Roman Caesars now rested in German hands.

Otto immediately set about to unify the Germanic tribes under the leadership of a central government. However, the fiercely independent spirit that had kept the *Germani* unconquerable for so many centuries was not so easily quelled. Powerful kings and princes were on the rise in other countries. Ruling dynasties brought stability and consistency to their subjects, often over many generations. Not so in Germany. As the centuries came and went, Germany remained a hopelessly fragmented, impossibly crazy patchwork of over 300 separate states.

The Protestant Reformation swept across Europe with hurricane force beginning with Martin Luther nailing his Ninety-Five Theses to the door of the Castle Church in Wittenberg on October 31, 1517. But Luther's impact on Germany went far beyond his Protestant vision of Christianity. His German Bible provided a standardized language for the people and became a powerful unifying influence. His doctrines of the freedom of individual conscience electrified the people and changed the culture profoundly. People were motivated to study and learn for themselves. Literacy rates increased. The arts and commerce thrived. Prosperity rose. Many of the Protestant German princes extended new freedoms to their people. A new sense of German pride and German nationalism began to develop.

Inevitably, the Reformation also brought war. These were considered issues of eternal consequence. The divisions became so bitter and acrimonious that both sides took up the sword to defend their faith. Rulers all across Europe were forced to decide where they stood. Soon all of Europe was divided into two major religious camps.

About a hundred years after Martin Luther's bold action,

one of the most devastating of the religious wars began. In this case it was not solely about religion. Competing dynasties were jockeying for power. Savage war raged across Europe off and on for three decades, earning the conflict the name the Thirty Years' War.

Germany lay right in the center of the conflict and was hit the hardest. Entire regions were utterly devastated. Thousands of towns and villages were destroyed. One-third of the population was lost to war, famine, disease, or being hauled off as slaves.

In the end, the Thirty Years' War virtually snuffed out every sign of the surge in culture, learning, arts, and commerce that had resulted from the Reformation. The Germany that was rapidly becoming one of the fountains of European civilization disappeared as a tidal wave of barbarism returned. Civilization came to a standstill in Germany while the rest of Europe moved forward into the new age. In these circumstances, it is not surprising that the German character became ingrained with a fatalistic acceptance of tyranny, autocratic and capricious rule, and suppression of law and human rights.

Prussia and Frederick the Great

In that dark and bewildering time, one German state, Prussia, began to slowly rise in prominence above the others. During the Crusades, a religious/military order called the Teutonic Knights, a fierce warrior class reminiscent of the earlier *Germani,* invaded Prussia and gradually wrested power from the native Slavic populations.

This was a kingdom built primarily on military prowess. It was far distant from the political centers of Europe. It had few natural resources of its own. The population was small and scattered. There were no big cities and no substantial industry. Even the noble families were poor by the standards of other European ruling families.

But the blood of those early *Germani* ran deep in the Prussians. Their determination to conquer was like hammered steel. Their organizational ability was remarkable. Their armies became some of the best in Europe, and their reputation for fierceness and courage spread rapidly. Where conquest was not likely, they made treaties and alliances with powers that threatened their success. When peace was no longer expedient, they tore up the treaties and invaded their former allies.

In Prussia, it was expected that the finest minds and the greatest talents would become military careerists. About three-quarters of the state's annual revenues went to the army. As one French leader later said, "Prussia is not a state with an army, but an army with a state." Thus, the state, which was run with the efficiency of a well-oiled machine, became everything. The people were little more than cogs in that machinery. Even the great German philosopher Immanuel Kant declared that the duty to the state demanded the suppression of human feeling.

In exchange for that total submission, the German people once again began to discover pride in being German, something they had not felt for over two hundred years.

In 1740, Frederick the Second became king of Prussia. A brilliant general and an astute statesman, he would soon come to be called Frederick the Great. Like the kings before him, he had absolute ruling power over Prussia. But unlike those before him, Frederick was wise enough to see that if he was to achieve his goal of bringing Prussia into the modern world and becoming a true political power, he couldn't rule in an autocratic or dictatorial manner. His guiding principle became, "What is best for

Prussia?" and he made it clear to his subjects that he expected them to ask themselves that same question.

Frederick's statesmanship became evident when he instituted a series of domestic reforms that strengthened the country. He established universal religious freedom and granted freedom of the press. The judicial system was reformed, and Prussia's judges came to be known as the most honest in Europe. He required general education throughout the country. He set up agricultural reforms, financed the rebuilding of towns, and built thousands of miles of road throughout the kingdom.

By the time he died in 1786, not only had Frederick the Great turned Prussia into one of the strongest states in Europe, but he also had created a loyalty and devotion to the Fatherland among the citizenry that would carry into the next century and shape German history forever.

Otto von Bismarck

After Frederick's death, weaker leaders tried to carry on his legacy but fell far short. In 1805, Napoleon put an end to the Holy Roman Empire. Ten years later an attempt to unify Germany led to the creation of a confederation of thirty-nine separate states. It was too weak and fractured to have much influence.

Once again, a natural leader stepped forward. Otto Eduard Leopold, prince of Bismarck and a son of one of Prussia's leading families, came to power. More commonly known as Otto von Bismarck, he got himself appointed to the *Reichstag*, the confederation's parliament. Already seen by others as a man of great ability and insight, he electrified the group on September 30, 1862, with a simple sentence that quickly became a rallying cry. After recounting their continuing failure to create a German state of any consequence, Bismarck stunned the chamber with these words: "Prussia must concentrate and maintain its power, for the great questions of our time will not be resolved by speeches or majority decisions. *That will come only by blood and iron!*"

It was straight from the spirit of the *Germani* chieftains of old. Only war put things right.

With armies largely financed by his own family and those of princes in league with him, Bismarck quickly defeated Denmark and Austria. That sent France into a panic, and war clouds began to gather—which was exactly what Bismarck wanted. Of all their enemies, France had been the most hated for centuries. Prussia's defeat by Napoleon was the final humiliation, and there was a deep and lasting animosity between the two nations.

With some clever diplomacy and through misrepresenting the truth, Bismarck deliberately provoked France into declaring war against Prussia in 1870. His brilliant leadership of the armies brought victory in under two years, crowning Prussia the third most powerful nation in Europe. It was a tremendous victory, and the German people were united in a way they hadn't been for centuries. Bells rang across the land, and celebrations broke out in the towns and villages.

A short time later, the German states were formally unified at last into a real German state. The head of state—which was largely a ceremonial office—would be called the *Kaiser*, or Caesar, invoking the grandeur of the Roman Empire. But the head of government, the real power behind the throne, would be the chancellor. To no one's surprise, and by virtually unanimous acclamation, Otto von Bismarck became the first chancellor of what was called the new German Empire. And thus, the Second German Reich was born.

After centuries of darkness, defeat, humiliation, and

oppression, at last there was an empire equal in power and glory to that of Imperial Rome.

Chapter Note

The information on German history comes from many Internet sources and also draws heavily from William Shirer's classic study of Nazi Germany (see *Third Reich*, 90–97).

CHAPTER 1

February 20, 1896—Graswang Village, Bavaria, Germany

It was snowing steadily on the day Hans Otto Eckhardt was born.

When it all started at 3:30 that morning, only a few flakes were floating down from the starless sky. That was when Inga Eckhardt shook her husband awake from a deep sleep. "Hans, go!" she whispered through clenched teeth. "Go to the village and fetch Frau Hemmert."

He rose up on one elbow. "What about the milking? Can you wait?"

"Not while you milk ten cows, *dummkopf!*"

"But . . ." Cows didn't wait either. "I can be done in half an hour."

"Go!" she cried. Grumbling to himself, her husband got up and began to dress.

Approximately twenty hours later, with six inches of snow outside, Inga gave one last piercing scream as she felt the contraction peaking again. "Push!" Frau Hemmert cried. "Push! It's coming!"

There was no need to yell at her. Nothing could have stopped her now. Biting her lip, gripping the bed frame so hard she felt she would leave fingerprints in the wood, Inga bore down one last time. And suddenly there was a euphoric feeling of release, of deliverance. She fell back, gasping as a lusty wail split the air. It was 11:47 p.m. on the 20th day of February.

"It's a boy!" the midwife exclaimed. She held up the baby for his mother to see, then turned and shouted over her shoulder. "Herr Eckhardt. It's a boy! You have a son."

There was a cry of exultation from the main room. "Give us five minutes," Frau Hemmert called, "then you can come in."

"My, my," she said to Inga as she turned back and went to work. "No wonder it took so long. Over nine pounds I would guess. Maybe ten. He is as strong as a horse! Oh, you poor woman." The baby was howling, arms and hands and legs and feet thrashing wildly. "And such mighty lungs," she laughed. "He is quite outraged at what just happened to him."

Inga barely heard her. Never had she felt so utterly exhausted, so utterly spent. She murmured something, not sure whether it was an appropriate response, but not caring, and then closed her eyes and slipped into a deep sleep.

• • •

Inga Jolanda Bauer had been born the oldest child of a *Schweinehirt*—a swine keeper. The family lived on a small farm in Unterammergau—or Lower Ammergau—in Southern Bavaria, just a few miles north of the Austrian border. Unlike most of their neighbors in the valley, the Bauers lived in wretched and perpetual poverty. Josef Bauer was one of those men whom life seemed to take particular delight in holding back. As one of his neighbors noted, if you gave Josef a bar of gold, he would manage to turn it into a brick of tin before the week was over. The fact that he was a heavy drinker, like so many men who failed miserably at life, didn't help.

Unterammergau was about two miles downstream from Ober—or upper—Ammergau, and it benefitted considerably from Oberammergau's "rich cousin" status. Set at the foot of the Bavarian Alps, the two villages and the stunning scenery of the valley around them drew a lot of summer tourists, particularly from Munich, just thirty miles to the north. But that only partially accounted for the valley's booming tourist industry.

In 1633, the Black Death—bubonic plague—was ravaging Europe. The villages watched in dread as the disease marched relentlessly southward. In desperation, and at the urging of their parish priest, the villagers made a sacred vow. If the Lord would spare them from the disease, they would put on a dramatization of Christ's Passion—the common name for the final week of the Savior's life—and would do so every year thereafter.

In a matter of weeks, death rates dropped dramatically and new cases almost disappeared. In July, only one adult was lost. Filled with a profound gratitude, the villagers staged the first play the following summer in a hastily constructed outdoor theater just outside the village.

Now, 232 years later, they were still doing it every ten years and bringing in tens of thousands of paying visitors. The fame of their little community—its fabled beauty, its charming houses, and a collection of wood-carvers the likes of which few other villages could boast—spread far and wide. The whole area had been blessed with a steady, reliable economy thanks to that simple vow of gratitude.

Unfortunately, not much of that prosperity touched the

Bauers. By the time Inga was six and ready to attend primary school, there were three other little Bauers to feed. So even though the schools were state-supported, Inga attended just long enough to learn to read and write and do some basic arithmetic. By the time she was twelve, there were seven children to feed. Her father's drinking problem had only deepened, and the Bauers were desperate.

One day when she was thirteen, Inga's father returned from Oberammergau, called his wife and Inga into the kitchen, and announced that starting the following day, Inga would become an indentured servant to one of the most prosperous men in the village—Herr Hermann Kleindienst. The Kleindiensts owned not only Oberammergau's largest wood-carving shop but the restaurant next door as well. In return for Herr Kleindienst's promise to buy every pig that Josef could bring to him, Inga moved into the family's household to help with their three children and do menial housework.

And there she had stayed until she was seventeen. For all her lack of education, Inga had a keen and quick mind. Impressed with her abilities, Herr Kleindienst started her waiting tables in the restaurant when she was fourteen. From there he taught her how to clerk in the store. She learned quickly, and people liked her ready smile and pleasant manner. By the time she was sixteen, she was working full time in the store and he was paying her a small wage in addition to her bed and board.

Inga accepted early on that she would not be what people called a handsome woman. She found her features to be plain, and her shy manners, especially around boys, did not do much to overcome that handicap. Ten years of slopping pigs had left her short frame muscular and stout. But when Herr Kleindienst started Inga working in his shop, Frau Kleindienst had taken her aside and coached her on how to present herself more favorably. She grew her hair out, reminded herself to smile until it became a habit, and chose dresses that complemented her figure.

And that changed everything.

Two miles west of Oberammergau and about four or five from Unterammergau, Hans Eckhardt lived with his family in the small village of Graswang. His father, Karl Eckhardt, was a *Milchbauer,* a dairy farmer. The village was not much larger than Inga's village, but like Unterammergau, it had prospered because of its near proximity to Oberammergau. Nestled between pine-covered hills, Graswang was situated on land that was flat and well-drained and grew sweet meadow grass in abundance.

The Eckhardt family of six consisted of Hans's parents, Hans, two sisters, and a younger brother. Though they considered themselves poor, compared to the Bauers they were very prosperous. They owned about twelve acres of land, which had been in the family for several generations. Their home was of stone and had a two-story barn attached to it. They owned twelve cows, several goats, an assortment of chickens, geese, and ducks, and a horse that pulled their milk cart.

Because of the sweetness of the grass, milk from Graswang was always in demand. And their cheese—from both the goats and the cows—was famous as far east as Garmisch-Partenkirchen. The Eckhardts were also suppliers to Herr Kleindienst's restaurant and store. It was almost predetermined that sooner or later, Hans Eckhardt and Inga Bauer would meet.

Since the Middle Ages, towns all over Germany had held *Christkindlmarkts* every year in the few weeks leading up to Christmas. Oberammergau's "Christ Child Market" was known to be one of the finest in all of Bavaria. Farmers and merchants, toy makers and artists, shoemakers, dressmakers, tinsmiths, blacksmiths, and glassblowers—all would come from miles around, even from as far away as Munich, and set up their booths and tents in the town square. It was almost more of a fair than a market, and as much for celebration as for selling.

Vendors sold bratwurst and pretzels, Bavarian crostini, sauerbraten, breads of every kind, a dozen kinds of cheeses, chicken, pork, and beef schnitzels, spaetzle with sauerkraut. Beer was brought in by the keg full and flowed more freely than water. Children darted everywhere, screeching for their parents to buy them this or that, their eyes dancing with excitement.

It was the Christmas after he turned twenty-one that Hans Eckhardt delivered a fresh supply of cheese blocks, cheese curds, and milk to the Kleindiensts' store at the height of the *Christkindlmarkt.* Inga saw him immediately and saw to it that she was the one who checked it off and gave him payment.

She had first learned of him when two of the other single clerks kept talking about the devilishly handsome son of a prosperous dairy farmer from Graswang. Though she hung back the next time he came in, she found a place where she could study him. There was no question that he was handsome. He was well over six feet tall, with broad shoulders and a trim waist. His forearms were like cords of wood, a sure sign of a man who milked cows for a living. His hair was a light brown, almost blond, and his eyes a dark blue. He seemed somewhat sober of mien, but when he did smile, it transformed his face into something very nice. She was impressed with the air of quiet confidence he carried with him and the fact that he could barely tolerate being fawned over by her fellow clerks.

To Inga's surprise, as she was checking in the things he had brought, she found herself overcome by the shyness she thought she had conquered. She smiled at him and thanked him but said little else. Only later did she learn that it was that, as much as anything, that had caught his eye.

Though he left that day without saying much more than *guten Tag*, when he returned to Graswang, Hans determined that he would find a reason to return to Oberammergau as often as possible before the market closed.

When they married that next summer, Inga was eighteen and Hans was twenty-two. The people of Unterammergau were all abuzz over Inga's astonishing good fortune. Both families were of the peasant class, but when the Bauers came to Graswang, they stood openmouthed before the Eckhardts' home and marveled at how many round stacks of hay were in the meadow. That their daughter had married so well was cause for great jubilation. Inga's father, warmed with a bellyful of beer, held forth at great length on how it had been *his* decision to send Inga to Oberammergau as a servant girl that had brought her to this happy day. Twelve years and three children later, whenever Hans and Inga went to visit Inga's aging parents, the Unterammergauers still treated their son-in-law's family like visiting nobility.

And then the children had stopped coming. Hans and Inga went five years with no new babies, and Hans had begun to despair over ever getting an heir.

February 21, 1896

Hans Eckhardt smiled to himself. Inga's village would be ecstatic to learn that Inga had finally blessed her husband with a son. As would all of Graswang and many in Oberammergau.

He sat in the rocking chair, looking down at the baby cradled in the crook of his arm. Frau Hemmert was gone. As she was preparing to leave, well after midnight, he had started to get up to give her payment, but she waved him back down. "We can make settlement tomorrow," she said wearily. Lines of exhaustion were etched deeply in her face. "Let Inga sleep as long as possible," she said. "This was a very difficult labor."

"*Ja, ja,*" he said, still filled with wonder. He brushed the back of one finger across the incredibly soft little cheek. "I have my boy. My Inga has given me a son."

"Yes, Herr Eckhardt. You should be very proud."

Now, an hour later, he still sat in the rocking chair looking down at his newborn in wonder. This was far more than the normal pride a father feels for a newborn. He could scarcely believe it. After three daughters, a boy. And a strapping one at that. No, not just a boy. An *heir!*

In the state land records at Garmisch-Partenkirchen, the administrative center for this part of Bavaria, there were land records showing that Eckhardts had owned this plot of land for five unbroken generations. Now there was a sixth generation. Now the land would not pass over to the husband of one of his daughters. For a moment, he felt like he was going to weep—something unheard of for the males in his family. It was like a huge burden had been lifted from his shoulders.

No, he thought, shaking his head. Five generations were only the ones they could document. His grandfather had told him that the Eckhardt name went back a thousand years. "And that blood," Hans murmured to the baby, "now flows in your veins, my son. That heritage is now your heritage."

Hans pulled back the blanket a little and nodded with deep satisfaction. You could see the strength in his face. You could feel it just looking at him. His head was flattened a little from the birth, but the face would be square, with strong features: wide-set eyes, a prominent nose—*my nose,* he thought with a smile—a firm and determined mouth above a strong jawline. He lifted his free hand and stroked the blond hair with the tips of two fingers. It was softer than the down of a goose and would remain blond the rest of his life. Hans was sure of that.

"What name shall we give him?"

Hans looked up in surprise. "You shouldn't be awake yet."

Inga turned over so she was fully facing him. "I've been watching you." Tears of joy came to her eyes. "You and your little boy."

"No, my little man," he said proudly. "Thank you, Inga. Thank you for giving us such a son."

"*Ach!*" she said. "I thought for a time that we would have to tie a rope around him and drag him out with a horse."

"Yes!" he cried. "He is a determined one. This one will not let anyone push him around."

Smiling, she asked him again. "And what shall we call him?"

"I have already picked a name." He wasn't looking at her, but at the baby. He didn't see the momentary flash of disappointment on her face. Even if he had, it likely would not have made much difference. Naming a child was the father's responsibility. Especially naming a son. "I should like to call him Otto von Bismarck Eckhardt."

It wasn't really a surprise to Inga. Hans had often talked of this, and always it was with a consuming passion. Von Bismarck was no longer Chancellor of the German Empire—he was in his eighties now and rumored to be in failing health—but that did not lessen his stature one iota. But to put such a ponderous name on an infant seemed . . . was it too pretentious? Too pompous? She wasn't sure. She just didn't like it.

"Well?" he prodded. "What do you think?"

She jumped a little, realizing she had gotten lost in her thoughts. What was it he had asked? *Ah, yes. A name for their son.* She nodded, choosing her words very carefully. "I think Otto von Bismarck is a grand name. He was a great general."

"*Ja, ja,*" Hans blurted. "That and so much more."

How could she say what was troubling her? She wasn't sure, but she had to try. "Hans?"

"Yes?"

"How old were you when your father went to France?"

"In the Franco-Prussian War, you mean?"

"Yes."

"The war began in 1870, so I would have been ten. Why?"

"Do you remember much about the war?"

"*Ja,* I do. I remember how handsome Father looked in his uniform, with gold braid on his shoulders and this enormously long saber at his waist. I thought that he was the grandest thing I had ever seen. Every day after he went off to war, my friends and my younger brother and sisters and I would play games. I was the oldest, so I was always von Bismarck. We made the youngest ones be the French."

"With a name like Otto von Bismarck, what if our son grows up wanting to be a soldier?"

He gave her a blank look. *Where had that come from?*

Seeing his reaction, she decided to change the subject again. "Do you think Germany will ever go to war again, Hans?"

It worked. Inga knew her husband prided himself on his knowledge of history. Turning to fully face her, like a teacher preparing to address a struggling pupil, Hans reached out and took her hand. "*Nein.* Bismarck has made Germany strong. No one dares attack us now. I read in the paper just the other day that Kaiser Wilhelm is determined that Germany shall have its own navy so that the Fatherland can defend itself from the other naval powers like France, England, and Spain."

"And America."

"*Nein*," he laughed. "America is not a naval power, *mein Liebling*." The very thought of that made him laugh. "Never."

Totally oblivious to the fact that he had just made his wife feel foolish—a common habit of his—Hans suddenly guessed where she was going with this. "Are you thinking that perhaps our little Otto may have to go off to war as well?"

"Yes."

"Perhaps he will," he mused. "But that may happen no matter what we name him. And if it does, then he shall serve his Fatherland well." He gave her a pointed look. "And we will *both* be proud if he does, *ja?*"

Inga took a quick breath. It was not her nature to stand up to Hans, especially when he was so sure that he was right, but this was important to her. And the fact that he refused to even consider her feelings irritated her. "But what if he chooses to be a career soldier instead of a dairyman? What then?"

Incredulous, Hans just shook his head. "All because of a name?"

"If the name makes no difference, why do you insist on calling him that?"

But his mind was already racing ahead of her. "Besides, Bismarck was so much more than a great general. He is the father of the German nation. What if our son decided that was what he wanted to do with his life? Think of the social insurance programs Bismarck initiated—old-age pensions, accident insurance, state-provided medical care, and unemployment insurance. He has made Germany a model for other countries. He is not only the father of the German Empire, he is the father of the first government to care for its poor and needy." He flashed her a smile. "I would even let my son leave the farm if he were to do something like that."

She sniffed, knowing that she had lost, but she was not yet quite ready to let it go. "When you called yourself von Bismarck when you were ten, was it because he was a great statesman?"

Before he could answer, she slipped out of bed, went to him, and took the baby from his arms. "He will be waking soon, and hungry." She sat down in the other rocking chair, smiling as the baby frowned at being disturbed. "He looks so much like you, Hans. I would like to name him after you."

That did what she had hoped. It totally took him aback. He had thought of that, of course, but the birth of this little boy was such a glorious thing in his sight that he felt the infant needed a name grand enough to inspire him to greatness. Hans was a very common name. He couldn't think of anyone famous or great named Hans, other than Hans Christian Andersen, the Danish writer of fairy tales. There was hardly any glory in that.

"Do you really think we should?"

"Yes! I want him to look up at you and think, 'I am named for my father. I want to grow up and be like my father.'"

"Go on," he laughed. "Boys don't say things like that." Then, after a moment—"Do they?"

"Of course they do. I want him to. What if we called him Hans Otto Eckhardt. Then, when he's older we could tell him that he was also named for Otto von Bismarck."

There was a soft grunt. It wasn't a sound of surrender. Not yet.

"Or," she cut in before he could protest further, "we could call him Hans Otto von Bismarck Eckhardt if you like. But I fear other boys will make fun of him with a cumbersome name like that. But whatever else, I want to call him Hans."

He peered at her, his eyes hooded as he mulled the idea over in his mind. Then abruptly he got to his feet, looking up at the clock. "I think I will get dressed and go out and do the milking. It's almost five."

"Does that mean yes?" she teased.

To her surprise, he walked over, bent down, and kissed her on the forehead. "*Danke schön,*" he murmured. "Thank you for giving me a son. If you wish to name him after me, I will not object."

· · ·

The irony dawned on Inga only as the years passed. The morning after Little Hans had been born, she had stubbornly resisted her husband's desire to name their son Otto von Bismarck Eckhardt because she dreaded the idea that it might inspire him to become a professional soldier. So they had finally compromised and called him Hans Otto.

And yet, almost everything the father had done since then seemed to set his son's feet on a path that would eventually take him out of the milking stalls. They tried for another son or even a little sister for Little Hans, but it never happened, so Little Hans got all of his father's pride and affection. He was also shamelessly spoiled by his older sisters. It surprised Inga how easily her daughters accepted that Little Hans was somehow superior to them and held a more important place in the family.

It quickly became evident that he was an unusual boy. His habit of eating like a little piglet every time he nursed soon had him rolling in baby fat. The village grocer's wife called him "Thunder Boy," which delighted his father to no end. But beneath the fat was a strong, muscular body, and, to everyone's surprise, he started to walk at nine months. By the time he reached his first birthday he was running everywhere. Or perhaps more accurately, he was falling forward and his feet had to run to keep him from going down, but either way, the baby fat quickly melted away.

On the other hand, Little Hans didn't start talking until he was nearly two. That was not because he wasn't intelligent. Just the opposite. He quickly learned to get people to do his bidding by pointing and uttering a series of grunts and growls. This so delighted his father that he started calling him *Kleine Bär,* Little Bear. Inga didn't like it, but it quickly stuck, and before long even she started calling him *Kleine Bär.*

The blond hair came in thick and long. The light blue eyes never darkened. His hands were huge like his father's, and by the time he was six he could milk three cows, one after another, without stopping. That was something his father had not been able to do until he was eight. "He'll be milking the whole herd before he's ten," he would tell anyone who would listen.

So what did his father do? He left the milking to the three older sisters and sent Hans to elementary school in Oberammergau. The girls attended the much smaller school in Graswang just long enough to learn to read and write, like their mother, and then they were brought home to help run the farm.

But the school in Oberammergau had a real schoolmaster who had been trained in Munich. And they separated the students by age to give them more individual attention. It cost five marks per term. Inga protested. Despite how much she wanted a good education for her son, she felt that was well beyond their means. Hans refused to listen. "He is gifted, Inga. We both know that. How can he achieve his destiny if he is not educated?"

She tried one last shot. "I thought his destiny was to inherit the farm when you and I are too old to carry on any longer."

"This is not a woman's concern," he snapped. Then, glaring at her, he turned away.

• • •

Little Hans started school in the fall of his sixth year. The following year his father bought him a bicycle so that he would not have to walk the two miles each way. He became the only child in the village to have his own bicycle.

Somewhere around that same time, his father dropped the Little Bear nickname, considering it too childish, and began calling him Hans Otto. Inga was wise enough not to fight him on it, but she stubbornly refused to do so herself. As her son left babyhood and became a strapping young lad, she changed "Little Hans" to "Young Hans," to distinguish him from his father, but she never once called him Hans Otto. Sadly, Young Hans liked the double name, and soon everyone was calling him that except Inga.

Though she resented the money it took to keep Hans in school, Inga had to admit that he was thriving on his education. His appetite for learning was insatiable. He was forever asking questions, to the point that his sisters would sometimes beg their mother to make him shut up. On the other hand, the schoolmaster, Herr Holzer, encouraged the curiosity by giving Hans his copy of the weekly Munich newspaper after he was done with it. Hans devoured each copy, and soon the family conversation around the supper table changed significantly in nature. Young Hans was forever sharing fascinating tidbits of information he had gleaned from the papers.

"Mama, do you know what a hamburger is?"

"*Nein.* Someone from Hamburg?"

"No, Mama, it is a new food. It was introduced in America at a great exhibition. It is chopped beef made into a patty and then fried. It is served between two slices of bread. Doesn't that sound good, Mama?"

"And why do they call it a hamburger?" Papa asked, a twinkle in his eye, thinking he might stump the boy.

"Because it was invented by German immigrants from Hamburg, I think."

A few months later, he had just stuffed some fried eggs in his mouth when he turned to his father and blurted, "Papa? Guess what? In America they have made a new motor bicycle. They call it a hog."

"A hog?" his youngest sister said, wrinkling her nose. "You mean like a pig?"

Irritated at the interruption, Hans quickly went on. "Yes. It doesn't say why they call it that. Its real name is Harley-Davidson, after the names of its designers. But it says one of the engineers was from Germany. Why wouldn't they put his name on it too?"

"I'm sure I don't know," his father replied. "Perhaps the Americans do not wish to give anyone from Germany the credit."

January 25, 1904—Graswang Village

Anything mechanical particularly fascinated Young Hans. One weekend morning a few weeks before Hans's eighth birthday, Inga came downstairs to start the fire in the cooking stove. When she looked up to check the time, the cuckoo clock was gone from the wall. Puzzled, she asked her husband about it. He was as baffled as she was. The girls knew nothing either. Then they realized that Hans Otto was still in his room. That is where they found the clock, totally in pieces carefully spread out on the bed. Threatened with decades of punishment, a tearful Hans kept saying over and over, "I just wanted to see how it works,

Papa. I can put it back together again." It took two days of Hans sleeping on the floor so as not to "mess up" the parts, but when the clock appeared back on the wall, to everyone's astonishment, it worked.

On this particular day, with the afternoon sun already low over the horizon, Young Hans came bursting through the door waving the newspaper wildly over his head. His face was red with the cold, and he was puffing heavily. He stopped, bent over for a moment to catch his breath, and then looked up.

"They flew, Mama! They flew through the air!"

His father stuck his head out from the bedroom. "Who flew?"

Hans Otto opened the paper and spread it out on the table. Everyone gathered around. "Some men named Wright. In America. They own a bicycle shop and built a machine with great wings made of cloth, with a petrol engine to pull it. And it flew through the air, Papa. Can you believe it? Men flying like birds."

His oldest sister snorted in disgust. "Cloth wings? You can't believe everything you read in the newspaper, Hans Otto. Don't be such a *dummkopf*."

He gave her a pitying look and then stabbed at the newsprint. "Look! There is a picture."

As they all leaned over to look, Hans turned to his father. "They flew 852 feet, Papa. They were in the air for almost a full minute." His eyes were bright with excitement. "Can you believe it, Papa? Men flying through the air like birds."

"I still think it is a hoax," his sister said.

"Of course you would," he said in disgust. "You have no imagination whatsoever."

The next day, Hans Otto had a quick bite of supper then

disappeared, saying something about homework. But when Inga went up to see how he was doing, he wasn't in his room.

They found him in the barn, a kerosene lantern hanging from a nail above him. His father's toolbox was to one side, with tools scattered all around it. But that was not what made his father swear as he pulled up short. "Hans Otto! What have you done?"

Kind of a foolish question, Inga thought, as she gaped at what lay before them. The bicycle had been completely disassembled and laid out in neat semicircles around Young Hans.

"I'm trying to figure out how to make a flying machine from my bicycle," Hans explained.

In this case, putting it back together was beyond him. That Saturday, Hans Senior and Hans Junior loaded the whole of it into their milk cart and drove into Oberammergau to the bicycle shop there. *More money!* Inga thought as she watched them drive away. And yet, there was this quiet pride as well. Hans was right. This was an unusual boy.

The bicycle shop owner could hardly believe his eyes when they showed him what Young Hans had done. Then he started to laugh. In a moment, he was laughing so hard that tears came to his eyes. "What is so funny?" the older Hans snapped, not much amused.

"I did the same thing when I was a boy," he said. "And I got a whipping for it. Now I have my own bicycle shop." Then he turned to Young Hans. "If it is all right with your parents, you can come here on Saturdays and I will teach you how to put your bicycle back together."

That night, with great solemnity, Hans Otto announced to his family that he had found his life's occupation. Inga couldn't help it. She laughed merrily. "What? To assemble bicycles?"

"No, Mama. I'm going to be an engineer. And I am going to

make a motor bicycle that is the best in the world. Better than the Harley-Davidson. And it's going to have a German name on it. I'm going to call it the Eckhardt Cycle."

Chapter Notes

Passion Play

The history of how the Passion Play came to be in Oberammergau is accurately portrayed here. It was last performed in 2010, when 102 performances were given over a period of five months. The production takes place in a covered outdoor theater that seats over 4,700 people. In all, about half a million people attended the play that year. The performances involved more than 2,000 performers, musicians, and stage technicians. Only those born in the village or those who have lived there at least twenty years can participate. It is considered a great honor to be chosen to play the role of Jesus.

The stage itself is large enough to accommodate flocks of sheep and Roman soldiers riding on horses. The performance takes about five hours—three hours in the morning, then two more in the afternoon after a three-hour meal break. It will next be performed in 2020, and tickets are already available for reservation. That performance will celebrate 386 years that the villagers have been keeping their vow.

In 1934, shortly after the Nazi Party came to power in Germany, a jubilee performance of the Passion Play was held, it being the 300th anniversary of its origins. The Ministry of Public Enlightenment and Propaganda saw it as a wonderful opportunity to propagandize and insisted that the official poster include the message *Deutschland ruft dich!* (Germany is calling you!). The official party line described it as "a peasant drama . . . inspired by the consecrating power of the soil." Hitler attended one performance and wholeheartedly endorsed it as being one with the Greater Anti-Semitic Agenda of the Nazi regime. An attempt to have the script rewritten to bring it in line with Nazi ideology was rejected, however.

It is generally agreed that up to that time, the play had strong anti-Semitic elements that blamed the Jews for the "murder" of Christ. Following World War II, numerous changes were made in the script, which softened the role the Jews played in Christ's final days and put the blame for His actual death on the Romans.

The only time the Passion Play has not been performed as scheduled was in 1940, one year after World War II began (see http://en.wikipedia.org /wiki/Oberammergau_Passion_Play#Nazi_exploitation).

German Language Issues

This first volume in the series centers on a German family living in Bavaria in the late 1800s and early 1900s. Clearly, they speak German and are culturally German. But the vast majority of my audience speaks primarily English, so I have made several adjustments for the convenience of the reader.

Even though the German characters speak English in the novel, I wanted to gently remind readers that these people are German. So I have sprinkled some German words that are generally familiar to readers throughout the book.

Also in deference to the majority of readers, who are American, the German characters use the standard terms of measurement that are used in the United States rather than the metric system. This is to avoid the tediousness of having readers mentally convert kilometers into miles, meters into yards, grams into pounds, or hectares into acres. Europeans would likely suggest that it is time for Americans to learn how to make those conversions, since the vast majority of the world is on the metric system. That's a hard argument to set aside, but my primary concern is to avoid distracting readers by pulling them out of the story to try to figure out just much or how far something is. Clearly, I am aware that Germans use the metric standards of measurement.

CHAPTER 2

February 20, 1908—Graswang Village, Bavaria, Germany

As it is throughout the world, a child's birthday in Germany is a big occasion laden with tradition. This is especially true of the twelfth birthday. Children look forward to their birthdays with great anticipation. In addition to the house being decorated in their honor, on that they day they are excused from any of their normal obligations—homework, chores around the house, laying wood in the stove. And for the Eckhardts, no milking the cows that day. Exquisite joy!

One of the favorite traditions was the birthday wreath. Normally this consisted of a simple wooden ring about a foot in diameter. Often the ring was made of four curved pieces of wood that lay flat and were about two inches wide and half an inch thick. These snapped together to form an outside ring and a large open space in the center of the ring. Twelve holes were drilled into the wood. Here candles were placed for each year of life, with one more being added each year until the child's twelfth birthday. In the center of the ring, usually in its own holder, was a larger, more ornate candle. This was known as "the candle of life."

Once lit, all of the candles were left to burn out on their own. None of this blowing them out, as in America. That would not be seen as a good omen.

The family—usually the mother and perhaps older female siblings—would be awake before sunrise to decorate the house and put out the birthday wreath. In the Eckhardt home, that was how it was with the birthdays of their three girls. But for Hans Otto, his father always insisted on not only helping out, but taking the lead. On this, his twelfth birthday, Young Hans awakened early, but he was not allowed to come out of his room until all of the candles were lit.

His mother cooked him a special breakfast, and shortly after noon the guests began to arrive with their gifts. Young Hans reveled in being the center of attention and begged his father to let him open the presents first, but his father held firm. The two biggest ones on the table were from his father. He wouldn't tell Inga what he had spent on them, but it was probably two or three times the combined total of what he spent on his three daughters each year.

Early on, Inga had tried to reason with her husband about the need for equity in the way he treated his children, but Hans had dismissed that out of hand. A boy had a different role in life, especially an only boy and the heir of the family. The interesting thing was that even now, though they were getting older, the girls accepted that without any visible rancor or resentment toward their little brother. It wasn't that Inga disagreed, but it bothered her that Young Hans was coming to believe that somehow he really was better than them by nature. All of this, of course, she kept to herself.

A sharp rapping on the table brought Inga's attention back to the party. The senior Hans stood up, holding up his hands for silence. When he got it, he looked at his son. "Before we cut the cake, let us sing the birthday song to our boy who is no longer a child. Ready? *Wie schön, dass du geboren bist.*" He raised one hand as if he were leading a choir, and they all sang together.

> *It's great that you were born.*
> *Otherwise, we would have missed you very much.*
> *It's great that we're together.*
> *We congratulate you, birthday boy.*

Hans Otto was absolutely beaming when Inga bent down and kissed him after it ended. "Happy birthday, son."

He quickly wiped the kiss off, but he smiled up at her. "*Danke*, Mama."

As she stepped back, Inga's eyes were shining. Her son had turned out to be just as his father had predicted. He had passed her up in height last year and looked as if he would be even taller than his father. His hair had remained a light blond, his eyes were large and expressive and so blue they looked like chips taken from the sky. Even older girls at school and in the village shamelessly flirted with him.

"May he never be found on the steps of city hall with a broom!" his grandfather called out from the corner. That brought a roar of laughter and red cheeks from Hans.

In Germany, if a man reached the age of thirty without either being married or having a girlfriend, on his birthday he had to go to the city hall and sweep off the stairs. Usually his friends would throw rubble on the stairs to give him something to sweep. And when he finished, they would throw more. This was so every single girl in the town could see that here was an eligible bachelor who could clean a house very well.

It seemed a little strange to say that to a twelve-year-old, but then, he was becoming a man this day. It was a subtle reminder that finding a wife and having a family were major parts of his coming responsibility.

Inga had long ago given up trying to talk Hans out of giving such lavish gifts to Young Hans on his birthday. But each year it galled her. "If you keep it up, Hans," she had said last year, the night after their son's eleventh birthday, "we are going to end up with a son who is spoiled, arrogant, and who thinks special entitlements are his natural due."

Her husband, of course, had scoffed openly at such a notion. "If a man is to make something of himself in this world, he must have supreme confidence," he said. "And our Hans Otto is going to make something of himself." If she tried to reason with him, he always erupted and started yelling at her, so she now kept her concerns to herself.

Since this was the twelfth birthday, Inga decided she would say nothing. Hans had been hinting that their present this year— he always called it "their" present, so as to make Inga party to the deed—would be something truly fantastic. She had told him that Hans Otto needed a new pair of boots and wanted a new *fussball*. To her surprise, her husband had gotten both. But she knew that wouldn't change the gift that *he* had picked out. So when her husband and Grandfather Eckhardt went outside to retrieve the special gift, Inga held her breath.

When they came back in, she gasped. They staggered under the weight of a large, shiny, black metal box. It was rectangular, about two feet long, with a hinged lid and a clasp with a place for a lock.

Young Hans shot to his feet. "What is it, Papa? Is that for me?"

"Yes, for you. But not *just* for you, Hans Otto. This one is for the whole family. And especially for Mama."

That caught her completely off guard. She gave him a sharp look.

He ignored it. "As you know, two days ago I sold two of our heifers to the butcher in Oberammergau, and therefore . . ." He let the silence stretch out, smiling at the eager faces before him.

"What, Papa? What?" That was from the girls, who were squirming excitedly.

"Our family is going on a little trip."

Inga whirled. "*What?*"

Young Hans shot to his feet. "Really, Papa? Where?"

Very much looking like a little boy himself now, the older Hans let the suspense build for a moment before he spoke. When he did so, it was with great solemnity and great elation. "When school is out in June, we shall go to the train station in Oberammergau and catch a train to . . ." He let it hang for several seconds. "To Hohenschwangau."

Inga's jaw dropped. There were gasps from every side. But it was Young Hans who spoke first. "To see Mad Ludwig's castle, Papa?"

Inga was so utterly stunned she just gaped at her husband. He laughed aloud. "Yes, Hans Otto, to see the fairy-tale castle of King Ludwig II. Would you like that?"

In answer to that, Hans Otto launched into a wild dance around the table, pumping his arms in the air and singing out, "*Ja, ja, ja!*"

The only thing that a dazed Inga could think of to say was, "What about the milking?"

Triumphant that he had for once achieved total surprise with her, the older Hans was smug. "Ilse and Heidi are both married now. And they and their husbands will help *Grosspapa* and *Grossmutti* take care of things for us while we are gone."

When she turned and looked at his parents, they were beaming and nodding. Ilse and Heidi, though not happy about being left behind, also nodded. Which meant that they had all known all about it. Grandfather Eckhardt, seeing her dismay, chuckled. "We are getting old, Inga, it is true. But we are not too old to take care of the farm for a few days."

"It is all arranged," Hans said.

"And where shall we stay?"

He laughed again, and then took her face in both hands. "I have arranged for us to stay in a hostel in the village there. It is very reasonably priced." Then he kissed her soundly and whispered softly in her ear. "This is for you too, my Inga. For giving us such a son and such fine daughters as this."

It was a brilliant move on his part. Inga had seen pictures of the fairy-tale castle just outside the village of Hohenschwangau all of her life. It was certainly the most famous castle in Germany, and perhaps even in all of Europe. It was exactly like the castles she had pictured as a young girl when she and her sisters and friends had played Cinderella or Sleeping Beauty or one of the other princesses from the fairy tales of the Brothers Grimm. It was only about thirty miles to their west, but for poor farmers that was still out of reach. As she had grown older she had come to accept the fact that it was likely she might go her whole life and never see it for herself. Tears suddenly filled her eyes. She kissed her husband on the cheek as her children applauded wildly. "I am speechless."

He clapped his hands in delight. "Then I have achieved a first."

CHAPTER 3

June 22, 1908—Hohenschwangau, Bavaria, Germany

The moment the train pulled out of the Oberammergau station headed west, Hans Otto stood up and cleared his throat. "Ahem," he said. "May I have your attention please?"

This was the first train of the day, and there were only a few other passengers in the car with them. But they all turned to look and then smiled. Young Hans had a folded paper in one hand and a short stick in the other, which he now rapped sharply on the back of the bench beside him.

Inga, never one to call attention to herself, blushed a little at his boldness. But she also found it amusing.

"In preparation for our visit, I have prepared a short lecture on King Ludwig and his castle at Neuschwanstein," he began.

"Yes, Herr Holzer," Inga murmured.

Anna, who was five years older than her brother, started to giggle, but one searing glance from her father cut that off instantly.

He leaned in closer to his wife. "Was that really necessary?"

It was her gentle way of chiding her son for his pride, and it irritated her that her husband took Hans Otto's side in it—as always. "Is it really necessary that he be so pompous?" she retorted.

He harrumphed something and then looked at his son. "Proceed, Hans Otto."

"Thank you, Papa." He opened his paper and began to read.

"King Ludwig II assumed the royal throne of Bavaria in 1864, shortly before his nineteenth birthday. Unfortunately, two years later, Bavaria lost its independence when the German Empire was formed and Otto von Bismarck was appointed chancellor. King Ludwig retained his title, but sensing it was little more than that, he steadfastly ignored state affairs and devoted himself to two things. He became a patron of the arts, most notably as a major supporter of the famous German composer Richard Wagner. He also commissioned the construction of two lavish palaces and a fantastically beautiful castle perched atop a rocky crag above the village of Hohenschwangau. He called it Neuschwanstein Castle, meaning 'New Swanstone Castle,' a reference to Wagner's Swan Knight in his opera based on German legend, *Lohengrin*.

"The castle turned out to be fantastic. Astonishing. Breathtaking. *Magnifique,* as the French would say. Its white stone blended into the mountaintop so that it looked like someone had carved it out of the native granite. Its turrets and round minarets pierced the blue sky like gigantic spears. Even before it was finished it was dubbed the 'fairy-tale castle,' and Ludwig came to be known as the 'fairy-tale king.'"

Young Hans stopped as the man three benches ahead of them stood up and came back. He removed his hat and briefly bowed, speaking to the boy's father. "Excuse me. I am sorry to interrupt, but is your family going to Neuschwanstein?"

"*Ja*," the senior Hans said in surprise.

"My family also. Would you mind terribly if we came back and joined you? I would like my children to hear this too."

Young Hans was beaming as his father turned to him. "Is that all right with you, Hans Otto?"

"Of course."

The man turned and motioned to his family, which included a woman about Inga's age and two daughters about ten and twelve. They came hurrying back and took the benches behind the Eckhardts. The older daughter was blushing furiously as she looked at Young Hans and did a little curtsy.

As the mother sat down, she leaned forward to Inga. "How old is your son?"

"He is twenty-eight and a college professor in Munich."

The woman's jaw dropped, and her eyes flew open in shock. Smiling, Inga turned clear around and leaned closer. "He's actually only twelve and just out of primary school," she whispered, "but don't tell him that. It would come as quite a shock to him."

Laughing, the woman stuck out her hand. "We are the Ballifs. I am Katrin, and these are my daughters, Eleanore and Ellspeth."

Inga's husband looked around, frowning. "Shall we continue?"

Young Hans picked up right where he left off as if there had been no interruption at all.

"King Ludwig's extravagance became an embarrassment for the government, and Ludwig's ministers and court advisers strongly counseled him to restrain himself. His answer was that he built his castle using only his own royal revenues and money he had personally borrowed and not state funds. But by 1885, he was 14 million marks in debt and still talking about additional projects. They felt it was time to take action.

"The government advisers knew that Ludwig's projects had captured the imagination of the Bavarian people and that, in spite of his eccentricities, he was a beloved monarch. So they hit upon a strategy that would allow them to constitutionally remove him from the throne. Ludwig was quite eccentric. He had never married. He was very shy. He would dine out of doors in bitterly cold weather and wear heavy overcoats in the heat of summer. So his advisers compiled a 'medical report' on his mental state, and Ludwig was declared incapable of ruling Bavaria. It was then that the nickname 'Mad Ludwig' began to circulate.

"The ministers sent a delegation to present him with the document and remove him from power. He tried to escape but was arrested a short time later and put under house arrest. The following day, King Ludwig and a friend were found floating facedown in a nearby lake. The death was ruled as either accidental or suicide, but most people believed that Ludwig had been murdered to stop him from creating further embarrassments. Within six weeks of his death, the still uncompleted Neuschwanstein Castle was opened to the public. It instantly became a huge tourist attraction, and Mad Ludwig's 'lavish excesses' now provide the single largest source of income for the Bavarian royal family."

Young Hans stopped and folded his paper. "I have more to say about the castle, but I think it is best if we do that after we reach the castle, so that will be all for now." With great solemnity he bowed once and took his seat.

Inga turned around to Frau Ballif. "Do you plan to visit the castle tomorrow? You are welcome to join us so that you can continue with the . . . lecture." She was smiling, but with pride as well as amusement.

There was instant disappointment. "No. My husband's brother is coming to Hohenschwangau, but not until tomorrow afternoon. We will wait and see the castle with him."

"Then we wish you a good holiday, and perhaps will see you in the village."

June 23, 1908

When Hans Otto had returned to school after his birthday and told the schoolmaster about their upcoming trip, Herr Holzer had gathered books on King Ludwig and his architectural masterpieces, which Young Hans had devoured. It said much for his shrewdness that he had said nothing of this to his family, holding the surprise for when they were a captive audience on the train.

But to the clear annoyance of their tour guide, Young Hans kept interrupting her to either correct what she was saying or add to it, which did nothing to endear him to either the guide or the others in the group.

In a way, the visit was a disappointment to Inga, especially considering the price they had had to pay for tickets. If Ludwig had been allowed to finish the castle, there would have been about 200 rooms in all. Even though they were lavishly done, only fifteen rooms and halls had been finished, so the family really didn't get to see that much of the castle. But Young Hans was enchanted and prattled on until even his father surprised Inga by suggesting that Young Hans just listen for a time.

Outside they were allowed to wander around the grounds at their leisure, and there it was Inga who was enchanted. Perched atop its own mountain, the castle had a spectacular view of the

Hohenschwangau Valley to the southwest. It was enough to make even Bavarians, who lived with magnificent vistas on every side, exclaim aloud in wonder. Spread out below them were emerald-green meadows stitched together by the darker thread of hedgerows. Off to the south, beyond the village, were two lakes—the Alpsee and the Schwansee—whose blue waters were even bluer than the sky. And all of this was framed by pine-clad mountains. It was enough that even Young Hans was momentarily speechless.

As Inga let her gaze slowly sweep across the view below her, the daughter of the *Schweinehirt* from Unterammergau was once again struck with a deep sense of wonder. What if she had not been indentured to the Kleindiensts? What if Herr Kleindienst had not put her to work in his store as a clerk? What if she had not been there to meet Hans Eckhardt at the *Christkindlmarkt* in Oberammeragau that day? Where would she be now? Back in Unterammergau feeding pigs? She shook her head in reverential awe. One thing was for sure. She certainly would not be here at the castle of Mad Ludwig with her husband and children.

That pensive mood was still on her when Hans Senior came over and told her that he had something he wished to say to the family before they returned to the village. It took her aback a little, but she smiled her encouragement and called for Anna and Young Hans to assemble in one of the courtyards behind the castle. Hans had Inga sit on a stone bench and placed the two children on the ground in front of her.

He waited until they were settled and then solemnly cleared his throat. "I have something I wish to say, especially to Hans Otto." Then, to everyone's surprise, he reached inside his jacket and withdrew a folded piece of paper.

Inga straightened. He wanted to say something to his own

34

children and he was going to *read* it from a piece of paper? That meant he had been planning this before they ever left home.

She frowned as a shadow seemed to pass across her vision.

Clearing his throat, Hans smiled nervously as he unfolded the paper. Then he decided perhaps a word or two of introduction was in order and lowered it again. "As we all know, our Hans Otto celebrated his twelfth birthday a few months ago. This is the age when a child is no longer a child but becomes an adult."

He looked at Inga and frowned. "As you all know, when Hans Otto was born, I wanted to call him Otto von Bismarck Eckhardt, but your mother thought it was too pretentious, too much for a little boy just come into the world."

"That's not what I—"

He hurried on. "She thought that our new little one looked much like me—and as we see now, she was right—and so she insisted on calling him Hans, for his father."

"I like being named after you, Papa," Young Hans broke in.

Thank you, son. Inga could have kissed him for that one. As Hans glanced at his paper, Inga's puzzlement deepened. *Where are you going with this?*

"I then suggested that we call him Hans Otto von Bismarck Eckhardt, but that was still too much for his mother. She worried that such a name might lead him to become a great soldier like Bismarck was."

"I only wanted to—"

His smile, which was a little pinched, cut her off again. "It's all right, *Schatzi*. I see now that you were right. Hans Otto Eckhardt is sufficient for our son."

"I tell everyone that I am named for Otto von Bismarck, Papa," Young Hans sang out. "They think it is a very important name for me."

"It *is* a very important name," his father agreed solemnly. "A very important name."

Inga winced. Probably a third of the boys in his school were named Otto, but only her son turned it into a name of grandeur.

"Which brings me to what I would like to say." Hans raised the paper and began to read. "Today we are here in Hohenschwangau to complete the celebration of the twelfth birthday of Hans Otto Eckhardt. Our son—" he glanced down at Anna, "and your brother—was named after Otto Eduard Leopold, prince of Bismarck, commonly known as Otto von Bismarck. It is a noble name, made so by the accomplishments of this man who almost singlehandedly was responsible for the creation of the German Empire."

He glanced at his wife and then looked away and went on. "Over a hundred years ago, Franz Joseph Haydn, one of the many brilliant composers that Germany has produced, wrote a hymn for the emperor of the time. Years later, another man wrote words to that hymn, which has now become the national anthem of our Fatherland."

"*Deutschland, Deutschland über Alles*," Young Hans sang out.

His father smiled down at him. "Yes. *Germany above all.* We all know the words well, but as an introduction to what I am about to say, I would like to read them to you again."

He straightened, holding the paper out in front of himself, and for a moment Inga thought he was going to sing to them. But he didn't. He read the words slowly and with great feeling.

> *Germany, Germany above all,*
> *Above everything in the world.*
> *When always, for protection,*
> *We stand together as brothers.*

36

From the Maas to the Mernel,
From the Etsch to the Belt*—
Germany, Germany above all,
Above everything in the world.
Germany, Germany above all,
Above everything in the world.

Sitting behind her children, Inga couldn't see their faces, but she sensed they were deeply moved, as she was. It was a song that inspired the soul, and she had sung it in her mind as Hans had read the words. But she was still completely baffled as to where he was going with all this.

"As we all know, Otto von Bismarck took the Fatherland from a backward, medieval society to a great empire and made Germany part of the modern world. By the power of one man, we can now truly sing, 'Germany above all.' As Bismarck recently said to the *Reichstag*, 'We fear God, but nothing else in the world.' How wonderful it is that our glorious leader has brought us to this point in history."

Inga looked away. This was for her. Young Hans might understand, but Anna would likely not. This was his way of saying, "You should have let me name our son Otto von Bismarck Eckhardt." But, gratefully, he didn't say it out loud.

He lowered the paper and looked up at the towering walls and graceful minarets that pierced the sky above them. But only for a moment. He lowered his head and began to read again.

"And now today, we are here to admire the works and accomplishments of another man whose name was also Otto." He

---

* These are geographic features that defined the breadth of land in which German-speaking peoples lived at the time it was written.

looked at his son. "Did you know that, Hans Otto? That King Ludwig's full name was Ludwig *Otto* Friedrich Wilhelm?"

Young Hans shook his head. "I did not, Papa. Is that really true?"

Laughing, Hans looked at Inga. "Mark this day well, *Schatzi*. I know something that my learned son does not."

"Amazing," she said, smiling back at him.

"So, my son, you bear the name of two great men, von Bismarck and King Ludwig. Both accomplished great things. Both are still honored in Germany today. But—" He leaned forward, his voice turning sharp. "But to which of these shall you look as your mentor and example? Shall you be a Bismarck, who formed a new nation and forever changed the destiny of our Fatherland? Or shall you be like the king, who shunned his responsibilities to rule and built fairy-tale castles in the sky, only to end up being murdered by the hands of those he trusted?"

The boy was stunned by the sudden fierceness in his father. "I shall be like von Bismarck, Papa," he stammered.

"Yes, you shall!" He almost shouted it. He took a step forward, looking down at his son. "Hans Otto, you have greatness within you. I feel it. Your mother feels it." There was a fleeting smile. "Oh, we don't expect you to be Germany's future chancellor. Or even someone of great fame and fortune like these two men were. But you will make a difference. You *must* make a difference. You must rise to your full potential and become all that you can be."

"Yes, Papa."

"I want you to never forget this day."

"I won't, Papa."

Hans turned to Inga. "Nor shall we." He folded the paper

38

and put it away as Inga just stared at him. "I have spent much time with Herr Holzer at the school of late, Inga."

So that was it, she thought. The schoolmaster had helped him write his speech. "Yes?" she said slowly.

"Starting this fall, he has agreed to tutor Hans Otto after school and to prepare him for university when he graduates."

"*What?*"

"He has agreed to do so in exchange for three marks per week plus providing his family with milk, cheese, and butter from this time forth."

"But, Hans . . ." She trailed off, too astonished to find words.

"Herr Holzer has important contacts at the University of Munich. He assures me that he can find a sponsor who will pay for Hans Otto's room and board and tuition." Before she could answer, he turned back to his son. "So come September, son, you will no longer have chores around the farm. Your every effort is to be devoted to your studies, to preparing for university. Do you hear me?"

"Yes, Papa." But now there was joy and amazement in his voice. "Of course, Papa. Thank you."

As Inga saw the eagerness in his eyes, it all came together for her. This was what the speech about von Bismarck and Mad Ludwig was all about. Perhaps this was even the ultimate motivation behind the trip. To set her up. To *soften* her up. How long had her husband been negotiating this with Herr Holzer? The bitterness was bile in her mouth. "And will he ever return to the farm?" she asked. She couldn't bear to look at her daughter or wonder what her two eldest would think when they heard this.

Anger darkened her husband's face. "No, not in the way you mean. But the farm will always be his." He reached down and gripped the boy's shoulders and shook him roughly. "Do you hear me, Hans Otto? You shall never give up the farm. But that doesn't mean you have to be a *Milchbauer* for the rest of your life. After you graduate from university, you will make enough money to pay others to run the farm for you."

He turned to Anna as a thought hit him. "You, lovely daughter, shall marry a strong man who loves the land, just as your older sisters have done. They shall run the farm for us when we are too old to run it ourselves. And Hans Otto will pay them so they do not want during hard times."

To Inga's surprise, Anna was nodding. She leaned over and touched Young Hans's arm. "When you are rich and famous, can we come and visit you, Hans?"

"Of course," he said, grinning broadly. "But I shall be very busy, I'm sure. You won't be able to stay for a long time."

"Where do you think I shall live after university?" Hans asked his father. "In Munich?"

"Of course not in Munich. Berlin will be your home. That is where all men of influence gather." He shook a finger at his son. "I expect perfect marks on your exams when you graduate from high school. You cannot disappoint Herr Holzer. This is a great thing he is doing for us."

"I won't, Papa. I promise."

Inga wasn't sure whether to laugh or cry, whether to yell at Hans and try to make him see what he was doing to their son or to embrace Hans Otto and tell him how lucky he was to have a father with such vision.

In the end she got to her feet, moved around to face her son, and then pulled him up to face her. She drew him close to her and held him tight, bending down to kiss the top of his head. Finally, in a choked voice, she whispered in his ear. "Your father is right, Hans. You can go far if you work hard at it. It is up to you."

"Thank you, Mama. I will."

The tears started again, and Inga quickly turned away as Anna moved in to congratulate him. *Three marks per week? Twelve marks lost out of their income each month? Are you mad, Hans?* But she said nothing more as she turned and started back toward where the carts that had brought them up to the castle were waiting.

Suddenly, she spun around and walked back to her son. Startled, Anna stepped back. Hans Senior was instantly wary. She ignored them all. Taking Young Hans by the shoulders, she shook him gently. "Listen to me, son. What your father has done for you is a great honor. But you must never, *never* start thinking that you are better than other people. You are the son of a *Milchbauer.* You come from a long line of people of the soil. That is your heritage, and there is no shame in that. If going to university makes you ashamed of who you are, then I shall ever regret what has happened here this day. Do you understand me?"

"Inga, I . . ."

She ignored her husband even as he stepped forward. Lifting her son's chin, her eyes bored deep into his. "Do you understand me, Young Hans?"

"I . . . Yes, Mama."

"You are the son of a *Milchbauer.* Never forget that. NEVER!"

Chapter Notes

Bismarck's statement about fearing God and nothing else was made in Berlin in the German parliament on February 6, 1888 (see *People's Chronology,* 586).

Deutschlandlied (Song of Germany), also known as *Deutschland Über Alles*, from the lines of the first stanza, did not become the German national anthem until 1922. The music was written by Joseph Haydn in 1797, but the words *"Deutschland, Deutschland, über alles, über alles in der Welt* (Germany, Germany, above all, above all in the world) were written by August Heinrich Hoffmann in 1841. This was at a time when there were thirty-five independent monarchies and four German republics. Hoffman's lyrics were a call to unify this hodgepodge of fragmented states into a unified German Empire.

During the Nazi era, the first stanza was the only one sung, but it was sung at events of great national significance. In the 1936 Olympics held in Berlin, a chorus of 3,000 Germans sang the song as Hitler and his entourage entered the Olympic stadium. Thus, the song became closely associated with the Nazi party.

At the end of World War II the Allies banned the song, along with other symbols of the Third Reich. But in 1952, it was made the national anthem again, with the third stanza being the only one sung at official occasions. The lyrics for the third stanza are:

> *Unity and justice and freedom*
> *For the German Fatherland!*
> *For these let us strive*
> *As brothers with heart and hand!*
> *Unity and justice and freedom*
> *Are the pledge of fortune;*
> *Flourish in this fortune's glory,*
> *Flourish, German Fatherland!*
> *Flourish in this fortune's glory,*
> *Flourish, German Fatherland!*

"Unity and justice and freedom," the opening line of this stanza, is now widely considered to be the national motto of Germany. It is found engraved on the two-Euro coins minted in Germany (see http://en .wikipedia.org/wiki/Deutschlandlied#Historical_background).

42

CHAPTER
4

April 18, 1910—Oberammergau Secondary School,
Oberammergau, Bavaria, Germany

H ans Otto? Please. Would you stay behind for a few
moments?"

Friedrich Rhinehart jabbed him with his elbow
and sniggered as he stepped around him. "Told you not to pass
that note to Ulla," he whispered.

Hans shot his best friend a dirty look, but Friedrich just
laughed.

"Herr Rhinehart? Are you seeking an opportunity to stay after class as well?"

"No, Herr Holzer. Sorry, Herr Holzer." And he shot out the
doorway before the schoolmaster could say more.

Ulla Rasbauer, who sat right behind Hans, was gathering her
books. As she stood up, she said *sotto voce*, "Teacher's pet."

Hans ignored her. His mind was racing. What could he possibly have done wrong? He was never in trouble with the schoolmaster. In fact, it was just the opposite. It was tempting to blurt
out a blanket apology, but Holzer didn't look angry, so Hans
sat attentively, waiting to be spoken to before he spoke. He had

43

learned very early on that the prime rule in Herr Holzer's classes was never to speak until you are spoken to. Hans had made it a point never to violate that rule.

His teacher waited until the classroom was empty except for the two of them, and then he motioned Hans to come forward and take the chair beside his desk. Just before Hans sat down, Herr Holzer motioned for him to turn it around so it faced him directly. Hans did so and then slowly took his seat.

The older man was watching him steadily. Finally he opened a drawer, brought out a folded newspaper, and laid it on the desk between them. Hans glanced down and saw that it was yesterday's edition of the *Münchner Neueste Nachrichten,* or *Munich's Latest News.*

"Are you through with it so soon?" he asked, fighting back the urge to snatch it up.

"Ach!" the teacher exclaimed, throwing up his hands. "As you know, the Passion Play begins in a few weeks' time. We are rehearsing every night, and I am learning my lines every morning."

"And what part do you have?"

Herr Holzer smiled proudly. "I was hoping to be Peter the Apostle, but that almost always goes to one of the master wood-carvers. But I am James the Apostle, who was also one of the fishermen called by Jesus at the Sea of Galilee."

"A very important role indeed," Hans ventured, hoping it truly was.

"Indeed. Anyway, I have no time for newspapers until fall, when the last performance is done. So they are yours. If I forget to bring them to school, please remind me. Once school's out, I will put them in a pile by my woodshed. Anytime you are in Oberammergau, you may stop by and pick them up."

"*Danke*, Herr Holzer. Thank you so very much. I love to read them."

To his surprise, that won him a strange look. "Do you have work for the summer, Hans Otto?"

"*Jawohl.* I will be working at my father's dairy."

"But with thousands of people coming to our village for the play, there will be many work opportunities. Surely you can make more money by coming into town."

Frowning, Hans looked away. "With all the people coming for the play, Papa already has many, many orders for our milk and cream and cheese. It will take all of us to fill them."

The schoolmaster nodded absently, looking troubled, so Hans rushed on. "It will be a lot of work for our family, but it will be a profitable summer too, no?"

"*Ja*, very profitable. For all of us."

"Papa hopes to buy one of those new mowing machines for our hay."

"So perhaps there would be enough to . . ." But he shook it off. He sat back, making a steeple with his fingers and studying Hans over them. Finally, he sat up, as if he had just made up his mind about something. "Hans Otto, do you still keep a notebook of things you have learned from the newspaper?"

Taken aback a little, Hans nevertheless nodded. "*Ja,* Herr Holzer."

"Do you have it with you?"

Turning, Hans lifted his rucksack off the floor and reached inside and brought out a worn notebook. "I started out putting clippings in it, but I found they were filling up my notebooks too fast. So now I just make notes." He held it out. "Would you like to look at it?"

"No, no. I was just wondering. Can you give me some

examples of what you have written in there? You don't have to read them, just tell me in your own words."

"Can I look at them to remind me?"

"Of course."

He half closed his eyes as Hans opened the book and flipped to near the back. "In 1908, there were 127,731 automobiles manufactured in America. That was almost double the number from the year before. The number-one car sold that year was Henry Ford's Model T flivver. It was–"

"And what is a flivver?"

"It is an American word. I could not find out what it meant. I'm sorry."

"But you tried?"

"*Jawohl*. I found an English dictionary in the library, but the word wasn't in there. I think it is a new word in America."

"Good boy for trying. Go on."

"The flivver has a wooden body attached to a steel frame. In American dollars, it cost $850.50."

The schoolmaster was trying hard not to smile. "What do you suppose the fifty cents paid for?"

Hans gave him a mischievous grin. He had asked himself the same question. "Maybe it is the commission paid to the salesmen." As his teacher chuckled, he went on. "Henry Ford, the president of the company, says that people can have the Model T in any color they want as long as it's black."

"Really? Only black?"

"*Jawohl*. And their sales motto is, 'The steel frame is stronger than a horse and easier to maintain.'"

"Very catchy. I am tempted to buy one myself."

Hans smiled briefly and then quickly consulted his notebook again. "Wilbur Wright, who, along with his brother, Orville, designed and flew the first flying machine, has designed a new aeroplane—that's what they're calling them now. It is for the United States War Department. The US government gave him a contract to build several machines. Each plane has to be able to carry two men, fly up to forty miles per hour, and stay in the air for at least one full hour."

"My goodness, forty miles per hour. Did you know that there was a time in the early history of the railroads when people said that if a man went faster than thirty miles per hour, all the air would be sucked out of his lungs and he would die?"

Hans hooted. "At thirty miles an hour? People can be so stupid sometimes." He started flipping pages quickly, looking for a specific article. When he found it, he held it up for his teacher to see. It was a black-and-white photograph of a man wearing a tight-fitting leather cap and goggles. He was sitting behind the wheel of a sleek-looking automobile with no top. The caption read "Barney Oldfield—Fastest Man on Earth."

Hans read to himself for a few seconds and then looked up. "What would those people say now if they knew this Barney Oldfield man recently set a new speed record at a track in Florida?" He looked up. "Guess how fast he drove?"

"Um . . . seventy-five—no, eighty miles an hour?"

"No!" Hans was elated that he knew something his teacher didn't. "He drove his car at an average speed of 131.25 miles an hour. Can you believe that? And guess what else? He was driving a car called the *Blitzen* Benz."

One eyebrow raised slightly. "*Blitzen* is lightning in German. A good name for a car a car that is so fast. But what is Benz?"

"Benz, Herr Holzer. Benz! Have you not heard of the Benz and Cie Motor Company in Mannheim? Have you never seen the Benz Patent-Motorwagen? Many consider it to be the very first automobile." He was racing in his excitement. "Everyone thinks that the Americans invented the automobile, but the first one was here in Germany."

"Ah," Holzer said, impressed. "So this Oldfield was driving a German car?"

"*Ja!*" He nearly shouted it. "And do you know why?"

Trying not to smile, he shook his head.

"Because we have the best engineers in the world. And someday, I'm going to be one of them."

He flipped some more pages, but his teacher reached across and shut the notebook. "*Danke*, Hans Otto. I am glad my old newspapers are good for something other than wrapping fish."

"No, Herr Holzer, thank you. I have learned so much from them."

"So let me ask you some questions. Why did you think the story about Herr Wright was important enough to include in your book?"

"Because that means they're going to start using aeroplanes in war."

"You really think so?"

"*Ja, ja!* Think of it. You could take a bomb up in the aeroplane and drop it on someone's head, and boom! Just like that, he'd be gone."

The schoolmaster sobered as he leaned forward. "That is a very wise observation, Hans Otto. I agree. I think we shall see the aeroplane change the whole nature of warfare. Profoundly so."

"If I were an engineer," Hans said, pleased with the praise, "do you think they would let me fly an aeroplane?"

"*Ja*, I think they might." He sat back again, his face thoughtful. Hans was bursting to share more, but he remembered the rule, so he bit his tongue. After a minute or more, without warning, Herr Holzer got to his feet and leaned down to face him. "Hans Otto, always remember this. The man who looks out on his world and sees nothing but what is before his eyes is destined to labor for others all of his life. But the man who looks out on his world and sees what is possible is a man of vision. And men of vision are always in high demand."

Hans stared at him for a moment and then grabbed his notebook and got a pencil from his knapsack. "Would you say that again, Herr Holzer? I should like to write that down."

Obviously pleased, the teacher did, speaking slowly and distinctly. He watched as the boy put his pencil away and read the words again. The teacher then asked, "Why do you like that saying, Hans Otto?"

"Because if I am going to be a man of great vision, I must start now."

"Do you believe you can be?"

Hans seemed surprised by the question. "If I set my mind to it. I can be whatever I set my mind to."

"*Ja!*" the schoolmaster cried. "You can, Hans Otto. Never forget that." Then a slow smile stole across the teacher's face. "If you are going to be an engineer with vision, you must learn how things work, right?"

"Most certainly," Hans Otto replied.

"Good. That is why I have called Herr Lehnig, who owns the auto mechanic shop on the north end of town."

"Herr Lehnig?"

"*Ja.* More and more people are coming to Oberammergau in private automobiles now. And the roads between here and Munich will cause them many problems. He told me that he is looking for someone who understands how machines work to help him for the summer."

Hans shot out of his chair. "Really? You think he would consider hiring me?"

"I think a better way to say it is, 'On my recommendation, he has already hired you.'"

"But . . ." Sitting slowly down again, Hans started to shake his head. "*Wunderbar*, Herr Holzer. But what about Papa?"

"Don't worry about your papa. I shall talk to him. I think it is your mother who will be the one we need to convince."

May 2, 1910—Oberammergau Secondary School

Two weeks later, when class ended, again Herr Holzer singled Hans out and asked him to stay after. Again the students sniggered, but having learned what had happened the last time, this time they reacted as much from envy as from mockery.

"Did you get to visit Herr Lehnig on Saturday?" Holzer asked, not asking Hans to sit down this time.

"*Ja*. It was wonderful. He showed me all around the shop. He even had a Model T Ford that was shipped over from America to a buyer in Garmisch-Partenkirchen. It was amazing. I start the Monday after school is out. Oh, and he was pleased to learn that I have my own set of tools and wants me to bring them. Thank you so much, Herr Holzer. I am so excited."

"And how do your parents feel about it now? Your father actually seemed pleased."

"He was. And secretly, I think Mama is too, but the money is always a worry for her. She told me that she would agree to my working in town if I would agree to use my wages to pay half of the salary of the person they hire to do the milking. She said that was only fair to the family."

"And did you agree?"

"*Ja*. That is our agreement."

"And how much will that be?"

"One mark per week."

"And how much is Herr Lehnig paying you?"

He grinned. "Three marks a week, which means I can buy more tools if I need them."

"*Das ist gut.* And does your mama know that?"

"*Ja.*"

"*Gut,*" the teacher said in soft satisfaction. "I knew that woman understood what is at stake here." He shook his finger at him. "It is important that you not hide anything from your mama, Hans Otto. Never lie to her, *ja?*"

"I won't, Herr Holzer. I promise."

"Very good." He waved his hand. "Sit down, please."

As Hans did so, once again the schoolmaster made a steeple with his hands, which seemed to be his habit when he was preparing to say something important. And once again, Hans waited patiently for him to speak.

Finally, his eyes focused on Hans. "I have a cousin in Munich who works with the Bavarian Ministry of Education. I went to Munich a fortnight ago and visited with him."

"Oh?"

He opened the drawer and pulled out another paper. Only this time it was not a newspaper but what looked like a letter. He dropped it absently on the desk. "I spoke to him at some length about you, Hans Otto."

"About me?"

"*Ja.*" The teacher was chewing thoughtfully on his lip. "You see, Hans Otto, our little visit a while back was actually somewhat of a test for you." A tiny smile played around the corners of his mouth, and his eyes were twinkling. "You might say it was like a final examination. It was after our visit that I decided to go to Munich and speak with my cousin. I took the liberty of giving him a copy of all of your school records and a recommendation from me."

Dazed, Hans could only nod.

"You are, without question, the most promising student I have ever taught. You have a gift for processing knowledge that is far beyond your age level. Your notebook and your answers to my questions that day made that very clear to me."

He opened the letter and extracted a single sheet of paper but didn't unfold it. "I told my cousin that you need much more than a humble schoolmaster in a small country village can offer."

"But Herr Holzer, I—"

"After seeing your grades and what you have done," he said, cutting him off, "he agrees with me. And he had a wonderful idea. Have you ever heard of Count Leopold Wilhelm Maximilian von Kruger?"

Hans reluctantly shook his head. Then a thought came and his eyes widened. "You mean like the von Kruger Palace? They say it is a magnificent estate to the north of Munich."

Herr Holzer smiled broadly, as if this only confirmed his convictions about Hans. "*Ja.* That is the summer home of the von Kruger family. They also have a winter palace in the south of Italy and a hunting lodge in Scotland. The von Krugers are one of the wealthiest and most influential families in Bavaria. In all of Germany, for that matter. The current Count is the ninth in a line of nobility that dates back more than three hundred years."

Hans nodded, impressed but growing increasingly puzzled.

"They were strong supporters of von Bismarck in his early political years, so when Bismarck became chancellor, they rose even higher in the circles of power. About forty years ago, Count von Kruger's father petitioned von Bismarck for permission to start a private school in Munich. His dream was to create a preparatory school for students of promise—regardless of their social class—that would help prepare them for the finest universities of Germany. The von Krugers felt that this was an important way they could influence the Fatherland for good."

He paused and then smiled at Hans's expression. "Bismarck, as you know, was very progressive in his thinking. He knew that having an educated population was critical to throwing off the shackles of ignorance that have bound down our people for so many generations."

"*Ja*," Hans said slowly.

"Bismarck was so pleased with the von Krugers' proposal that he not only gave his permission for the new academy, but he even provided funding to build several of the buildings they would require."

"Are you saying . . . ?" His mind was racing ahead, making connections, drawing conclusions. But still he didn't dare to hope.

"The current Count and Countess von Kruger have carried on with that dream, and the Von Kruger Academy is now considered to be one of the top ten private preparatory schools in all of Europe. Some of Germany's most influential families send their children there."

Hans was staring at his mentor, his jaw slack now. He saw exactly where his mentor was going, and a sick feeling was sweeping over him.

Holzer's hands shot up and gripped Hans's arms. "My cousin agreed that you would be an excellent candidate for the academy. He wrote to Count and Countess von Kruger and told them about you. He also sent them the records I gave to him."

Nodding numbly, Hans forced a sickly smile and then looked away again.

Triumphantly, Herr Holzer took out his reading glasses, unfolded the letter, and began to read. "This is dated two days ago. 'My dear Christof. It is with the greatest pleasure that I inform you that I received a response from Countess von Kruger in this morning's mail concerning your student, Hans Otto Eckhardt. She was very excited to learn about your protégé and was highly impressed with his records. The Von Kruger Academy is committed to doing whatever it takes to ensure that Hans Otto becomes one of their students. And—'"

The disappointment was so intense that Hans couldn't stand it any longer. "But Herr Holzer." It was almost a sob. "I am the son of a *Milchbauer*. Our family has no prestige whatsoever. And we cannot possibly afford such a school as this. And I would have to move to Munich. Where would I live? How would I eat? There is no possible way that—"

Holzer reached out and laid a hand on his student's arm, cutting off the torrent of words. "Patience, my boy, patience." He returned to the letter. "'Many in the academy come from upper-class families from all over Germany, but the von Krugers strongly believe that gifted people are not all born into high station. Therefore, one of the provisions of their original charter is that at least twenty-five percent of the student body must come from families from the lower half of Germany's socioeconomic classes.'"

"But—"

"'With that in mind, along with his acceptance to the academy, Hans Otto will receive a full scholarship, which will not only cover the tuition and housing but will also provide sufficient funds to cover his living expenses for the duration of his studies.'"

Herr Holzer sat back, removing his spectacles. He was grinning like a schoolboy now. "All right, Hans Otto. You may speak now."

"I . . ." He sat back, unable to get the words out. And then he couldn't hold it back. He lowered his head and began to cry.

Holzer watched him, so filled with joy and elation that he too could barely speak. After several moments, he cleared his throat and picked up the letter again. "There is one last paragraph in my cousin's letter, Hans Otto. Listen carefully as I read it to you. It is important that you do exactly as it says."

Wiping forcefully at the tears with the back of his hands, Hans nodded.

"'I am authorized by Countess von Kruger to have you share this information with Master Eckhardt, but details are still being worked out and so nothing is to be said to his family until a formal letter of invitation is prepared and sent directly to Herr and Frau Eckhardt. With warmest regards,' etc., etc."

He lowered the paper, and Hans saw that his eyes were suddenly shining. "Ah, Hans Otto," he managed to say in a choked voice. "It is all that I have dreamed for you. All that I could have wished for. I am so proud of you. Go forth and find your vision."

May 4, 1910—Graswang Village

The whole family went to the window of the Eckhardt cottage to watch the schoolmaster climb into his buggy and drive off, giving one last wave as he did. The moment he disappeared from sight, the family erupted into a delirium of shock, awe, and joy.

Except for Inga. She had to sit down as Young Hans was swarmed by his grandparents, his father, and his older sisters. He was hugged and pounded on the back and had his hand shaken so vigorously that she was afraid it was going to be pulled right off.

There was no lack of astonishment on Inga's part. Or joy either. She was as elated as the rest of the family. Her son—her Little Hans, accepted at such a school as this? Chosen by one of the noble families of Germany? It was unbelievable—too incredible for her mind to fully accept quite yet. It felt like she was in a dream.

But in that dream there was sorrow too. With a mother's natural intuition, she realized that all was not going to be roses and dancing around the maypole for Hans. He was about to enter a level of society with which he had absolutely no experience whatsoever. The educational opportunity was, without question, astonishing. But she sensed that he was in for another kind of education, and this one would probably come with a lot more pain. One part of her was amazed at how enlightened the count and countess were to recognize that talent could be found in all levels of society. Nevertheless, it still showed their inherent snobbery that only a quarter of the student body would be from the masses. Surely, the upper levels of German society did not constitute three-quarters of the population.

So, how would he cope, this son of a *Milchbauer?* How would he do with the children of the ultra-wealthy? Would they shun him? Point at him and make fun of his clothes, his accent, and his manners—or lack of manners—behind his back? Or worse, to his face? She remembered the days when she worked the *Christkindlmarkt.* She knew about the super wealthy from firsthand experience. They rarely looked at her like she was a living person. If they did, there was this oozing, condescending manner in their voices and on their faces, as if they had come across a particularly cute dog and wished to pat it on its head before moving on. And how would her son, who believed he was equal—if not superior—to anyone else he knew, take all of that? "Come!" Her husband's voice cut into her thoughts. "This calls for a celebration. Hans, hitch up the cart. We are going into Oberammergau to have the most expensive dinner that Herr Kleindienst has on the menu."

• • •

It was long past midnight, but Inga still was unable to get to sleep. When Hans turned over beside her for the third time in a minute, she decided that he hadn't made it either. "Are you awake, *Schatzi?*" she asked softly.

He mumbled something unintelligible and then turned over on his side to face her. "*Ja.* You too?"

"How can we sleep after something like this? I still can hardly catch my breath."

"I know, I know. It is like a Grimms' fairy tale. The son of poor dairy farmers is to become a prince of learning in the most exclusive school in all of Bavaria? It is hard to take in."

She didn't remember Herr Holzer saying that it was *the* most exclusive school, just *an* exclusive school, but she let it pass. "Hans?"

"Yes?"

"Will he make it?"

He hooted in derision. "Of course he will make it. You know how his mind works. It is a gift."

"I didn't mean academically, Hans. I have no worries there. It is with . . . Well, how will he do with the others?"

"Others? What others?"

"The students from the upper crust. You know how conceited they can be."

To her surprise, he didn't dismiss her concerns out of hand. He rolled onto his back and put his hands under his head. "It is a good question, and I worry about it too."

"So what do we do?"

He grunted something and then came up on one elbow. "Let me ask you this, Inga. Of all our family—you, me, *Grossvater* and *Grossmutter,* Ilse, Heidi, Anna—who has the highest opinion of himself and the greatest amount of self-confidence?"

"Hans Otto," she said with a laugh. "Far and away."

"And of all the children in Graswang and Oberammergau combined?"

"Undoubtedly, Young Hans."

"And maybe even in all of Germany, if not the whole European continent?" He was tickling her now as he threw the questions at her, and she was squealing with laughter. "Okay, okay. I get it."

He sobered. "So when those aristocratic brats turn their noses up at him, what will he do?"

She sobered as she realized that what he was saying was true. Not just true, it was profoundly true. "He will look at them with those wide blue eyes of his and scowl at them in utter contempt and wonder how anyone could be so stupid as to not see how truly grand he is."

He brushed a strand of hair back from her cheek. "*Jawohl, Schatzi.* That is exactly what he will do."

She felt a sudden lump in her throat. "And before he graduates, they shall come to know for themselves that he is not inferior to them. Not in any way." She tipped her head back and lifted up high enough to kiss her husband softly on the lips. "You are right. I must stop worrying about him. *Danke schön*, dear husband. Thank you for reminding me of how strong he is."

"And thank you," he said, kissing her back. "Thank you for giving us such a son as this."

Chapter Notes

The items that Hans reads from his notebook are all actual events (see *The People's Chronology*, 676).

Munich's Latest News was a leading newspaper in South Germany up until 1945, when it changed its name to the *Süddeutsche Zeitung*, "South German Newspaper," and operated under the permission of the Allied Occupational Forces. It is still published today and is Germany's largest subscription newspaper.

The von Kruger family and the Von Kruger Academy are creations of the author.

CHAPTER
5

May 22, 1913—Graswang Village, Bavaria, Germany

I f someone had asked Inga Eckhardt, or even her husband, Hans, whether they planned to go to Munich anytime in the near future to visit their son at the Von Kruger Academy, they would have looked at the person as if he were mad. Or laughed in open derision.

It wasn't just the cost of two train tickets. Nor was it the challenge of leaving twenty-one cows for others to milk—they now had three married daughters and their husbands helping with the dairy. Nor did the idea of traveling to the big city bother either of them. Inga's next younger sister's family lived in Munich now, and they went up about once a year to visit them. Last year, when her sister was very ill, Inga had traveled to Munich alone to stay with her for a couple of weeks.

But not once on those visits had they gone to the academy to see Young Hans. There was one primary reason for that: though he had never come right out and said it, Young Hans had made it clear that he would rather come home and see them at Christmas and in the summer than have them come to the academy for a visit.

Though it hurt Inga, it wasn't really a surprise to her. Nor did she want to change it. She had as much anxiety about walking on the campus and accidentally bumping into the von Krugers or some other catastrophically rich family as her son had about his friends meeting his parents and seeing just how humble his circumstances really were. Hans and Inga had told their son they would attend his graduation the following year, but that would be it.

Until the invitation arrived.

When Fritz Heinkel, their postman, brought the squarish, very fancy, very elegant-looking envelope, he didn't leave it in the Eckhardts' mailbox at the end of the lane. He brought it all the way up to the house. It was raining steadily, which made it all the more surprising that he would bring whatever he had all the way to the door. Their mailbox was sufficiently large to handle all but the biggest packages.

Inga, who was sitting at the table preparing some schnitzel for their supper, saw him first. When he walked right by their mailbox, she immediately got up and went to the back door. "Hans, you'd better get in here," she called. "The postman is bringing something to us."

"What?"

"He has something for us," she hissed.

Wiping his hands on his trouser legs, he gave her a strange look. "He's bringing it to the house?"

"*Ja*," she shot back, "and if you don't hurry, I'll have to let him in. And then he'll stay to find out what it is so he can tell the whole village about it."

That spurred him into action, and he hurried around the house. As Inga sat down again at the table, Hans appeared in front of the house and intercepted the postman just as he started up the stone walk to their door.

"*Guten Tag*, Fritzie," Hans called, smiling broadly. "What brings you to our door on this rainy spring morning?"

Surprised, and clearly disappointed, Heinkel reluctantly pulled up. Inga didn't hear his answer because Hans put his arm around the man's shoulder and turned him around so they were facing away from her. Even though she couldn't see his face, she could tell he was vexed at being so rudely turned aside. He reached in his bag and drew out a large, white envelope and handed it to Hans, who immediately stuck it under his jacket. He thanked Fritzie profusely but gave him a gentle push back toward the road. It was bad enough to turn him away on a good day, but when it was raining? She could tell by the way he walked that he was highly offended.

She didn't care. If the mystery envelope was important enough for Heinkel to bring to the house, Inga knew that news of it would be all over the village by nightfall. It still would be, but at least the postman wouldn't be able to tell the villagers what was in the mail. If it had a return address on the outside, that would be shared, of course. After all, wasn't that one of the unwritten functions of a postman?

"Who is it from?" Inga asked as her husband came into the house and removed his raincoat, holding the envelope out so it didn't get wet.

He stopped, a look of grave concern on his face. Then he looked at the envelope. "It is from the Von Kruger Academy in Munich."

She dropped the knife and jumped up. "What?"

Hans was shaking his head. "Why would they send us a letter? What has Hans Otto done that would make them write to us?" Knowing his son as he did, he wasn't worried about him pulling off some silly schoolboy prank that would get him expelled. He was picturing something more like blowing up the chemistry lab or maybe tearing apart some expensive piece of equipment. He shoved the envelope at her. "I don't have my glasses. You read it."

Inga wiped the knife on her apron and then slit the envelope open and removed what was inside. It was not a letter but a square piece of expensive card stock, folded in half. She lifted the flap. A smaller, folded piece of paper fluttered out and fell on the table. She barely saw it. Her eyes were not as bad as Hans's, but she still had to hold the card out at arm's length to read it. Then she softly gasped. "Oh, my!"

"What? What is it? What has he done?" Her husband fell into the chair across from her.

Sensing his alarm, she tried to keep her expression serious, but she couldn't. A huge smile broke across her face. "It's not a letter, Hans. It's an invitation." In reverential awe, she sat down across from him and began to read, speaking very slowly.

THE VON KRUGER ACADEMY
CORDIALLY INVITES
HERR HANS & FRAU INGA ECKHARDT
TO THE ANNUAL CAMPUS OPEN HOUSE
AND COMMENCEMENT EXERCISES

SCHEDULE OF EVENTS
Friday, June 13, 1913
Awarding of Academic Honors
Kruger Hall
6:00 to 7:00 p.m.

Reception and Tea
Hosted by Count and Countess von Kruger
Memorial Gardens (weather permitting)
7:00 to 9:00 p.m.

Saturday, June 14, 1913
Grand Processional
9:00 a.m.
Assembly at Biesinger Chapel
Commencement Exercises
9:30 a.m.

Stargardt Auditorium
Banquet and Grand Ball with Promenade
Ballroom, Weissmuller Sports Arena
8:00 p.m.
Semiformal dress suggested but not required

By that point, Inga's hand was to her mouth. "Oh, my," she whispered again. Half dazed, she set the invitation down and picked up the smaller paper. Unfolding it, she read that to Hans as well.

"'Dear Herr and Frau Eckhardt,

"'Just a brief note of explanation. This letter may come somewhat as a surprise to you, since your son, Hans Otto Eckhardt, will not be graduating from the Academy for another year. However, it is a long tradition of the Academy to invite the parents of all students who are receiving academic honors to participate with us in all of the activities noted on the invitation.

"'Your son will be receiving an award as the outstanding student in the Department of Science and Engineering. We sincerely hope that you can be in attendance to see him receive that honor. Kindly RSVP to the address on the envelope to my attention by June 1st. If you need any help in arranging housing or transportation, please so indicate at that time. We will be happy to assist you in any way possible.

"'We look forward to meeting you in person. We express our gratitude to you for allowing your son to attend our academy. Please bring this invitation with you and present it at the gate and you will be directed from there by our highly competent staff.

"'With warmest good wishes,

"'Frau Dagmar Schramm

"'Secretary, Graduation Activities'"

Very slowly, Inga laid the letter beside the invitation and smoothed it out. Hans came around and sat down across from her. He looked as dazed as she felt. "Outstanding student in Science and Engineering? Our son?"

"Can you believe it?" She wanted to cry and laugh and shout out loud. She was so proud.

Hans picked up the invitation and held it at arm's length. "What does semiformal dress mean?"

She shook her head. "I'm not sure. We'll have to ask Herr Holzer. He'll know."

He was watching her closely. "But it says that formal dress is not required."

"Of course it is," she exclaimed. "If we go, we will not be the only people there dressed like peasants."

"*If* we go? Surely you want to be there when our son receives such an honor as this."

She was rereading the invitation and didn't look up.

"When is Paula's baby due?" her husband asked.

"The week after this." Finally, her head came up. "But you

said you didn't want me to go help her this time—that we couldn't afford to hire someone to help with the milking this year."

He shot her a sly smile. "I don't remember saying any of that."

She hooted. "You were very firm about it."

"We're going," he said firmly. "Hans Otto will be devastated if we don't. And Paula will be delighted if we do."

"You shall have to get your suit cleaned."

"*Ja*, Mama."

She slowly got to her feet and turned to face him. "All right, we shall go. On one condition."

"And what is that?"

"I get a new dress."

Laughing, he took her in his arms. "If I am paying for it, do I get a say in what you buy?"

"Of course not," she teased. "Do you think I am a fool?"

June 12, 1913—#16 Herrenstrasse, Menzing, Munich, Germany

Wolfgang Groll, Inga's brother-in-law, was a junior civil servant in the Bavarian Ministry of Public Works, which was housed in Munich. His wife, Paula Bauer Groll, was Inga's next younger sister and was three years younger than Inga. Like Inga, Paula had left the pig farm in Unterammergau in her early teens to be indentured to a merchant in Oberammergau. She had also followed the example of her older sister and accepted a marriage proposal from a man who would help her escape the overcrowded Bauer household with its numerous children and surrounding pigsties.

Wolfgang had been the youngest son of the more successful of the two greengrocers in the village. He had started calling on

Paula when she was still sixteen. They had married when he was twenty-two and she was seventeen. Paula and her husband had experienced some disappointments when it came to having children, just as Hans and Inga had. Paula had given birth to a girl a year after their marriage and a boy two years after that. Then everything shut down for many years. After they had seen several doctors and offered many prayers, their delightful little Gretl came along when Hans Otto was ten. Then several months ago, Inga had received a letter from her sister announcing that, much to her shock, she was once again with child. They were praying for a boy, whom they planned to name Bruno, after Wolfgang's father.

Wolfie, as Paula always called her husband, had clerked in his father's store all through his teenage years. After their marriage, he went to work for the Oberammergau Town Council as a clerk. Three years later he applied for the job in Munich and was accepted.

Of all her sisters, Inga was closest to Paula. When Paula had moved to Munich, it had been a great loss to Inga. But they corresponded often, and in those years when Paula wasn't having babies, Wolfgang would take the family south to visit their families or Hans and Inga would take their family north, so they saw each other at least twice a year, sometimes more. Inga had been in a high state of anxiety ever since the invitation had arrived. Yesterday morning, the day of their departure, she had told Hans that she was too sick to travel. Though he was not renowned for his sensitivity, fortunately that morning he had understood exactly what she was going through. Assuring her over and over that all would be well, he pulled her out of bed and gave her a gentle shove toward the bathroom.

He had been right, of course. As always with such things.

They had arrived at the train station in Oberammergau half an hour early. The train was on time. Wolfie was waiting for them at the sprawling station in Munich and guided them through the dizzying maze of a city to his home in Menzing, a western suburb. After an evening of catching up on Paula's condition and playing with the children, Inga and Hans retired early. To her astonishment, she slept deeply all through the night.

This morning had dawned clear but cool. The worst of the summer heat was not yet on the city, and it promised to be a perfect day to be out. At breakfast, Wolfie announced that the academy, which was on the eastern outskirts of the city, was too far for them to walk and that getting there would require several changes of trolleys. Inga had felt her anxiety instantly spike, but her brother-in-law calmed her when he told them he had asked his supervisor for permission to be a little late for work. He would take them to the academy and then go on to work after that. Paula and the other children waved good-bye from the doorstep and wished them well as they left for the trolley stop, which was just two blocks from their home.

Wolfie was almost as excited as Hans and Inga were. This was a great honor for all of the family, and he had done considerable research on the von Krugers and their academy. As soon as they were settled in their seats he began sharing what he had learned, much like a professor addressing his captive class.

Inga only half listened. She liked her brother-in-law, primarily because he adored his wife and doted on her much more than Hans did on Inga. He was also a good father to his children. Hans liked him too, but he had a habit of finding fault with Wolfie when they were not in his presence. He was "a little dull," he would say. "A plodder, with no great vision for his family."

Hans never openly added, "unlike myself," but it was clearly implied.

But on this morning, there was none of that. Wolfie dutifully acknowledged what an honor this was for the whole family, which pleased Hans no end. Hans had been pumping him with questions ever since they had left the house. Now, as they approached their final destination, he was still going on about what he knew about the von Kruger family.

Inga decided to break in. "What does Count von Kruger do?"

"Do?" Wolfgang was taken aback by the question. "What do you mean?"

"What does he do for a living? How does he make his money?"

He laughed aloud and then quickly lowered his voice. The trolley was about half full. "People like that don't work for a living, Inga. They are born into money—huge, obscene amounts of money. They have estates and properties and investments that other people run for them. In fact, I've been told that people like that believe that any kind of manual labor is demeaning and far beneath their station. They don't even dress themselves."

"No!" Inga peered at him to see if he was teasing her.

"*Ja*," he replied. "They have servants who lay their clothes out for them. They actually hold them out so that all the aristocrats have to do is stick out their arms."

Hans broke in, determined not to be outdone by his brother-in-law. "And when they eat, they never serve themselves. They have dozens of servants hovering around to pour their wine and serve their food."

Openly skeptical, Inga turned to her brother-in-law to see if he agreed. He did. "*Ja, ja*," he said eagerly. "Only people like the von Krugers don't eat, Hans. They *dine*. And they wear formal clothes all the time. When you attend the banquet, you'll see that for yourself."

"I'm not going to the banquet."

Hans jerked around. "What?"

Inga set her jaw. "I'm not going to the banquet. In fact, I'm not going to any of it. You and Wolfie go. I'm going to go back to stay with Paula in case the baby comes today."

Laughing, Wolfgang took her hand in his. "You'll be fine, Inga. The aristocrats live very differently than we do, but you'll find that they seldom descend from their divine thrones to mingle with the unwashed poor like us." There was a touch of bitterness in those last words. "I'm afraid you must do this," her husband coaxed. "Hans Otto would be crushed if you didn't come."

"I know," she said bleakly. "I know."

Wolfie leaned forward. "This is our stop coming up. Come." He stood up and dragged her to her feet as the trolley clanged in warning and others began getting up too.

To her surprise, as she stood, Hans reached in and kissed her on the cheek. "You are a good woman, Inga Eckhardt," he whispered in her ear. "And no one can take that away from you. You are no longer the daughter of a *Schweinehirt*. You are the wife of a prosperous dairyman and the mother of a remarkable boy. Just think about that and let the servants pour your wine. *Ja*?"

She laughed in spite of herself. "*Ja*," she said, squeezing his hands. "I am the mother of the best science and engineering student in the school."

CHAPTER 6

June 12, 1913—Von Kruger Academy, Bogenhausen, Munich

The academy was four blocks from the trolley, through a quiet street filled with a mixture of small but pleasant homes, two- and three-story apartment buildings, and a few small businesses. Though it was straight up the street from the trolley stop, Wolfie felt compelled to escort them all the way there. *Or,* Inga thought wryly, *perhaps it was to finish sharing all that he had learned.*

"What is now the campus of the Von Kruger Academy," he was saying, "was once a small, private monastery in one corner of the vast summer estate held by the von Krugers. So the whole campus is surrounded by an eight-foot wall."

"Really?" Inga exclaimed. "Young Hans has never said anything about a monastery."

"He probably doesn't know that. I only found it out by accident. The chapel and one other building are all that's left from that time. The church is over three hundred years old, but all of the classrooms and other buildings are under fifty years. I couldn't find out how old the walls are, but they look ancient.

71

They are all covered with ivy and are actually quite wonderful. It's like entering a park when you pass through the gates. The sounds of the city are shut out, and it's so quiet and peaceful."

He stopped as he saw Hans's questioning look.

"I . . . uh . . . I actually wanted to make sure I knew how to find the school, so I came here last week on my way to work."

"And just how big is the campus?" Hans asked.

"Not that large—perhaps twenty or twenty-five acres in all. They say the monks kept bees here and also had vineyards outside the walls that supplied the estate with wine. But all of that is gone, of course. As Munich kept growing in population, the family sold off much of the estate and turned it into highly lucrative rental properties. They probably own everything you see around here."

"Really?" Inga was starting to have second thoughts again. Without realizing it, Inga's pace had started to slow. The jitters were back, and the prospect of what awaited them was filling her with dismay. Realizing his mistake, Wolfie hurriedly took his pocket watch from his vest. "Oh, dear. I'm going to be late for work. I'd better go back before I miss the next trolley. Just keep going straight up this street and you'll see the school on the left. You can't miss it."

He bent down and kissed Inga's cheek. Then he took her hands and squeezed them softly. "It will be all right. Hans Otto is waiting for you. That's why you're here."

"*Danke*, Wolfie. Thank you so much for showing us the way."

He took a piece of paper from his inside jacket pocket and handed it to Hans. "Here are detailed instructions on how to get back. I could come back for you, but I have no way of knowing when you will be through. Probably late. I need to be with Paula."

Hans took the paper and put it in his pocket. "We'll be fine, Wolfie. *Danke schön*. We are in your debt."

The walls around the school were made of stone, now plastered over, and seemed higher than eight feet. The main entrance consisted of two massive bronze gates—which were closed—with a bronze arch spanning the width of them. On the arch in large, wrought-iron letters painted gold was the name of the school. Just to the left of the gate was a small guardhouse.

As the couple approached, a liveried footman stepped out and took his post beside the gate, watching them without expression.

At first, Inga thought he was glowering at them and felt her heart start to thump a little faster, but as they drew near, he smiled pleasantly. "*Guten Tag.*"

"*Guten Tag,*" Hans answered. He pulled the invitation from his side pocket and extended it to him. "We are the Eckhardts."

The footman took the card, gave it a perfunctory glance, and then smiled again. "Thank you for coming, Herr Eckhardt." He looked at Inga and inclined his head. "And to you as well, Frau Eckhardt. Welcome to the Von Kruger Academy."

He turned and opened a smaller gate behind him that Inga hadn't seen earlier and then stepped back. "The students are in a meeting with the provost in the chapel. They are receiving last-minute instructions for the ceremonies tomorrow. They should only be a few more minutes. In the meantime, you are welcome to look around the grounds. Oh, and just inside the gate on the left you will find a large bronze plaque with a map of the campus. If you have questions, please don't hesitate to let me know."

"Yes," Inga answered. "Our son told us to meet him at the plaque."

"Very good." He stepped back and shut the gate behind them after they passed through.

"You see," Hans whispered. "That wasn't so bad, was it?"

Inga said nothing. Her head was turning back and forth in wonder. Her first thought was that her brother-in-law was right. The noise of the city had mysteriously faded away. There were some sounds, but they were faint, almost imperceptible. The hush was reverential. And Wolfie was also right about it feeling like a park. Some of the trees were huge, towering forty and fifty feet above the walls. But what caught her eye and nearly took her breath away was the splash of brilliant colors.

The walkways, which spread out in several directions, were lined with flowering bushes that were nearly as high as the walls. She recognized several different colors of azaleas but couldn't begin to identify the dozen or so other kinds of flowering shrubs that joined in the dazzling display. Here and there, a few students sat on large expanses of grass. It had been recently cut and in the morning sunlight was of such a brilliance as to almost hurt the eyes.

"Oh, my," she breathed. "That boy! Remember? I've asked him several times what the grounds were like, and all he's ever said was that they had lots of grass and flowers."

Hans was still studying the plaque. He looked up as she spoke, obviously not paying much attention to her. He raised a hand to point to the nearest building. "That's the chapel—the one with the small clock tower beside it. And just beyond it, that big building is the auditorium."

Inga barely heard him. She was staring at the church. The door had just opened and students were pouring out into the sunlight. The sound of their voices floated softly on the air. She took a step forward, squinting against the glare. There were so many. And they were compressed in a tight group as they came out.

"What is it?" Hans asked, seeing that she was fixed on something other than what he was saying. Then he too leaned forward. "Is it him? Do you see him?"

"Not yet. But that has to be the group the guard told us about."

"Well," he said, taking her arm, "then let's go and see."

As they started forward, Inga's hand shot out and grabbed Hans's arm. "Look! There he is. Just coming out of the door." She pulled him to a stop and raised her other hand and waved. "Hans! Hans! Here we are."

The students were dispersing quickly now, and she got a clear view of her son. All the students were talking animatedly, and no one seemed to have heard her. Their son had stopped on the top landing of the stairs and was looking back inside the building. "It's him," she confirmed.

"I see him. Let's go." Her husband broke free of her grasp and started forward, but as he did, Young Hans disappeared back inside the building. "Come, Inga," Hans called over his shoulder. "We must catch him before he goes another way."

She fell into step beside him, surprised by the intensity of her joy at the mere sight of their son. They had only gone about ten yards when Hans reappeared. Only this time he had someone with him. Inga slowed to a stop again. Hans did the same. "Who's that?" he asked.

She said nothing. She was peering intently now, trying to see better. They were still maybe thirty or forty yards from the chapel. There was no question that it was a girl. She wore a dark skirt and a bright red blouse with long sleeves. Her hair, which came halfway down her back, looked like it was jet black. Even from this distance, it gleamed in the sunlight. At the bottom of the steps, the pair turned in the opposite direction. They were walking together, but not particularly closely. Their shoulders weren't touching.

"Hans Otto!"

Inga cuffed her husband on the shoulder. "No, Hans. Don't shout." She was staring at the two figures moving away from them. "Has he ever said anything to you about having a girlfriend?"

He glared at her. "No." Then he gave her a sharp look. "Why do you ask that? It's just another student. Look, they're not even holding hands."

Inga said nothing. She didn't know why she felt that way. There was just something about the way Hans had been looking at her as they came out the door.

"Come on," he said gruffly. "Let's catch them before we lose sight of them."

"All right, Hans. But no more yelling."

He grunted something unintelligible and started off. She ran quickly to catch up and then fell into step beside him. Neither of them spoke.

Students were going every which way now, some coming directly toward them, and it was hard to keep Young Hans in an unbroken line of sight. He and the girl were not strolling; they were setting a pretty swift pace. They disappeared behind a large azalea bush and reappeared moments later. They entered a large archway covered by what looked like wild roses. The archway curved and was surprisingly long, and Hans and Inga couldn't see the other end of it. As husband and wife quickened their pace, Inga's lips set in a tight line. She wasn't sure, but she could have sworn that just as the two students had entered the shaded archway, Young Hans had reached out and taken the girl's hand.

"We have to hurry," Hans said, "or we'll lose them." Instead, his wife stopped and pulled him to a stop as well. She suddenly had a bad feeling about what they were doing.

"No, Hans. I think we need to wait here for them."

He gave her an incredulous look. "No, Inga. We're here to see Hans Otto. We've waited long enough." He grabbed her hand and pulled her into a fast walk beside him. "I want to meet this girl."

The rose-covered trellis was the entrance to the campus gardens, and by the time they reached it, no one was in sight. The pathways that branched off from the main walk were empty.

"I think we need to wait here for him," Inga said again. "We don't know where he's gone."

"Stay here if you like," Hans retorted as he grumpily started away. Bad feeling or not, Inga quickly fell in beside him.

The gardens were quite extensive, with the one main walkway that went through the center joined by several smaller stone pathways that branched off in different directions. It was breathtaking. Almost every bush was heavy with blossoms. Perennials bloomed along the walks and between the larger shrubberies. A small fountain with a nymph pouring water from a jug into a watering trough murmured softly to their right. Another life-sized sculpture of a man in a naval uniform stood in the center of a small sitting area with four low benches.

They moved slowly, staying on the main path but searching the side paths as they walked. They saw no one. It appeared as though none of the students were seeking solitude this day.

Except for our son.

"It looks like the path goes all the way through," she ventured at the halfway point. "Maybe it leads to the dormitories. I think we need to go back and wait for him where we agreed to meet."

Her husband said nothing, but from his expression she could tell he wasn't going back anywhere. Not until he found his son.

The far corner of the garden consisted of two rows of perfectly aligned yew trees spaced out across another expanse of manicured lawns. The trees were well over twenty feet high. Each was the exact same size and had been trimmed so it was perfectly pear shaped, each without a leaf out of place, each exactly like the other nine.

They slowed their pace. "Can you believe the amount of work it must take to keep these looking like this?" he whispered. "Amazing."

"Shhh!" Inga hissed, squeezing his hand.

They listened intently, and in a moment they heard it again. It was laughter. A girl's laughter.

Pressing a finger to his lips, Hans moved forward very carefully. The first thing they saw beneath the canopy of the first tree was two sets of legs—one in trousers, one in a black skirt. They were standing close together. Once again, Inga tried to pull her husband to a stop. Young Hans would not be happy to be discovered like this. But her husband wouldn't let go of her, and he kept moving, though more carefully now. In four more steps they came around enough to see who belonged to the legs. Even Hans stopped dead at what they saw next. Young Hans and the girl were standing close to the tree, obviously hoping not to be seen by anyone. His back was to them. She was in his arms, facing them, but fortunately her head was tipped back and her eyes were closed.

As her son leaned in to kiss the girl, Inga's first thought was that she was incredibly beautiful. Then as their lips met in a long, lingering kiss that quickly turned passionate, Inga saw it wasn't just Hans kissing the girl. She was kissing him back, one hand behind his head, pulling it down hard against her.

Grabbing her husband by the coattail, Inga pulled him sharply backwards until the tree was between them and the couple again. She went up on tiptoe and whispered in his ear. "We can't let him see us," she said. "He'll think we were spying on him."

For one long moment, she thought he was going to jerk free and go barreling over to their son. She could see that he was seething, but something in her eyes got through to him. Nodding, he carefully followed her as she backed away until they could no longer see the two young people—or be seen by them. Then they turned and hurried out of the garden, returning across campus to the bronze map. There they found a bench and settled down to wait for their son.

For several minutes, neither of them spoke. Finally, Hans muttered one sentence. "That was not their first kiss."

Inga shook her head. "No, it wasn't."

Neither of them spoke again. It was fifteen minutes more before Young Hans appeared, coming across the campus toward them, shouting and waving his hand in greeting. And he was alone.

For what seemed like forever, Inga held her breath as she watched father and son embrace. She could see the anger in her husband's eyes and the thunderclouds building on his face. But as they hugged each other and slapped each other on the back with blows hard enough to fell a horse, she saw the clouds roll back. And she realized, gratefully, that her husband didn't want to spoil this moment any more than she did.

She was next. "Oh, Mama," Young Hans said as he swept her up in his arms. "I was afraid you wouldn't come."

She pulled back, her eyes narrowing. "You were?"

"*Ja*, with the milking and all. And Aunt Paula. How is she?"

"She's good. The baby is not ready to come quite yet."

"*Wunderbar*. I've been so afraid it might come early and you would have to miss the awards ceremony."

"Did you really think we would miss the crowning of our son as smartest boy in the school?" his father asked.

Hans Otto laughed. "I don't think there will be a crown, Papa. And I am only the smartest in science and engineering. But I was second in mathematics and in history. And that's in a school that already has the best students in all of Bavaria."

"So you are the best of the best," his mother said proudly. *And proud of it.* And that was all right too. She moved in and slipped her arm around his waist. "Come. Let's sit down and you can tell us all about it. Then we want you to show us around the school. I want to see everywhere that you go so I can picture it when we return home again."

"I've got a better idea," he said, taking them both by the hand. "I haven't eaten yet this morning. There's a wonderful little *Ratskeller* just two blocks from here. Let's talk over lunch." Then before his father could respond, he added, "My treat. I never spend all of my weekly allowance, and what I don't spend is mine to keep. So I have over three hundred marks in the bank now. It will help when I go to university."

The senior Hans stared at him for a minute and then turned to Inga, pride lighting his eyes. "Did you hear that, *Schatzi*? Our son is going to buy us lunch. Will the surprises never stop?"

Der Ratskeller, or "the council's cellar," is a name commonly given in German-speaking countries to a bar or restaurant located either in the cellar of city hall—the *Rathaus*—or close by. This one obviously catered to students from the academy, because Young Hans was greeted warmly and shown to what the host assured them was their best table.

Inga was much too excited to eat, but finally, at her son's insistence, agreed to a plate of *Apfelstrudel* with a cup of strong, dark coffee. Hans gallantly conceded that it would not be as good as the *strudel* she made at home, but promised that it was the best he had found in the city. When she bit into the delicate and flaky rolls of pastry wrapped around diced apples flavored with cinnamon, raisins, and powdered sugar, she was surprised to find it nearly equal to her own.

Hans and his father chose heaping dishes of *Käsespätzle*, cheese and noodles, served straight from the pan and boiling hot. They also ordered large steins of pale lager, a beer very popular throughout Germany. With their food served, the parents sat back and ate while their son regaled them with a summary of his life in Munich. He got so excited that from time to time Inga had to remind him to pause long enough to take a bite of food and wash it down with his beer.

And she marveled as she watched him.

She had known things were changing for her son from his occasional home visits and Christmas holidays, but now she could see just how much he was changing. No. *Had* changed. He was not a boy any longer. He had filled out even more than when they had seen him at Christmas. And maybe added another inch in height. He was now a good foot taller than she was. He was seventeen and already a man—a thought that brought back into her mind the image of him kissing the girl behind the yew tree.

She kept waiting, wondering if he would eventually get around to that, but he did not. He talked about his friends but mentioned only male names. He spoke of his classes and how challenging they were and how he excelled in all of them. He spoke of his professors in almost reverential tones, describing how he often spent time with them outside of class hours.

In some ways, his unabashed self-confidence made her wince a little, but she said nothing. It would have done her no good, because his father reveled in it. "That's what I always told you, Hans Otto," the senior Hans would say again and again as his son told them of another of his accomplishments. "I told you that you were a gifted boy, *ja?*"

"*Ja*, Papa," he would answer. "You always said that. But I didn't believe you."

"But now you do."

"*Ja*, Papa."

They left the *Ratskeller* shortly before noon and returned to the campus. Young Hans proudly introduced his parents to the guard at the gate, whom they had encountered earlier. Then as they entered through the gate and started their tour of campus, he stopped constantly to introduce them to students, all of whom greeted him warmly and welcomed his parents to the school. Three different times he also introduced them to one of his professors.

Just outside the main administration building they met the Dean of Students, and Hans Otto introduced them to him as well. All the time, Inga's amazement grew. Her son was not only gifted academically, he was gifted with people. As she watched him interact with others, she could tell that they genuinely liked him. They enjoyed being in his presence. Adults and fellow students alike—they just liked him. Her mother's instincts told her that such a gift might be of even greater importance than his academic prowess. And what warmed her heart even more, there was not the slightest hint of him being embarrassed by the fact that his parents were peasants from a small farming village. He would speak of their dairy farm proudly and tell others how his father had built it up from ten cows to almost two dozen now.

They ended their tour with a walk through the gardens and past the yew trees and then returned to the chapel, which was at the hub of the campus. Young Hans looked up at the clock tower steeple. It was five minutes to two. "Oh, dear," he exclaimed. "I've lost track of the time. I have to meet someone at two o'clock."

Inga felt a quick stab of jealousy. The raven-haired beauty they had seen earlier? But she managed a smile. "That's all right, son," she said. "Your father and I should get an early start back. We need to figure out how to make three different trolley changes."

He spun around in surprise. "No, Mama. You can't go yet. It's not something with the school. In fact, I want to introduce you and Papa to someone. Then I plan to ride the trolley with you back to Uncle Wolfie's and Aunt Paula's house. I'm staying there tonight. Didn't they tell you?"

"No, I . . ."

"Good. I told them I wanted to surprise you. Tomorrow we don't have to be back here until just before the reception and the awards ceremony, which are not until evening, so Uncle Wolfie is going to take us downtown to the *Marienplatz* to show us the world-famous *Glockenspiel* there. Have you seen it before?"

Inga shook her head. Her husband did as well, but added, "I've heard much about it."

"It is the most wonderful clock in the world. The tower is very high, and the clock has forty-three bells and thirty-two life-sized figures that come out while the clock is chiming the hour."

"That's nice," Inga murmured. Then, still catching up with his torrent of words, she asked, "You have to meet someone?"

"Yes. I want to introduce you." And he turned and started away.

Falling in behind their son, Inga and her husband exchanged knowing glances. *At last*, she thought. So he wasn't hiding the girl from them; he had just been saving his best surprise until last. She smiled, more relieved than she had expected to be. Yes. Their son had become a man, and now he was going to introduce them to his girlfriend.

• • •

"Mama. Papa. I would like you to meet two friends of mine from America."

As Young Hans had led them into his dormitory and taken them to the lounge on the main floor, Inga had been rehearsing what she would say to the beautiful young woman they had seen in the garden. But as they entered the lounge, the only two people there were two men in suits and ties. They also carried Homburg hats in their hands. Inga was still looking around for the girl when Hans went up to them and shook their hands. Now she just stared at them, thoroughly confused.

"This is Elder Jackson from Salt Lake City, Utah. And this is Elder Reissner, from Idaho." He grinned. "Wherever in the world that is."

The second young man stepped forward, "*Guten Tag,* Frau Eckhardt. *Guten Tag,* Herr Eckhardt. We are honored to finally meet you. Your son has told us all about you."

It barely registered. Inga's gaze swung back and forth between the two young men and her son. They were clearly older than Young Hans, probably in their early twenties—hardly what you would call elderly. In German, the name for an elderly person was *Älterer*, a description that certainly didn't fit these two men. But Young Hans had used a different word. He called each of them *Kirchenältester,* which meant "elder priest," or "elder in the church." It was used only of officials in the church. And her mind was still trying to process the fact that they were not the beautiful young woman she had been expecting.

Seeing the bewilderment on his parents' faces, Young Hans laughed. "These are missionaries, Papa. From America. They are Mormons. Come, let us sit down."

Once they were settled, Hans Senior spoke. "Mormons?"

"*Ja,*" the one called Reissner said. "That is what people sometimes call us. But the official name of our church is *Kirche Jesu Christi der Heiligen der Letzten Tage.* The Church of Jesus Christ of Latter-day Saints."

This boy's German was much better than Elder Jackson's, who spoke it well but with a heavy American accent. Reissner spoke with the accent of north Germany, perhaps Berlin, but his German was flawless.

Reissner went on. "We have come from America to share a message about our Savior Jesus Christ. We met your son a few weeks ago in the town square and quickly became good friends."

"They are helping me with my English, Mama," Young Hans said. He took his mother's elbow.

"Ha!" Elder Reissner exclaimed in mock horror. "So your only interest in us is self-centered and selfish?"

Hans thought that was enormously funny. "But of course. I am a self-centered and selfish person. Ask my mother if you do not believe me." He turned to her, smiling. "Right, Mother?"

For a moment she was completely taken aback by this sudden

turn in the conversation, but then a smile slowly stole across her face. "I never said you were selfish."

That actually startled him for a moment, and then he feigned deep hurt. "I am shocked, Mama," he cried. "So you think I am self-centered?"

She reached out and touched his hand. "Let's just say that I don't think you are burdened with an overabundance of humility."

"Can I be blamed for being prideful when I have so many excellent qualities to be proud of?" he shot right back.

Even Inga had to laugh at his impudence. She felt a warm rush of affection for him. No wonder people liked him. He had a quick wit, an open and happy manner, and he was right. He did have so many gifts that it was only natural that his confidence was pretty near unshakable.

But even as those thoughts came, she saw her son turn and look at his father. Instantly, the laughter in him died. "Papa, we were only joking with each other."

Inga turned and saw the deep creases in her husband's forehead. He glared at her for a moment and then turned back to the others. "I see no humor in belittling the gifts and abilities of another."

Elder Reissner quickly spoke up. "Herr Eckhardt, let me assure you that my companion and I only spoke in jest."

Irked at his ill humor, Inga said, "It's all right, Elder Reissner. My husband was speaking more to me than to you."

He went on anyway. "We treasure our friendship with your son. We find much in him to be admired. We are blessed by our acquaintance with him."

"Are you trying to convert him to your religion?" Hans Senior asked bluntly.

"No, Papa," Young Hans cried. "We have talked much about religion and God, and they know that my beliefs in those directions are not strong. But I find much in their feelings about the nature of God to my liking. They see him more as a loving Heavenly Father than the harsh and punitive deity that we often hear preached in the churches."

Inga could sense that this was not mollifying her husband. "We are a God-fearing family," he said tightly, speaking to the missionaries, "but we have little patience for organized religion."

She knew that given his present mood, Hans would not appreciate what she was about to say, but she felt compelled to say it anyway. "My husband speaks for himself, and perhaps for our son," she said quietly. "But he does not speak for all of our family. I attend church in our local parish each Sunday with our three daughters and their children."

Hans swung toward her, but she turned to Elder Jackson and spoke to him before her husband could say any more.

"Do you have given names?" she asked. "I assume your first names are not *Kirchenältester.*"

Jackson laughed aloud. "A lot of people ask us that. But yes, my first name is Charles."

"And where is this Lake of Salt?" Hans Senior asked.

"Salt Lake City? It is in the state of Utah. That's in the western part of the United States."

Reissner leaned forward. "And my name is Jacob Reissner. Jacob Heinz Reissner, to be precise." He pronounced his first name as *Yah-kohb* in the German way.

"But that is a German name," Hans Senior said in surprise.

"*Ja.* My grandfather and grandmother joined our Church back in the 1860s and emigrated from Germany to America. I am named for my grandfather."

"Is that where you learned to speak such excellent German? From them?" Inga asked.

"No. They both died while I was still little. But my father was a boy of ten at the time they emigrated. He learned English very quickly and spoke it with only a hint of an accent. So he always spoke English in the home. But he also used a lot of German too. I just kind of picked it up, I guess."

"I am sure your grandfather would be very proud of you," Inga said warmly, "for your German is very nearly perfect."

He nodded and smiled. "Papa always said that *Deutsch* was the language of heaven. All other tongues were from the lower regions."

"Well spoken," Hans Senior said, actually laughing. "Well spoken, indeed."

Elder Reissner stood up, saying they had another appointment they had to get to. They shook hands all around, promised to see Young Hans again soon, congratulated him on his coming award, and then said farewell.

As they watched them go, Young Hans turned to his parents. "I'm so glad you liked them. I find them to be excellent company."

His father gave him a long, probing look. "We are not sending you up here to study religion."

To Inga's surprise, her son bristled at that. "I am here to study many things, Papa," he said tartly. "You don't need to tell me what I should or shouldn't study." Then, turning to his mother before Hans Senior could respond, he said, "Let me run upstairs and get my things, and then we will go. I'm anxious to see Uncle Wolfie and Aunt Paula again. And Gretl. It will be good to see Gretl too."

Chapter Note

Though it will come as a surprise to many members of the Church, there were about 200 missionaries in the Swiss-German Mission at this time, and they were having great success. In spite of persistent and widespread opposition, convert baptisms in the mission kept increasing. For example, in the six-year period from 1898 to 1904, a time of great persecution, the number of members in Germany went from 1,028 to 2,863, nearly a 300% increase. And in 1924, the Swiss-German Mission was the top baptizing mission in the world and had the largest number of members of any mission in the Church (see *Mormons in Germany,* 51, 62). Even with considerable emigration of converts to America, in that year there were 11,102 members in the Swiss-German Mission, which was almost 2,400 more members than were in California at that time.

CHAPTER
7

June 13, 1913—#16 Herrenstrasse, Menzing

As it turned out, they didn't go into Munich to see the *Glockenspiel* the next day.

During the night, Paula went into labor. Inga was certain that it was early, or false, labor, which was confirmed when everything stopped by morning. But with Gretl, Paula had been in labor for only three hours before the birth, so they all decided it wasn't worth the risk of being that far away from home. At Paula's urging, Wolfie went to work so that he didn't have to take a day off before it was necessary. Young Hans, who didn't need to be back at the academy until later that afternoon, promised he would take the trolley in and fetch Wolfie if things changed.

They spent a quiet day together. Inga made Paula sit and watch while she cleaned the house and prepared food. Gretl was out of school for the summer and went over to a friend's house nearby. Young Hans and his father went into the sitting room and talked together for over two hours.

When they came out, though she was curious, Inga said

nothing. She waited until Paula went upstairs to take a nap and Young Hans said he had to study. When she heard the doors shut, she immediately cornered her husband. "Did he say anything about the girl?" she queried.

He shook his head. "Not a word. Not even a hint."

She sighed. It was not a surprise, but it was a disappointment. "I've decided it's nothing. Just a harmless flirtation."

The look she gave him was a mix of incredulity and irritation. "A flirtation?" she exclaimed. "You saw how they were kissing. How can you say that is a flirtation?"

"Hush, Inga," he hissed, looking toward the stairs. "Hans Otto will hear you."

Biting back a retort, she turned away. Why should she be surprised? This was how it always was with him. Hans Otto could do no wrong in his father's sight. He readily turned a blind eye to things he didn't want to see. And he hated confronting their son with anything unpleasant, which was so out of character for him. With merchants or customers buying their dairy products, his style was blunt, hard-nosed, and often filled with angry confrontations. Even with their girls he was quick to correct, often in a way that left them in tears. But with Young Hans his role was to be the ever-supporting, doting father. His look had said it all. *If something needs to be said, it is going to have to come from you.*

She spun back around. "Did you see her clothes? Did you even notice her hair and that necklace she was wearing?"

That took him aback. "Of course I saw her clothes. What about them?"

"They shout money, Hans. The necklace was gold. She wore silver bracelets. Everything about her reeked of money."

"So?"

"She's out of his class, Hans. She's out of *our* class. She's miles above him."

His face instantly darkened. "That may be true of us, Inga, but not of Hans Otto. He left our so-called class the day he was accepted into the academy. We knew that was one of the benefits of his coming here. It's not just his education. It's the connections he's making, the friends that he's associating with. That's part of what a prep school is all about, *Schatzi*. Connections. He has broken free from the peasant's life." He suddenly grinned. "Maybe he'll marry into a rich family and take care of us in our old age."

She didn't think that was funny in any way. "There will be no connection here. She comes from a very wealthy family. A girl like that doesn't marry into a family like ours. He's going to be hurt, Hans. And if he doesn't say anything about her, I'm going to say something to him before we go."

"No!" Hans growled in an angry whisper. "You'll say nothing to him unless he brings it up."

Inga's head came up. "Either you say something to him, or I will." Then she whirled and went into the kitchen before he could answer her—or before she said something to him that she would later regret.

• • •

Nothing more was said of the girl that day. After an early supper, Young Hans dressed in his suit and came down to join them. Any resolve to confront him about his romantic involvement melted away as Inga watched him come into the kitchen. Tears sprang to her eyes as he stopped and did a little pirouette. "How do I look?"

"Oh, Hans," she said in a choked voice, "where has my little boy gone? You are so handsome. And I am *so* proud of you."

He came to her, bent down, and kissed her cheek. "Thank you, Mama." His voice was a little choked now too. "I love your dress. You look beautiful. I'm so glad you came."

She pulled a face. "I wish I could say the same. I don't want you to be ashamed."

"Ashamed of what?" his father said as he entered the room, still tugging at his bow tie.

"Nothing," she murmured. Her son gave her a quick glance, smiling, and then moved to his father. "And look at you, Papa. You? In a tuxedo? This is a wonder."

To Inga's astonishment, she saw that her husband was coloring too, something that she couldn't remember ever seeing him do before.

"*Ja,*" he said, waving a hand dismissively. "I almost came in my milking boots and coveralls because I knew you would never recognize me in a tuxedo."

Young Hans slipped an arm through Inga's arm and then turned her so he could do the same with his father. He pulled them both close against him. "I have never been more proud than I am right now," he whispered. "So let's go introduce the world to the Eckhardt family."

• • •

The awards ceremony was not as large as Inga had expected. But then she remembered that the academy had fewer than two hundred students, and only a small percent of those had earned an award. She wasn't sure why she had expected more.

The ceremony was held in Kruger Hall, which seemed to be a combination student center and lecture hall. The auditorium was not that big, but it easily held the crowd that had assembled. Hans and Inga found seats near the back and sat down. Young Hans and the other honorees were expected to sit in the first two rows, so he left them and went down front. As he moved away, Inga noticed that there were eight chairs behind the podium, but none of them were occupied yet. She would have to wait for her first live glimpse of the von Krugers.

She already knew what they looked like. Virtually every building in the school had a near life-sized portrait of them hanging on the wall. In every case, Inga had found it difficult to take her eyes off of them. They were a strikingly handsome couple. In most of the portraits, the count was dressed in some kind of military uniform, with a saber at his side. His chest was covered with various medals and ribbons. He had not been smiling in any of them, but Inga decided that his face was quite pleasant nevertheless.

The countess was stunningly beautiful, of course. Weren't all nobility? Long, dark hair framed a round face with large, dark eyes and translucent skin. In two or three of the portraits she had the tiniest smile on her face, as if she knew something that the rest of the world didn't. Inga liked her immediately.

Finally, she turned back to watch her son. He was still standing with several of the other students. She watched him proudly as they congratulated him on his accomplishment. Adults were also stopping by to acknowledge him. He seemed so at ease, so confident with it all. She laughed silently to herself. Hadn't his father predicted this on that day at Neuschwanstein Castle? On another occasion, Inga had expressed concern that he would be hurt because he would be out of his class. Hans had suggested that with their son's level of confidence, it would never occur to him that he was outclassed. Now here they were, and she had been wrong and Hans had been right.

She turned as Hans nudged her with his elbow. He was looking back toward the main door to the auditorium. He said nothing, just jerked his head in the direction of a cluster of young women who had just entered. Inga saw what he was looking at immediately. The "girl" was in the center of the group, laughing happily at something one of them had said.

"Oh, dear," she murmured. The girl wore a white dress of some very expensive-looking fabric that clung softly to her figure as she walked. The gold necklace had been replaced by a string of black pearls that perfectly accented her dark hair and eyes. Even though she was in a group, she moved with a natural grace that made her stand out from the rest. She was even lovelier than she had been yesterday. People in the audience, especially the men, were turning their heads to watch as she passed by.

No wonder you're smitten. Oh, Hans. You are in so far over your head here.

The girls moved down several rows and filed in to the seats. The girl sat in the middle of the group, where Inga could see only the back of her head. But she watched closely to see if Young Hans would turn around and acknowledge her, or vice versa. To her surprise, he did not. Nor did she seem to ever look at him.

Suddenly, those in the audience rose to their feet and began to applaud. Hans pulled Inga up to stand beside him. "It's Count and Countess von Kruger," he whispered.

And with that, Inga forgot about the girl and her son's infatuation and began to clap as well. As she did so, a sense of great wonder descended upon her. In her wildest dreams she had never pictured herself in the same room with a real count and countess. She was the daughter of a *Schweinehirt*—a pig farmer—and the wife of a *Milchbauer*. She was of the peasant class from the tip of her toes to the top of her head. Yet here she was in the same room with nobility. And a little later this night, she would briefly shake their hands. And all because of their son.

Tears sprang up as she pounded her hands together with even greater vigor than before. It was all she could do not to shout out, "Bravo! Bravo, my son! Bravo!"

The awards took longer than the planners had evidently expected. It said on the Eckhardts' invitation that the event was scheduled for 6:00 to 7:00 p.m., with the reception and tea with the von Krugers to follow in the gardens at 7:30. Only two speakers were scheduled on the program, the Dean of Students and the graduating class valedictorian, but both spoke for far longer than their allotted time. Inga watched as the von Krugers kept glancing at the clock and then looking at each other. They were clearly getting frustrated.

But all was finished by 7:15, so the person conducting the ceremony reminded the audience that they were quarter of an hour behind schedule and asked them to move immediately to the gardens for the reception.

"I don't care if we make it to the reception or not," Inga told her husband as they made their way down the aisle toward the front. "Let's take Hans out somewhere."

One look from him put an end to that. She sighed. Hans had bought his tuxedo for one reason and one reason only, and that was for meeting the count and countess in person. There was no way he was going to let that opportunity pass.

Inga suddenly remembered the girl and searched the crowd in front to see if she was there congratulating the honorees. After a moment, she spotted her. And the girl was doing just that. But to Inga's astonishment, as she watched, she saw that the girl never got within three people of Hans. After shaking several hands, she and her friends went up the other aisle and left the hall.

Inga glanced at her husband to see if he had noticed, but he was talking to another parent, so she said nothing. But her lips set in a tight line. Before this night was over, she would either meet this girl in person or she would wring the information about her out of her son. This whole thing was getting stranger by the minute.

As they left the hall with Young Hans and headed for the gardens, Inga tried to hang back. She did not want to be the first in line—or even in the first hundred. But son and husband were eager for refreshments and pulled her along.

She needn't have worried. By the time they got there, the line came clear out of the garden, through the rosebush archway, and back into the main quad. It took them thirty-five minutes to even get close enough to tell where the greeting line had formed. It was in the grassy area in front of the yew trees, not far from where she and Hans had stood and watched their son and the girl. She saw at once why the von Krugers had chosen that particular place. It was open enough that people could easily move on to where the refreshments were being served without having to push their way back through crowds still waiting.

As they inched their way forward, still too far away to see the count and countess, Young Hans and his father conversed back and forth. They would occasionally ask Inga a question and try to draw her in, but with every step, her anxiety shot up another few notches, and she ignored them. But as the line crawled forward with infinite slowness, the waiting became unbearable, and she knew she had to do something to take her mind off of her nerves. So she moved up beside Young Hans and joined the conversation.

They inched forward for another fifteen minutes, and then Young Hans raised his head. "Ah, there they are." He looked down at his mother. "See. I told you they were out here somewhere."

Inga turned to look. "Finally," she breathed.

She saw Count and Countess von Kruger immediately. The provost of the college was first in line so he could introduce the people to them, but they were next. Both had changed their clothes since leaving the awards banquet. The countess now wore a shimmering gold ball gown covered with something shiny. The skirt was so full that her husband had to stand a good two feet away from her. He had changed from his uniform to a perfectly-tailored tuxedo with a red rose in the buttonhole. Up close, Inga could see that they were even more stunning than they had seemed before.

And then Inga gasped. She leaned forward slightly, her mouth agape. Her feet felt like they had suddenly taken root through the sidewalk.

She jerked around and looked up at Hans. One look at his face and she knew he had seen it too. He looked like an apparition had suddenly materialized before his eyes, causing the blood to drain from his face.

Slowly Inga turned back and stared at the third person in the line. She had not taken time to change her clothes. She still wore the white dress and the string of black pearls. Seeing her standing shoulder to shoulder with the countess, Inga recognized what she had missed before. The resemblance between the two of them was striking.

She felt a nudge on her arm. "What is it, Mama? What's wrong?"

She turned to Young Hans. She had to take a quick breath before she could speak. "Who is that?"

He looked around. "Who is what?"

"The girl standing next to the countess."

"Oh, her?" He peered more closely, a puzzled frown twisting his face.

"The girl in the white dress and black pearls." It was all she could do not to shout it at him. *The one that you were kissing so passionately yesterday.*

He shrugged. "I think that's the von Krugers' oldest daughter. Her name is Lady Magdalena Margitte Maria von Kruger." He said it easily, as if he had pronounced it many times before. Then he shrugged again. "Come," he said. "It looks like we'll get to meet her tonight too."

"Do you know her?"

He was momentarily startled. "The young Lady von Kruger?"

"Yes," Inga said. Her eyes were pleading. *Don't lie to me, Hans. Don't lie to me.*

It was as if he found the question amusing. "I know who she is, but that's all. She's a student here at the school, but in the class a year below mine."

"But you don't *know* her?"

He sniffed as if the thought were ridiculous. "People like me don't *know* people like her. She's strictly in a class all by herself."

Inga couldn't hide her astonishment. Those blue eyes of his were as innocent as a child's. The stab of disappointment was so sharp that she had to look away to hide the pain.

After a moment, she turned and looked up at Hans. "I'm sorry, *Schatzi*, but I'm not feeling very well. Can you take me home, please?"

Without a word, her husband gave one curt nod and turned to his son. "I'm sorry, Hans Otto. Don't worry about us. We'll take a trolley back to your aunt's place and—"

"What is it, Mama? Can I help you?"

"No. You need to stay. You know the way to Paula's place. We'll see you in the morning."

Not waiting for him to answer, she blindly groped for her husband's arm and then, together, they walked away.

CHAPTER
8

June 14, 1913—#16 Herrenstrasse, Menzing

During the night, Paula again started into false labor, but it went away even more quickly than it had the night before. But it was enough. It was a perfect excuse for Inga.

All students were required to attend graduation, so Young Hans was up early. He had to be at the chapel to watch the processional by nine o'clock.

When Inga told him about Paula's late-night episode and asked him how important it was for her to attend the graduation, he assured her it was not required, at least not for them, since he wasn't graduating.

"Papa and Wolfie are going, but if it's all right, I think I'll take a rest now so we can have time together this afternoon before we have to go back."

She didn't wait for him to object or assent before she hurried up the stairs.

The men arrived back home shortly before noon. All three of them seemed to be in good spirits. When Young Hans agreed to play cards with Gretl, Inga asked her husband the question that had been on her mind all morning. He shook his head. "I didn't say anything to him," he whispered. "And he didn't say anything to us."

Relieved, Inga immediately set to work preparing lunch for the family.

While Gretl helped Inga with the dishes, Paula sat with Wolfie and Young Hans and made her nephew tell her all about the award he had received and about meeting the count and countess in person. Then, though he wasn't graduating, she made him tell her all about the commencement ceremony. After all, he would be graduating the next spring, and she had promised that she would be there for that.

At 1:30, on receiving a nod from Inga, Wolfie stood up. "I'm going to go for a walk for a while, *Schatzi*. Why don't you try to get some sleep?" Paula agreed instantly, excused herself, and was gone before Wolfie could even get his shoes on. As he went out the front door, promising to be back in an hour or so, Young Hans got to his feet too. He stretched and yawned. "I didn't get home until nearly midnight last night. And we've got a late night tonight. I think I'll grab a nap too."

Inga was up and in front of him in two steps. "Not just yet, son. Can we talk for a few minutes?"

His eyebrows lifted slightly, but then he shrugged. "Sure, Mama." As he sat down again she could tell that he still had no clue what was about to descend on him. His father got a drink of water and then came and sat on the sofa beside Inga.

Inga had thought of little else all morning, rehearsing in her head all the possible directions the conversation might take. She knew that her approach and Hans's approach would be very different. She had hoped that they might get a chance to talk it through, but that hadn't happened. Though one part of her hoped that her husband would lead out, another part of her worried about him losing his temper. It was a worry that quickly became a reality. The moment they sat down, he launched his attack.

"Hans Otto, you need to know that your mother and I are extremely disappointed in you."

His head jerked up. "*What?*"

"*Schatzi*," Inga said, looking at this man she knew so well, "can I explain something first?"

He ignored her. "Why are you lying to us, boy?" he snapped.

Young Hans shot to his feet, his face instantly flushed. "Lying? What are you talking about?"

"You know what I'm talking about. I'm talking about that young woman. Young Lady von Kruger."

Hans Otto's face was instantly a brilliant red. He went to speak, but nothing came out. Inga decided it was time to jump in.

"Sit down, dear," she said. Then she shot a warning look at the man beside her. "I'll try to explain what your father is saying."

He didn't sit down. His fists were clenched so tightly that his knuckles were white. His eyes darted back and forth between the two of them.

"Please sit down, Hans. Please."

Finally, he dropped back into his chair. But the fight wasn't out of him. Those blue eyes that were usually so filled with laughter were flashing pinpoints of fire. His chest was rising and falling as he glared at his father.

Inga took a quick breath and began. "Hans, when we first arrived at the school, you were still in a meeting with the provost."

"So?"

"So your father and I were standing near the gate, studying

the bronze map of campus, trying to orient ourselves. Then we saw you come out of the chapel—"

"Wait! You were here that early? You told me you wouldn't be there until about noon."

She explained that Wolfie had worried about them not finding their way and that he had come with them to show them where to make trolley changes. With all of that, they had arrived more than an hour early.

He nodded, but she could see that he was tensed for flight—rocking back and forth, fists clenching and unclenching.

"We saw you come out of the meeting. We called to you, but we were too far away for you to hear us. You didn't see us and then went back in again."

"*Ja*. I had left my books on the pew. I went back in to get them and take them to my dorm room. Is that such a crime?"

"Watch your tongue, boy," his father snapped. "You're in enough trouble already."

Inga frowned. They had seen him pretty clearly when he came out of the church, and she was almost certain he wasn't carrying anything. "When we saw you again," she went on quietly, "you were walking with a girl."

At that he visibly flinched. She waited, watching his face as he tried to decide how much to say. "A girl? Oh, yes. I remember now. That was Rachel, a girl from my physics class."

Inga's eyes half closed. She heard Hans draw in his breath beside her.

"We followed you, Hans Otto," he blurted.

"You *what?*"

"We tried to call out to you," Inga explained, "but you didn't hear us."

"How far did you follow me?" His voice was suddenly shrill.

"All the way into the gardens," his father snapped. "All the way to where you took that girl behind the yew tree. We were close enough to see you kiss her. So you can stop lying now. Her name isn't Rachel, it is Lady Magdalena von Kruger."

Hans Otto's head dropped and he stared at his hands. He started to say something but then changed his mind. Finally he looked up at his mother. "That's what upset you so much last night in the reception line, isn't it? I knew it was something more than you just being embarrassed to meet them. It was when you saw Maggie and realized who she was, wasn't it?"

"Maggie?" his father shouted incredulously. "You call her 'Maggie'?"

"All right, Magdalena." He was still looking at Inga. "That was it, wasn't it?"

"Yes."

"Why did you lie to us?" Hans shouted.

"Why didn't you say something last night?" he shot right back.

Turning away, he stared out the window. After almost a full thirty seconds he answered. "I lied because I knew this was how you would react if I told you that we were friends."

"Friends?" Hans shot to his feet. "Friends don't kiss like that."

"All right. I knew you would overreact if I told you that she was my girlfriend."

"Do you know what hurts me the most?" Inga asked.

"What?"

"How easily the lie came to you. Like you've been doing it a lot lately."

He was like a cornered animal now. "I had to lie. *We've* had to lie, because . . . well, you can imagine what people would say. The daughter of a count and the son of a milkman."

"Do her parents know?" Inga asked.

"Of course not. Not yet. She's going to tell them after the ball tonight."

"No, she's not," his father roared. "You two are not going to say anything about this, because it's over. Right now. It's over and done with. Do you understand me?"

"No, Papa. I love her. We've even talked about . . ." His voice trailed off as he saw the look on his father's face.

"What?" his father roared. "What have you talked about?"

"Nothing." He was backpedaling frantically. "Just that we talked about her staying for summer school, like me."

It was such a pathetic lie that Inga felt her anger rising. But to her amazement, her husband accepted it. He nodded, seeming relieved. She was incredulous. Had he really bought into the summer school explanation? Could he not see that their son had nearly said, "We've even talked about marriage"?

His next words answered that for her, and her anger turned against both of them.

"You are *not* going to stay for summer school," Hans Senior said. "You are coming home. You are going to milk cows until you learn not to lie to your parents."

Now Young Hans shot to his feet. "Don't be ridiculous, Papa. I'm sorry that I lied to you, but I have two summer classes that I need to take before I can begin my advanced engineering courses. I told you that before. I'm not coming home until Christmas."

Inga's hopes plummeted as she watched her husband's face turn a mottled purple. *Oh, Hans, you are only making things worse.* But the damage was already done.

"You are coming home *now!*" his father shouted. "You will do as I say, or I will . . ." He sputtered to a stop, unable to think of something horrible enough to make up for the betrayal. Young Hans seized on it immediately.

"Or you will what, Papa? Cut off my funding? Oh, that's right," he sneered. "You don't provide any of my funding. That comes completely from the school. So then what? Will you take me out to the woodshed and put the paddle to me?" His arrogance was shocking. "Oh, dear. That won't work either, because I'm now taller than you and outweigh you by twenty-five pounds."

Inga leaped up and moved between them, her back to her husband. For a long moment, she stared at her son, who was having difficulty facing her down, and then she stepped forward and slapped his face with all the strength she could muster. His head snapped back and he cried out.

For an instant it was hard to determine who was the most shocked: Hans Senior, Hans Junior, or Inga. But she was the first to recover. She went up on her toes until her face was just inches from her son's. "You will not speak to your father in that way," she said, her voice trembling. "You apologize this instant or you will not have a place to come home to at Christmas."

One hand came up slowly and rubbed at his cheek. Inga was shocked to see her handprint in the flesh, bright red and clearly visible. Then her son's head dropped. "I'm sorry, Papa. Mama is right. I should not have spoken to you in that manner. Please forgive me."

Inga stepped back and then whirled to look up at her husband. "Well?" she snapped.

He looked confused for a moment. Her eyes narrowed even more. "I . . . uh . . . I accept your apology, Hans Otto," he stuttered.

"And?" Inga prodded.

"And I am sorry that I shouted at you."

"I'm sorry that I lied to you, Papa. And to you, Mama. It was a stupid thing to do. I'm sorry." Then his head came up. "Besides, there's nothing to worry about. Maggie's family—Magdalena's family—is leaving on Tuesday for their estate in Scotland. They'll be gone for a month, so she won't be in summer school. I probably won't see her again before fall term."

Hans and Inga exchanged relieved glances. "That's for the best," she finally murmured. As her husband opened his mouth to speak, she quickly went on. "I think we all could use a nap right now. Then we can talk about tonight."

• • •

Inga and Hans had not spoken a word to each other. Her husband was still brooding darkly. And while much of that was because their son had defied him, she knew he was equally angry at her for interfering. When the time came to get ready for the banquet and ball, both parents came to the room where Young Hans had a cot. There, Inga announced that neither of them would be going to the final gala of the graduation celebration. "I just can't," she said.

Trying not to show his immense relief, Young Hans nobly volunteered to stay with his mother and father. Inga would have none of it.

"You were honored as an outstanding student yesterday," Inga said. "Everyone knows you now, even if they didn't before. If you are not there, it will be noticed. So you must go."

"What if the count or countess asks why you are not there?"

"Tell them about your Aunt Paula. Tell them she's been in

labor for the last two nights—which is true," she added pointedly, "and that we dare not leave for that long."

Young Hans turned to his father. "And what about you? What do I say about you not being there?"

His head came up slowly. His mouth was pinched into a tight line. "Tell them that I have never been more sharply disappointed in my son than I am at this moment and that I couldn't bear to be with you."

Hans Otto rocked back as if he had been struck.

Inga quickly stepped in. "*Schatzi,*" she pleaded. "We will work this out later, but not in this way."

He turned on her, eyes blazing. "That's right. Take his side, Inga, like you always do. No wonder the boy is so headstrong and out of control."

"Like *I* always do?" she cried. "Am I the one who said this was a harmless flirtation? Am I the one who didn't want to talk about it anymore?"

"That's enough!" he roared, one hand coming up as if to strike her.

She fell back a step, stunned at his rage.

"You will not speak to me in that manner," he shouted. "Do you hear me?"

Inga dropped her head as tears sprang to her eyes. Suddenly, she felt hands on her shoulders, pushing her out of the way. She turned and saw that her son had taken her place. He was standing toe-to-toe with his father, eyes wide, nostrils flaring. "And you will not speak to Mama that way either, Papa! I am the one to blame here. Leave Mama out of it."

His father's fist cocked back. "You dare talk to me like that?" he shouted.

"No!" Inga cried.

But to her horror, her son didn't flinch. He actually stepped closer, thrusting his face next to his father's. "You want to hit me? Do it! But you'd better make it hard enough that I can't get up again."

At that moment, two things happened simultaneously. Wolfie rushed into the room, his face a mask of horror. And Inga thrust herself in between these two raging bulls and shoved them roughly apart. "Stop it!" she cried. "Stop it this instant!"

Wolfie grabbed his brother-in-law's arm and pulled him toward the door. "Come, Hans. I think maybe you need some time alone to cool down."

To Inga's surprise, after staring at Wolfie for a moment, her husband nodded and let Wolfie lead him out of the room. For a long moment, mother and son stood there, still too shocked to speak. Then finally, Young Hans stepped toward her and tried to take her in his arms. "I'm sorry, Mama. I am so sorry."

She jerked free of him, and tears came again. "Oh, Hans. Can't you see that your choices have consequences? You can't just go blithely on your way not caring how things will come out in the end."

"Mama, I . . ."

"Go get ready. I think it's best that you leave for the academy now."

His head dropped. "Yes, Mama." He stepped around her and started for the door.

"Hans?"

He turned back. "Yes, Mama?"

"You will not dance with Lady Magdalena tonight. Do you understand that?"

The anger was instantly back in his eyes. "Do you take me for an idiot, Mama? We would never do something as public as that.

Not until after she's talked to her parents about us. And she's going to wait until they get to Scotland to do that."

"Oh, my dearest boy," she said, more hurt than she could ever remember. "I could never think of you as an idiot. You are far too brilliant." She turned and started away but then spun around again. "But what I can't understand is how someone with a mind like yours could be so utterly devoid of even the tiniest lick of common sense. It is like you are still four years old, Hans. Can you not even see that?"

She didn't wait for an answer before quickly leaving the room.

• • •

Inga was waiting up when Young Hans tiptoed through the front door and shut it quietly behind him. When he turned and saw her, he gave a little yelp and jumped back.

"Mama! You startled me."

"Sorry." She glanced at the clock on the wall. It was almost quarter to one in the morning.

He stopped. "Has Paula—"

"*Nein.* Paula is sleeping. No pains tonight so far."

"Then you should be in bed."

She took him by the hand and led him into the kitchen and then carefully shut the door.

"Is Papa asleep?"

"No. From the sounds he's making, I think he passed out shortly after his head hit the pillow."

Hans chuckled softly. "You mean that noise he makes that sounds like a passing freight train?" He dropped into a chair. "I don't know how you sleep with that."

She gave him a fleeting smile. "I try to snore as loudly as he does. How was the banquet and ball?"

"The food was unbelievable. Table after table of all kinds of exotic dishes."

"And the dance?"

"Well, I didn't dance with Magdalena, if that's what you mean."

"Did you dance with anyone?"

"Yes. Almost every dance."

"*Gut.* Good for you."

"Mama, I . . ." He shook his head and sat back again.

"I stayed up because I want to say something to you, Hans."

"I'm sorry I lied to you."

"I know, but that's not it. I want to talk about you."

"What about me?"

She drew in a breath and then sighed deeply. "Hans, you are a remarkable young man. You know that, and we know that. Everyone who knows you recognizes it."

"*Danke,*" he said warily. "But?"

"There are no buts about that," she said. "You are gifted. You are talented. You are extremely bright. Your father and I know that you will go far, that you will make something of yourself. Maybe you will even become rich and famous someday."

"Maybe I will marry someone who is rich and famous." He flashed her a defiant smile. "That would help, don't you think?"

"Ah, Hans. My little Hans. Can't you see it? This thing with the young Lady von Kruger will never work. It's a fairy tale, son. Only you are the Cinderella taking out the cinders and the ashes, and she is the beautiful princess. Only in fairy tales do royal families allow their children to marry the boy who cleans out the ashes and draws water from the well."

"It's different with us, Mama. I know you can't see that, but it is. People here don't care what my background is. You saw Lady von Kruger at the awards ceremony. You heard what she said about me. She praised me for who I am, not where I came from."

"And rightly so, but that is a very different matter from letting you marry her daughter."

"Maybe it won't come to that. I know that. And Magdalena and I are not saying we certainly will marry, only that it might be someday. It would have to be after I finish university and establish myself, make some money."

His mother wanted to weep. Oh, how blind were the young. How foolish were their hearts. Blind enough that they refused to see, foolish enough that they refused to listen. So she tried another approach. "Perhaps it will all work out as you hope, but you are only seventeen, Hans. She is only sixteen. If she tells her parents that you are talking about marriage now, one of two things will happen."

He was staring at the floor and refused to look up.

"Either they will pull her out of school and send her somewhere else, or . . ."

His head snapped up. "Or what?" He snorted in disgust. "They'll kick *me* out of school?"

"They are not going to let this happen, Hans. They are not."

"I am one of their top students. I plan to be valedictorian next year. The University of Berlin has already talked to them about giving me a full scholarship. That brings a lot of prestige to the academy. They are not going to kick me out of school."

"And who influences the university to give those scholarships?" she exclaimed. "Count and Countess von Kruger."

He said nothing, just clamped his jaw and stared past her.

"Will you do one thing for me, Hans?"

He didn't move. She leaned forward, eyes hard. "I am your mama, Hans. And I have a right to be concerned. If you don't want to talk to me, then I'll go wake up your father."

"What?" he grunted. "What do you want me to do?"

"Before Magdalena goes, you have to tell her not to say anything to her parents about the two of you. Not yet. Give it this next year. If you've managed to keep it a secret this long, then you can do it for another year. At this time next year, if you still feel the same way about each other, then you can tell them together. Then they can't stop your schooling. Then you'll be eighteen and a legal adult, at least."

She sat back. There was nothing more she could think of to say that might reach him. Now it was up to him.

His eyes searched hers as a wave of emotion played across his face. Then finally he gave a quick nod. "Okay, I will do this much. I will tell Magdalena not to say anything to her parents. We'll keep it a secret. But I promise to do that only for the summer. Come this fall, we will evaluate the situation and decide whether or not to keep our love secret. I'm sorry, but that's the best I can promise you."

Inga was actually elated. She hadn't expected to get anything from him. "I have your word on it?"

"Yes, Mama."

"No more lies?"

"No, Mama. And what about Papa? Are you going to tell him all of this?"

"When you go to the train station with him, you tell your papa that you've asked Magdalena not to say anything to her parents and that you're not going to see each other this summer. Then the rest—"

"Wait!" he blurted. "Who said anything about not seeing

her? I only promised that we wouldn't tell her parents. When she comes back from Scotland, I plan to see her. I'll just be really careful that no one sees us."

Inga sighed. She was very tired, and the lateness of the hour was only part of the reason. "All right," she conceded. "Tell your father that she's not going to say anything to the count and countess now. That will be a huge relief to him." Her voice became very earnest. "He worries a lot about you getting kicked out of school. You know how much your education means to him."

"I know." Hans sighed too. "I'll make sure he knows I won't jeopardize that."

"*Gut*. The rest can be between you and me for now."

"Are you sure he will accept that?"

"Yes. He won't like it, but he will accept it." She hesitated and then added, "Though he is very angry, he doesn't like confronting you." She sighed with some bitterness. "That's my job. Your job is to convince him that you are not going to throw this all away."

He slowly got to his feet. He came over, bent down, and kissed his mother on the cheek. There was very little affection in the gesture. "All right, Mama. You have my word."

CHAPTER 9

July 31, 1913—Von Kruger Academy, Bogenhausen, Munich

Hans Otto was at the small desk in his dormitory room. He was barefoot and wore no shirt, only his trousers. A small fan whirred softly from his small bookshelf, but it barely stirred the oppressive heat. His window was thrown fully open. That made no difference either. The leaves on the sycamore tree just outside his room were as motionless as if they were carved from stone.

He straightened and then leaned back to scratch his back against slats in the chair. His whole body was clammy with sweat. With a sigh, he reached over and shut the book he'd been studying, sticking his notebook inside to mark his place. How was he supposed to study when he was smothering to death?

He pulled a face. "Come on, Eckhardt," he muttered. "It's not the heat that's bothering you."

He had been at this for nearly an hour, and he hadn't comprehended more than a paragraph or two of his textbook, which for him was very unusual. It was a fascinating study, but the title alone was so ponderous that it was enough to put you to sleep: *Rudolf Diesel and the Sparkless Internal Combustion Engine.*

Normally Hans was enthralled by the brilliance of Rudolf Diesel's design for an internal combustion engine. He wasn't the one who first discovered that if air is compressed it generates heat, and that if it is compressed with enough pressure it gets hot enough to ignite fuel without using a spark plug. But Rudolf Diesel had taken the concept and developed it into an engine that generated the highest thermal efficiency of any internal combustion engine available. Since then, Diesel's engines had become part of engineering history. They were everywhere—in factories, on steamships, in railroad engines, in trucks. Hans found all of it so fascinating that he was now thinking he might make it his specialty when he went to university.

He groaned. But right now, all he could think of was Magdalena. Today was the last day of July. Today her family was scheduled to pack up their things in Scotland and start back for Germany. Magdalena had told Hans she would be back by the fourth of August. That was this coming Monday. And for the last week, he'd been able to think of little else.

They hadn't written, of course. At the graduation ball, they had been able to snatch a few minutes together behind the auditorium, where he told her that he had decided it wasn't wise to tell her parents yet. He had expected a fight but was relieved when she readily agreed. He had then asked if he could write to her. She had panicked. "No, Hans! The servants always get the mail, and they always take it straight to Papa. You can't do that."

He made no attempt to hide his disappointment. She had leaned in and kissed him hard. "I know," she said. "I'm going to miss you so much. But now that we're not telling my parents about us, we can't let them know we're writing. We just can't."

So he had not heard anything from her in almost six weeks. And with each passing week, his ability to concentrate on his studies diminished exponentially.

He looked up as he heard the murmur of men's voices and footsteps coming down the hall. A moment later there was a sharp rap on the door.

"Come!"

The door pushed open and two men stepped in. Hans leaped to his feet. "Hey, Elders!" he cried in English. "How are you?"

Elder Reissner moved forward and gripped his hand. "*Sehr gut*, Hans," he replied in German. Then in English, "We're very good."

Elder Jackson joined them and slapped Hans lightly on the back. "What are you doing sitting in here? Let's go find some shade. This is unbearable."

"You're telling me!" Hans grabbed his shirt and pulled it on without buttoning it and then shoved his feet into his loafers. "Let's go."

"Where have you guys been?" he asked as they started down the hall. "I was beginning to think you had gone back to America."

"Not America. Somewhere a little closer to home."

Something in the way he said it made Hans's ears prick up. "Like where?"

"Let's talk about it when we get outside."

"Okay. I'm all for outside."

Reissner laughed. "Your English is getting really good."

"*Danke.*"

"You've only got one problem."

"What's that?"

"You speak it with an American accent. And you're

picking up American slang. That won't make you very popular in Europe."

Hans brushed that aside as they exited the dormitory and headed for the deep shade of the sycamore tree. "Perhaps I shall go to America and make my fortune. Then when I come back filthy rich, no one will care what I sound like."

He threw himself down on the grass, kicking off his shoes, still not bothering to button his shirt. "Ah. This is much better. Thank you for saving my life." Then he squinted up at them. "Look, I know you have to look like missionaries, but can't you at least take off your jackets? If anybody sees you sitting here in suit coats, they'll think you are a couple of . . . How do you say it? Loo— uh—"

"Loonies?"

"*Ja*, loonies." He grinned. "And no one wants to talk to loonies."

He watched them take off their jackets and fold them up on the grass. "So," he said. "Back to my question. Where have you guys been?"

"Jail," Jackson said nonchalantly.

"Come on," Hans scoffed, "I'm serious."

"All right," Reissner said. "We were kicked out of our apartment by the police two nights ago, but we were able to find a place that gave us two nights of free lodging."

"Get serious, guys. What kind of place does that?"

"Jail," Jackson said again, grinning.

Hans stopped dead. "You *are* serious?"

"Yes," Reissner answered. "Very serious."

"Who did you rob?"

"Very funny. Actually, the charge was not robbery. It was being a Mormon."

"Go on, they don't arrest you for that. Bismarck secured freedom of religion for Germany."

Jackson pulled a face. "Things are getting better, but there are a lot of towns and cities that still think there's a law against our Church holding meetings in Germany. In Berlin—well, actually, in all of Prussia—you can be fined 300 marks or sentenced to six months in jail for even attending one of our meetings."

"I find that hard to believe, to be honest. Are you sure these are not just wild rumors?"

That clearly irritated Elder Reissner. "Okay, so how's this for a rumor? I've talked to elders who were there when it happened. It was in June of 1910."

"When did you come to Germany?" Hans interrupted.

"About fifteen months after that. So anyway, there was a meeting in Berlin and—"

"Wait. You've been here two years?"

"Almost."

"No wonder your German is so good. How much longer will you stay?"

"We normally stay three years. My tentative release date is in October of next year. So you've got me for a while."

"Good. Okay, go on."

"Okay. We have apostles in our Church, just as Jesus did when He was on the earth. An apostle is one of the most senior of our leaders. We view them with the greatest respect. Kind of like Catholics would a cardinal."

"I understand."

"So in June of 1910, one of our apostles, whose name was Rudger Clawson, came over from England to visit our mission. A meeting was called for all missionaries and members who could make it to Berlin."

Hans was listening intently, finally starting to take them seriously.

"So, they rented a big hall and all gathered there. There were several hundred missionaries, members of the Church, and what we call investigators—people who are learning about the Church to see if they are interested in joining. Elder Clawson was speaking. Suddenly, there was a commotion in the back of the hall and a bunch of policemen came busting in. One of them went up to the stand and very rudely shoved Elder Clawson aside, right while he was talking. He shouted that the meeting was illegal and was now ended. "If you can prove you are of German citizenship, you are free to go," he shouted. "All others will be immediately banished from the city of Berlin and the state of Prussia.

"Twenty-five Americans, mostly missionaries but also Elder Clawson and a few students who were here on valid student visas, were marched off to jail and held there overnight. The next day they were escorted to the Prussian border, warned never to come back, and dumped off to fend for themselves."

Hans was shaking his head. "If I didn't know you, I'd say you were crazy, but . . . Wow! It's really hard to believe that they're throwing you guys in jail."

"Hey," Jackson said, "getting thrown in jail here is so common that it's almost a rite of passage for us. If you haven't been in jail, you're not considered a real missionary yet. Now Elder Reissner here, he has four incarcerations under his belt including this latest one, so he's considered the elder statesman of incarceration." He giggled. "Get it? *Elder* statesman?"

Hans rolled his eyes and looked at Reissner. "How many times have you really been in jail?"

"Four times. Twenty-three days all together."

"Wow, I would never have believed that possible here. But you are out of jail now, so where are you going to stay tonight?"

"Actually, that's why we came to see you."

Hans gave him a sharp look. "You want to stay with me?"

"No, no. That could get you in trouble with the school. Not because we're Latter-day Saints, but because we're not students."

"*Ja*, I can't even have a fellow student sleep in my room without permission from the senior resident."

"So," Reissner said, taking a quick breath, "we had another idea."

"Go on."

"We've learned that local police don't often share information with other cities and towns, so if we're kicked out of one place, we just pack up and move to a new place and start again."

"I don't see any luggage."

"It's at a member's house. So, here's my question for you: don't you have a sister or something who lives over in the west part of Munich?"

"Not a sister. An aunt. And my uncle. Yes, they live over in Menzing. Know where that is?"

They both nodded. Reissner looked like he wanted to say something but then changed his mind and shook his head.

"What?" Hans asked.

"I . . . Look, I don't want to put you on the spot, so let me ask it this way. Would you have a problem with giving us their address?"

"You want to teach them?" he scoffed. "My uncle is even more agnostic than I am."

"No, no!" he said hastily. "It's just that we don't know anyone out that way. And we don't know the area at all. So I was thinking that maybe they could steer us to some places that would be available for rent."

"Oh, is that all? No problem, Elder. My aunt would be happy to help you. My uncle too. He's with the Public Works Department here in Munich, so he knows the city well. Remind me when we get back inside and I'll give you their address."

"That would be great. *Danke schön.*"

"You're welcome. I'll also write a short note introducing you if you'd like."

"All the better."

They talked for nearly half an hour, first about the mission conference, then about Hans's schooling, and then about life in general. Finally, Elder Jackson said, "I saw where Leipzig won your national soccer match last week."

Hans hooted. "Soccer? What kind of word is that? We don't 'sock' the ball. That's against the rules. We kick it or butt it with our heads."

Jackson looked crestfallen. "Oh, yeah. So what do you call it again?"

"*Fussball.*"

Jackson puckered his lips and pronounced it with a long ooh sound—"*Foohsbahl.*"

They all had a good laugh at Jackson's expression. Then Hans got to his feet and looked across the quad toward the clock tower. "Hey," he said. "It's 11:30. What say we go to the *Ratskeller* and grab some lunch? I'm starving. And I'm buying."

The two elders exchanged quick glances.

"What?" Hans asked.

"Uh . . . Actually, there's another reason we came to see you, Hans."

"Oh, brother. Not another jail story."

"No. Nothing is wrong," Elder Reissner said. "It's just that . . . Well, you know why we're here in Germany, Hans. We've come to teach the gospel. Our mission president talked to us about that at the conference. He said that sometimes we missionaries make friends among the German people and spend a lot of time with them, but we never get to teach them the gospel because they're not really interested."

Hans grunted. "Like me, *ja*?"

"*Ja*." Elder Reissner took a quick breath. "He didn't ask us to stop seeing you, but he did recommend that if you're not in-terested in our message, perhaps we should start spending more time seeking out others who might be."

Hans was pulling on his lower lip now, but finally he nodded. "*Ja*, I can see the sense in that."

"Any chance at all that you are interested?" Reissner asked.

"Sorry, guys. I wish I were. I like you two a lot, but religion just isn't my thing."

"The other problem is," Jackson added, "if we move over to the west side of Munich, it will be much farther for us to come over here to see you. We're on a limited budget, and . . ."

"I understand. That's no problem. I love talking to you guys, but . . . Well, I understand." He reached out a hand to Reissner and hauled him to his feet. "Okay, so *Ratskeller*, here we come."

The Ratskeller

The restaurant was busy, but not as packed as it was when school was in full session. They found a corner table inside to get out of the sun and ordered. The elders tried to settle for light fare, but Hans wouldn't hear of it. He was saddened to think that they wouldn't see one another as frequently as before. He had come to view these two young men as some of the best friends he had. So he ordered for them and chose the largest dishes on the menu. He also pulled the waiter down close and ordered a large stein of beer, telling him to put it in front of Elder Jackson. Hans almost fell off his chair laughing when Jackson turned a shade of green at the smell of the beer under his nose. Then Hans placed it in front of himself.

As they were finishing their food about half an hour later, Reissner's head came up. He was seated so that he was facing the door of the restaurant. Hans saw that he was staring at something and half turned to look. But he was behind a pillar and couldn't see the door or what had caught Reissner's attention.

Reissner took another bite and then lifted his head again. He leaned forward, squinting a little. "Hmm. That girl looks familiar."

Again Hans turned. Now he could see the back of a man but nothing more. He reached across and nudged the missionary. "I thought you elders weren't supposed to be looking at girls."

Reissner shot him a look and then stared some more. "Do you know her, Elder Jackson?"

"Nope," he said. "Never seen her before."

"Never mind. But I could swear I know her from some—" He stopped and snapped his fingers. "Oh, yeah. Remember, Elder? We saw her about a month ago at the *Johannistag* celebration."

"The what?" Jackson was blank.

"St. John the Baptist's Day. We went with the Arnheims. Remember? They had that huge bonfire."

"Oh, yeah," he said. "And she was on the grandstand with her parents. Count and Countess something or other."

Hans lunged across the table and grabbed Reissner's arm. "What did you say? You saw Magdalena?"

"If that's her name, yes."

"A month ago?"

"Yeah, about that."

"That's not possible. She's with her family in Scotland."

"Not that day, she wasn't," Reissner said. "I'm sure that's her. She's beautiful. You don't forget a face like that."

Hans didn't hear any of that. He nearly knocked his chair over as he leaped up and spun around. In two steps he cleared the pillar and had a full view of the room. For a moment he didn't see anyone that even resembled Magdalena, but then a movement caught his eye and he saw a waitress leading a couple toward one of the small back rooms where people could dine in private. He only got a glimpse, but it was enough. It was her! She was back! He felt like leaping into the air and shouting hallelujah.

Working his way through the tables and the thinning crowd, he followed after the waitress. She was just closing the door on the room as he entered the hallway, so he stopped and examined a painting on the wall until she was past him and out of view. Then he moved forward. Hesitating for only a moment, he knocked on the door.

"Come in." It was the man's voice.

Hans opened the door and stopped. They were sitting together, shoulder to shoulder, on the same side of the table so that they both faced the door. He could scarcely believe it. It was indeed Lady Magdalena Margitte Maria von Kruger. And she was as radiant and beautiful as he had ever seen her. The pair's heads were together, and they were talking softly to each other. Looking up in surprise, the man started to get up. Magdalena's head came up. She gave a little squeal and fell back. "Hans?"

Hans recognized the man—or boy, actually—instantly. He was a student at the academy as well. His name was Rolf Godecke. He was a year older than Hans and had just graduated with a specialty in European history. They hadn't had a lot of classes together, but Hans had always liked him because—his eyes narrowed—because he was the son of a clothing merchant in Augsburg. Like Hans, he was one of the twenty-five percent of the student body who came from lower-class families. All of that flashed through Hans's head in an instant.

Before he could process it, however, Magdalena leaped to her feet.

"Hans? What are you doing here? I thought you went home for summer break."

"No, Maggie. What are *you* doing here?" He started forward. "I didn't think you were coming back until Monday." He wanted to run to her and sweep her up in his arms, but she didn't move from behind the table, and Rolf was standing between them.

"When did you get back?" he finally asked, suddenly aware of how awkward this was.

"Uh . . . a little while ago."

"I am so glad to see you again."

Rolf looked back and forth between them, his expression a combination of awkward confusion and open irritation. Hans ignored him. "Look, can I talk to you for a minute?" He looked at Rolf. "Would that be all right? I'll bring her right back."

Turning, he looked at Magdalena. It was clear how Rolf felt about it, but she finally nodded. "I'll just be a minute, Rolf. All right?"

He nodded and stepped back, making room for Magdalena to come out around the table. As she came up to Hans, he went to take her by the arm, but she jerked away and hurried past him out into the hall. He quickly followed.

As soon as the door shut behind him, she turned on him.

"You can't do this, Hans. You just can't just barge in on me like this when I'm with someone."

He was looking around and didn't answer. He took a few steps and opened the next door. Another small dining room. And it was empty. He held the door open and motioned for her to go in. She did, her skirts swirling angrily as she pushed past him. He checked the hall once more to make sure Rolf wasn't going to follow them and then shut the door.

For a moment, he just stared at her, drinking her in like a dying man gulps down water. Then he moved to her, took her in his arms, and leaned down to kiss her. She jerked her head away and pulled free of him. "No, Hans! Not now."

"Aw, come on, Maggie. I haven't seen you for six weeks. I've missed—"

"Don't call me Maggie. I've told you. I hate that name."

"You never said that. You told me you loved it when I called you Maggie."

"Well, I don't. So say what you have to say. I need to get back with Rolf."

"I'm sorry," he said contritely. "I guess I shouldn't have barged in on you, but when I saw you, I . . ." He took a quick breath. "When can I see you?"

She looked away. "I'm not sure. I'm not in school, you know. And it's not like you can come to the house and visit me."

"But that's got to happen sometime, right? We talked about this before. About how someday maybe we might get married . . ." He let the thought die as he saw the expression on her face. She was incredulous. Shocked.

"You didn't think I was serious, surely?"

"I—"

"Oh, Hans. We had some fun, that's all. Lots of laughs. I like you. You're a great kid."

Anger flared inside him. "Kid? I'm a year older than you."

"It's over, Hans. That's why I didn't come see you when I got back." She reached out and let her fingertips brush his cheeks. "It was a lot of fun, but it's over."

Magdalena pushed past him and left the room, slamming the door behind her. He stood there, staring blankly at the door—hurt, angry, confused. And then, an image from years before flashed into his mind. One day, during recess at the school in Oberammergau, the boys had noticed a magnificent thoroughbred horse tied to the hitching rail at one of the wood-carving shops. In awe, the boys gathered around, admiring it. Then, as Hans had watched, a large, black horsefly had landed on its haunches. The horse's flesh rippled a little, trying to shake it off. The horse noticeably flinched as the fly bit in. Hans stepped in to shoo the fly away. The horse was faster. Its tail flicked up and knocked the horsefly away. When it flew back a moment later, the horse did it again. After that the fly disappeared.

Back at school, Hans had told Herr Holzer about what they had seen. Now he remembered his reply. "Hans, there is a lesson to be learned in that. A horsefly may bite the horse and cause it to flinch, but when all is said and done, the thoroughbred is still a thoroughbred, and the horsefly is still a horsefly."

Later, as he took Elders Reissner and Jackson to the trolley stop and gave them directions to find his Aunt Paula's house, Hans was still smoldering and still half dazed. Even though the missionaries could tell that something very upsetting had happened in the *Ratskeller,* Hans said nothing about it, and they didn't ask. Now, walking back to campus, he was muttering to himself under his breath.

"She's moved on. That's what it is. She's found some other poor working-class slob to bestow her radiant presence on. Does that give her some kind of perverse satisfaction? Stooping down to mingle with the unwashed masses? Seeing how the lower half of humanity lives? Tolerating the horsefly to see what it feels like?"

His next thought was grating on him even more than the first. "She didn't even say she was sorry. Not once. She never once said she was sorry."

Chapter Notes

During the years that the Church was waging a legal battle against the United States government to get plural marriage legally recognized, the negative publicity filled newspapers all across the country. It quickly spread across the Atlantic, and the missionary work in Europe was heavily affected. In England, the Church came under a lot of persecution, but generally the British protection of religious liberty prevented local governments from stopping the Church from functioning.

In Germany, however, though there were laws protecting freedom of worship, these were enforced with differing levels of vigor throughout the fragmented German states. In the 1890s and during the first decade of the twentieth century, many cities and states passed laws making it illegal for Latter-day Saint missionaries to proselytize and for citizens to join the Church or attend its meetings. Mormons were accused of preaching a religion that advocated immoral behavior and disloyalty to the government. The immoral charge was an irony, since it was very common for a German man to have a mistress. Everyone knew this and accepted it, but people were outraged at the idea of a man having two legal wives at the same time.

Nevertheless, so many missionaries were being banned from Germany that in 1904 the German and Swiss Missions were combined, and many missionaries were moved to German-speaking Switzerland. Eventually the persecution began to ease, but the missions were kept combined.

After World War I, things had changed enough that in 1924 a new German-Austrian Mission was divided from the Swiss-German Mission.

It was a common tactic during those years of persecution for missionaries who were thrown out of one location to move to another city or town where they could continue their work for months before the authorities caught up with them. Because this action was often precipitated by local magistrates enforcing laws that were in contradiction to German national law, missionaries felt that bypassing these laws was not contrary to the Church's commitment to honor and obey the law (see *Mormons and Germany: 1914–1933*, 26–34; and *Mormonism in Germany*, 40–60).

Banishment and jailing of missionaries became so common that it did become a bit of a badge of honor for missionaries. One elder joked that it was a good thing that he was banished to another area, because "the intention of the president was to transfer me anyway." Another wrote his family saying that he had been blessed with another night of "free lodging."

The story of Elder Rudger A. Clawson, of the Quorum of the Twelve Apostles, who was serving as European Mission President at that time, is found in *Mormonism in Germany*, 54.

CHAPTER 10

August 6, 1913—Graswang Village, Bavaria, Germany

Inga came through the front door and looked around. The house was empty. She turned toward the stairs. "Annalisa? Is anyone here?"

A head appeared at the top of the stairs. It was Annalisa, Ilse's first child and Inga's oldest granddaughter. "I'm here, Grandmama. Mama and the others are out in the barn with Grandpapa."

"Run and tell Grandpapa that I'm back from the village. And tell him we have a letter from Hans."

"Yes, Grandmama." She ran lightly down the stairs and out the back door.

Inga moved to the table and set down her bag of purchases. Dropping into a chair, she took the envelope from her apron pocket and tore it open. "I hope you remembered to tell us what train you will be on," she murmured.

But when she extracted the letter, she was taken totally aback. There were two lines of hastily scrawled words, with a signature dashed off below them. She let the letter flutter to the table and sat back. "No, Hans. Not again."

Two minutes later when her husband came in from the barn, she was still sitting there, staring out the window. "So what does he say?" he asked, coming over. "When is he coming?"

Slowly turning, she picked up the letter and, in a dull voice, read, "'Sorry. Can't make it home. Too much preparation for fall classes. I'm in the midst of finals. Got to run. Write later.'"

As he sat down at the table beside her, she took a quick breath. "Hans?"

"*Ja, Schatzi?*"

"I want to go to Munich."

He jerked up. "What? Now?"

"No. Not tomorrow either. I have to get things ready. But on Friday. I've saved enough money to purchase the train ticket. And I'll stay with Paula, of course. That will be good too. With Wolfie's new promotion, he's gone a lot more. I think she's struggling a little with the new baby."

He fell back in his chair, not answering. She waited, letting him sort it out in his head.

Finally, he took a deep breath and then let it out in a long, slow sigh. "You think this is about the girl?"

"What else?" she muttered. "He promised he'd come home for a whole week. Now this."

He said nothing.

"It worries me, Hans. What if those two foolish children take it into their heads to tell her parents they are talking about marriage? You know—" Her mouth fell open as a worse thought hit her. "Surely he wouldn't run off with her and get married?"

He scoffed openly. "*Nein*. He would never do that." But even as he said it, she could see the impact her question was having on him. "Would he?"

She looked away, wringing her hands. That did it. Her husband jumped up, "If I helped you, we could have you catch the afternoon train tomorrow."

Relief shot through her. "Tomorrow? Yes! That's good. I think time may be critical."

He reached out and found her hand. "I don't understand this," he said. "When I first saw you, I was smitten. But I never lost my head over you like he's done."

"No. You never did, Hans."

"Stupid boy! He could lose everything." He leaned over to give her a perfunctory kiss. "Go. Go quickly."

"*Danke, Schatzi.*" She paused for a moment, then, "I may stay as long as a week."

"Stay two weeks if that's what it takes. Do whatever you have to do. Just stop this nonsense once and for all."

August 7, 1913—Munich Main Station

Wolfgang Groll was waiting on the platform as Inga descended from the train. He rushed forward, all smiles. "*Guten Tag*, Inga." He bent down and kissed her on both cheeks and then took her bag. "So good to see you again. Paula is so excited to have you back so soon. And the children are too."

"*Danke*, Wolfie. I am excited to see them too."

He frowned slightly. "There is one slight problem. I have a new position at my work." The smile was instantly back. "I am the manager of my section now and supervise nine other people."

"That's wonderful." To her surprise, her voice was suddenly husky. She reached out and touched his arm briefly. "You are a good man, Wolfie. You are a good husband to Paula. And a good father to your children." She swallowed quickly. "And you are good to me as well."

She could see that her words had touched him. He looked down at the ground for a moment and then whispered, "*Danke schön*, Inga." Then he brightened. "But here is my problem. When I asked my supervisor if I could come and meet you here, he was very happy to let me go. But we are working on a report that must be turned in tomorrow."

"All right," she said, not sure what that meant.

"So, I have to go back to the office now. I'll be working late, so I can't take you home."

A stab of panic hit her. He rushed on. "But it's all right. I have arranged for a small carriage and driver. He will take you all the way to our home so that you don't have to worry about changing trolleys."

"But . . . That will be too much money, Wolfie."

He leaned forward, grinning as he cupped his hand and whispered in her ear. "Don't tell anyone, Inga, but with the new position, I got a ten percent increase in my salary."

• • •

As the carriage pulled up in front of number 16 Herrenstrasse, Inga began fumbling in her purse. The driver, a congenial, grandfatherly man, turned in his seat. "No, Frau. Herr Groll already gave me a generous tip." He wrapped the reins around a stubby post attached to the wagon seat and jumped down. "Here, let me help you with your bag."

He helped her down first and then retrieved her bag and set it on the sidewalk beside her. She waved and called out her thanks as he drove away. Immensely relieved that she hadn't had to traverse that much of Munich on her own, she picked up her bag and started up the steps. But she had only got halfway up when the door opened and a tall young man in a suit stepped out, followed by a second a moment later.

She stopped. So did they. The sun was low in the sky and shining directly in their eyes. The first man raised a hand to shade them. "*Guten Tag*," he said politely. Then almost instantly, he leaned forward, peering at her. "*Hallo!* Is that you, Frau Eckhardt?"

The sun was partially in her eyes too. Surprised at being called by name, she set her bag down. "And how is that you know me?"

But even as she asked, she looked up into his face and recognized who he was. "Ah, you are Young Hans's friends. Uh . . . *Kirchenältester* Reissner, right?"

His face lit up with pleasure. "And you remember my companion, *Kirchenältester* Jackson? *Schwester* Groll said you were coming, but she didn't expect you for another hour." He smiled warmly. "Here, let me help you with your bag."

She nodded, barely hearing. *Sister?* He had called Paula sister. Had he meant to say "your sister"? But his German was flawless, as she remembered from before.

She didn't have time to think about it. Elder Jackson had stepped back and was holding the door for her. Reissner was already entering the house with her bag. And then a thought struck her, and her heart jumped with joy. "Is Hans Otto with you?" That would explain how two missionaries she had met at the academy were now at Paula's home.

"No," Elder Reissner said regretfully, "but we were just on our way to see him. *Schwester* Groll has asked if we will go to the academy and tell him that you are here. She's hoping he can join us for supper."

Her head was swirling. *Us?* Would they be eating here too? And he had called Paula *Schwester* Groll again. She had heard correctly the first time. He was calling her *his* sister. How strange was that?

And then all was forgotten as she heard cries from inside the house and the pounding of steps on the stairs. "Auntie Inga, Auntie Inga!" Inga dropped to one knee and opened her arms as Paula's daughter Gretl came barreling through the door at her.

• • •

When Hans returned in company with the elders, it was as if none of their last time together had ever happened. Nor did he seem the least bit surprised that his mother was there. If there was any coolness in his manner, she could not detect it.

"Hello, Mama. How good to see you again." He gave her a quick hug and kissed her on the cheek and then immediately turned to Gretl, Paula's daughter, who was seven and absolutely worshiped her handsome, older cousin.

Young Hans had always liked his Aunt Paula and Uncle Wolfgang. Their first two children were both married now with children of their own. They lived in Garmisch-Partenkirchen, and Hans rarely saw them now. But he loved his cousin, who adored him, and took surprising joy in Bruno, the new baby who was two months old. With Magdalena out of his life now, he came over to stay with them every two or three weeks. They were, in many ways, his family now.

• • •

When Wolfie called just before supper time to say that he would probably not get home until after ten, Hans and the missionaries volunteered to help his mother and aunt with supper. Working together, they prepared a delicious dinner of Wiener schnitzel, sauerkraut, and a decadently rich chocolate raspberry Bavarian torte cake. Inga, surprised how easily the missionaries fit in, was dying of curiosity about how they had come to know her sister's family. But Paula was so eager to tell Inga everything about Wolfie's new job and all about her married children that she didn't interrupt her.

As they cleaned up the dishes, Inga's curiosity only deepened. The elders continued to call Paula *Schwester* Groll, and when they spoke of Wolfie, they always called him *Bruder* Groll. Brother and Sister Groll? And yet they unfailingly addressed her son as Hans or Hans Otto and her as Frau Eckhardt. And there was the fact that Gretl played with the missionaries almost as much as she did with Hans. That indicated to Inga that this was not the first time the missionaries had been there.

She finally pushed it all aside, determined to concentrate on what she was going to say to Hans when they were finally alone. But as they finished the dishes, Hans announced that he had to return to the academy tonight. Inga reacted immediately to that. "Do you have class tomorrow?"

"No. Classes are finished for the summer."

"Do you have a test tomorrow?"

Warily, sensing where this was going, he replied, "No. I finished my last final this morning."

"Then you are not going back tonight."

He raised a fork in protest and opened his mouth to say something, but one look from her cut him off. Finally, he nodded. "Yes, Mama," he grumped.

No one dared smile except Paula. She caught Hans's eye and pulled a face. "Now you know what I grew up with," she said.

Elders Reissner and Jackson left right after supper, saying they had another appointment. Paula bade them good night and went off to nurse the baby, telling Gretl to go up and take a bath. Once they left, Inga got up from the table and crossed the hall into the sitting room. She never said a word to Hans, nor looked at him. After a moment, he got up and reluctantly followed. She stood at the door until he entered and then shut it behind her and sat down across from him.

As she fixed her gaze on him, he half groaned. "Does this have to happen tonight, Mama? I am very tired."

"You said you have to leave first thing tomorrow." She cocked her head. "If that's not true, then we can talk in the morning. If so . . ." She shrugged.

"I do," Hans grumbled. "I just learned that a boy in math and physics is slightly ahead of me in the race for valedictorian. So I'm going to use this break time to push forward. I am determined to have it."

"That's wonderful, Hans. I'm very pleased."

"What? No comment on how self-centered I am?"

That surprised her, but only the timing, not his bitterness. "I'm not here to talk about your pride, Hans."

"Oh, really? Then what are you here for?"

That helped her make up her mind. "All right then. Maybe it's time we stopped dancing around the maypole. I'm going to come right out with what I want to say."

"I think it's time."

She plunged right in. "Have you and that girl spoken with her parents about your relationship yet?"

His mouth dropped open for a second, and then he burst

out laughing. "First of all, Mama, she's not 'that girl.' Her name is Magdalena."

"Or Maggie, as I remember."

"No," he snapped. "She doesn't like that."

One eyebrow came up, but she said nothing.

"In the second place, she didn't enroll in summer school. She hasn't been on campus all summer."

"Really?"

"Yes, really. And in the third place, 'that girl' and I broke up a long time ago. It's over. There's nothing to talk to her parents about."

Jerking forward, she almost blurted, "I don't believe you," but the pain in his eyes was too real. He was neither lying nor joking about this.

"What happened?" she asked softly.

"What happened?" he shot back sarcastically. "I'll tell you what happened. I thought a lot about what you and Papa said that day, and, though I didn't like it, I decided you might be right. Maybe the von Krugers were not as progressive and for-ward-thinking as I thought. Maybe they would be furious if they thought their daughter and I were talking about marriage. And I decided that my schooling is everything right now. I couldn't risk losing it."

She sat back, her mind whirling. It was not that she didn't believe him. His emotions were too raw to be an act. But some-thing didn't feel quite right.

"Well, say something," he pleaded.

"I . . . I am very pleased to hear that, Hans, and your father will be too. He has been very worried about you being expelled. So, while I know how hard that must have been for you, it's for the best." Then, still bothered a little, she added, "How did Magdalena take it?"

He shrugged diffidently. "She cried a lot. Like girls do. Begged me not to do it. Vowed that her parents wouldn't object. But I could tell she knew better." He shrugged again. "So it's over. I haven't seen her since that night. And I heard just today that her parents are sending her to a private school in Italy this fall. So I won't be seeing her in the future either, which is good. It just makes it harder for her to be here."

The relief was almost dizzying, and Inga tried hard not to show it.

He looked up, glancing at the clock, and then turned to her, though his eyes were having a hard time holding hers. "So is that really all you came up for, Mama?" His tone was a little accusatory.

"Yes, and to help Paula with the baby." Then she decided to be completely honest. "I came because your last letter to us was so abrupt. You knew that we were worried about you and Magdalena, so when you said you weren't coming, we naturally assumed . . ."

He nodded, and she saw that he was softening a little. "Of course you did. I should have seen that. I was simply on my way to a special tutoring session with one of the teachers here. It was stupid of me not to see how that would come across."

He looked at the clock again. She glanced up too. It was 9:20. "Are you thinking of going back tonight?"

"I would like to, but I don't want you to be angry with me."

"Will you give me your word that this whole thing with Magdalena is over?"

"Unreservedly. We both know it's over."

"Then go. Go study. Go get that valedictorian honor."

"Maybe I can come over on a weekend. Not this weekend. I've got to really hit the books. But next weekend. Will you still be here?"

"I will be if you promise to come see me."

For the first time he smiled, and it was warm and genuine. "No more talk about Magdalena?"

"Are there any other girls I should know about?" she teased.

"None."

"Not even one you flirt with a little?"

He bent down and kissed her cheek. "Maybe when I graduate. Not before, though."

August 9, 1913

The morning sunlight was coming through the kitchen window and bathing Inga with its warmth and light.

The house was quiet this Saturday morning. Wolfie and Gretl were still asleep. Paula had fed Bruno and was now burping him while Inga peppered her with questions about the missionaries. "So," she said in conclusion, "in answer to your questions, yes. Since you were here last, we've seen a lot of the missionaries. They've been teaching me about their Church."

"Yes, they evidently talked a lot about their Church with Hans too."

"No, Inga, I'm not talking about casual conversations about their Church. They've been teaching formal lessons to me and Gretl."

"*What?* Really?"

Bruno let out a belch that echoed off the walls, causing them both to laugh. Then Paula got up and laid him down in the bassinet in one corner of the sitting room.

"And what are they teaching you?"

Paula pulled a blanket over the baby and then stood up and went to the bookshelf. After taking down a book with a light brown cover, she came back and held it out in front of Inga. "About this."

Inga looked up. "*Das Buch Mormon*? What is that?"

"It's their book."

"Whose book?"

"The missionaries'. Well, they brought it to me, but it actually is their Church's book. Haven't you ever heard of the Mormons?"

Inga shook her head. "Not until we met the elders that day at Hans's dorm."

"It's because they only work in the large cities." She leaned closer. "And they prefer being called Latter-day Saints."

"They think they're saints? I thought you had to be dead for at least a hundred years to be a saint."

Paula laughed merrily. "That was exactly what I said the first time they said that. But they say it means someone who is trying to live a good life. In the New Testament, followers of Christ were called Christians, but they also called themselves saints. The official name of their church is *Kirche Jesu Christi der Heiligen der Letzten Tage*. But because of this book, the Book of Mormon, many people call them Mormons."

"I see," Inga said slowly, which was not true in any way. She didn't see why a church would have one name and be called something else. She didn't see why Paula was giving her a copy of this book. And she didn't understand the fervor and earnestness her sister was showing as she spoke. Her tone was almost reverential, and it made Inga uncomfortable.

"All right, start at the beginning. How is it that the two missionaries from America, who were teaching my son English, ended up here, obviously teaching you? Does Wolfie know about this?"

"Of course," she said. "Wolfie and I don't keep secrets from each other."

"And he's all right with it?"

"He doesn't like it much, but he says if it makes me happy, then he has no objection. As long as I don't ask him to get baptized too."

Inga rocked back. "*Too?*"

Tears came to Paula's eyes. "Yes. I am going to be baptized two weeks from today by Elder Reissner in a small lake just outside the city. Gretl wants to be too, when she turns eight."

"Baptized! But you have already been baptized. You were baptized as an infant in the Catholic church in Unterammergau. You can't remember that, but I can. I was almost four at the time."

"I know. But this is different. You have to be baptized, and not just sprinkled on, to become a member of the Church."

"And will you attend this church?"

"Not yet. The nearest branch is closer to the center of the city, and that's too far from here. But the elders are in the process of organizing a branch that will be just half an hour away from here."

Her mind whirling, Inga absently closed the book and handed it back.

"No," Paula said. "That's your copy. Elder Reissner left it for you."

"I'm not looking for a church."

"Do you still go to church in Graswang?"

"Um . . . usually."

"That's what I thought."

"So that's why you're giving me this book. You want me to become a Mormon?"

"No, Inga. I just want you to read it. Then it's up to you what you do."

"Read what?"

They turned as Wolfie came into the kitchen, still stuffing his shirt into his pants. Paula quickly slid the book back across to Inga. Inga leaned forward, folding her arms so the book was hidden beneath them.

Wolfie saw that and smiled. "Watch it, Inga, or my wife will turn you into a Mormon too."

Paula stood up and went over to kiss him. "Would that be so bad? You told me you think I'm a better person since listening to the missionaries."

"You are," he teased, "but it's only been a couple of months. I think we have to wait longer than that to see if it sticks." He kissed her soundly and then looked around. "What's for breakfast?"

"There's some bratwurst and biscuits in the pan. The mustard is in the icebox. Inga and I already ate." As he moved away, she chided, "You were a sleepyhead this morning."

He rubbed his chin. "I didn't get in until almost midnight."

"Did you get it finished?"

"Yes, and my supervisor was very pleased. He'll present it to the higher-ups this morning." He opened the icebox and started rummaging around in it. Sighing, Paula went over. "It's right here," she said, retrieving the sharp German mustard from behind a milk bottle. She winked at Inga and then pushed her husband gently toward the table. "Sit down, *Schatzi*. I'll get it for you."

She got a plate and cup from the cupboard, laid the table for him, and dished up his food.

No wonder he lets her do what she wants, Inga thought. *She treats him like a king.*

Just then there was a shrill ring. Paula started toward the phone, but Wolfie was faster. He took the receiver off the hook and put it up to his year. "*Hallo!*" Pause. "*Ja*, this is the Grolls'. Who? Ah, *ja, ja*. One moment." He turned to Inga. "It's Hans."

Taken aback, she got up quickly and took the phone from her brother-in-law. "Hans? This is Mama. Is something wrong?"

Through the earpiece the voice sounded tinny and distorted, but she could tell it was him. "No, Mama. Everything is fine. But I wanted to give you some good news."

"I like good news," she said.

"When I got back last night, there was a letter waiting for me."

"A letter? From whom?"

"Do you remember me telling you about my friend whose father is a member of the Junker family? The one who owns a big truck factory in Nuremberg?"

"*Ja*, I remember." *Vaguely*, she thought.

"Well, his father wants to meet me. He's asked me to come to his factory and work for him during the break. He hinted that if he likes me, he might have a job for me when I graduate next summer."

"*Wunderbar*, Hans. That's wonderful."

"I know. I am very excited. But he wants me to catch a train to Nuremberg this morning. He's paying for my ticket. I'm leaving in half an hour. If he likes me, maybe I can work there from now until school starts again."

"*Das ist gut*, Hans. Why do you make it sound like a problem?"

"Because I won't be able to come and see you next weekend."

"Ah, I see." That was a disappointment. "But this is important, Hans. Very important. Your father will be so happy."

"I know. I wish we had a telephone at home so I could call him and tell him myself."

"I'll tell him, Hans. But write us as soon as you can and tell us all about it."

"I will, Mama. I have to go. I love you, Mama. *Tschüss!*"

When the call went dead, Wolfie took the phone from Inga and put it back on its hook.

"Did you hear him?" she asked them.

They both nodded. That was one of the things about their telephone—anyone in the room could hear both sides of every conversation.

"Your boy is a wonder," Wolfie said. "We're going to see great things from him."

"I know," she said. "Oh, Hans is going to be so proud. And when I tell him no more Magdalena, he'll be deliriously happy."

"Have they brought phone lines to Graswang now?" Paula asked.

"Yes, but only two or three people have telephones."

"Could you call one of them and have them fetch Hans?"

She considered that for a moment, but shook her head. "No. I want to be there to see his face."

"But that will be another . . ." Paula stopped. "I can't believe I'm going to say this, but what if you went home today, Inga?"

"What!"

"Think about it. Young Hans is not going to come and see

147

you, and your Hans is going to want to hear this news as soon as possible."

"But what about you? I didn't just come for Hans. I—"

"I know, and I don't want you to go. But this is important, Inga. And—" She turned to her husband. "Can I tell her, Wolfie? What you're doing for me?"

"Of course."

"Wolfie is letting me hire a girl to help with Little Bruno. Maybe do some light housework too. She starts Monday. So I'll be all right, Inga."

Looking back and forth between them, Inga was torn.

Wolfie sawed off a slice of bratwurst and went to stick it in his mouth but then stopped as an idea hit him. "Because I worked so late last night, my supervisor said I don't have to come in this morning until noon. So if you want, Inga, I could take you to the train station on my way to work. You could be home by midday."

That sounded so good, and yet she felt guilty. "I've not even been here twenty-four hours."

"Go, Inga," Paula urged. "I'm fine."

A little dazed, she finally nodded. "All right. I shall."

"I'll finish eating while you pack," Wolfgang said.

"I don't have much. It will take me only a few minutes."

"And I'll be done and ready to go too."

Paula came to Inga and slipped an arm around her waist. "Come, I'll help you pack."

• • •

Not quite ten minutes later, Inga closed her suitcase and secured the leather straps. Then she looked around. "I guess that's it," she said.

"Not quite," Paula said, and from the pocket of her apron she pulled out the book. "Will you take this and read it?" she asked.

Inga hesitated, and then shrugged. "If it means that much to you, why not?" She took the book and bent down to undo the straps on her suitcase.

"Why don't you put it in your purse instead?" Paula said quickly. "Then you can read it on the train if you like."

Inga shrugged again and slid it into a side pocket of her purse.

"I wanted to tell you all about it," Paula said. "About the man who restored the Church and about how he got the book. It's an incredible story. I'll write you all about it."

"That would be good."

"But don't wait for that. Just start reading it now."

"You won't give me any clue about it?"

"You love reading the Bible, right?"

"I do."

"Then I think you'll love reading the Book of Mormon too."

"Inga?" Wolfie's voice floated up to them from below.

"Coming," she called back.

"I'm ready whenever you are."

"I'll be right down."

The two sisters stood there for a moment, knowing the moment had come that they both dreaded. Then they fell into each other's arms and held each other very tightly for almost a full minute before they started down the stairs.

CHAPTER 11

June 28, 1914—Sarajevo, Bosnia and Herzegovina,
Balkan Peninsula

Ask historians what sparked the Great War, the first of what would come to be known as the "World Wars," and most will point to a small country on the Balkan Peninsula, across the Adriatic Sea from Italy. It was June 28, 1914. Archduke Franz Ferdinand, heir apparent to the throne of the powerful Austro-Hungarian Empire, had come to Bosnia-Herzegovina to inspect the imperial armed forces stationed there. He was accompanied by his young and very beautiful wife, Princess Sophie, duchess of Hohenberg, who was much beloved by the people.

Europeans have a long history. They also have long memories. In 1389, the Serbians, next-door neighbors to Bosnia-Herzegovina, were defeated by the Turks. In the centuries that followed, one conqueror after another kept the Serbians under their thumbs. In 1908, just six years before this visit, the Austro-Hungarian Empire had annexed most of the Balkan Peninsula and subjugated its peoples to the emperor, Franz Ferdinand's father. The Serbians still seethed with rage over this latest humiliation. A group of nationalist fanatics, committed to using whatever means it took to win back their independence, saw this official visit by a member of the royal family as the perfect opportunity.

On the morning of June 28th, the archduke and duchess and their entourage were traveling in an open motorcar with very little security. Great crowds had come out to see the royal couple. Suddenly, one of the Serbian nationalists stepped forward and threw a bomb at the passing car. He missed his target by inches. The bomb bounced and rolled off the back of the car, exploding beneath the following car. The archduke and duchess were unharmed, but one of their security officers and several bystanders were injured.

The security detail evidently learned nothing from that close call, as later that same day the royal couple were once again in an open car, this time on their way to the hospital to visit the injured officer. How often it is that pivotal points in history are influenced by seemingly inconsequential things. So it was this day. The procession took a wrong turn and started down the same street they had traversed before. The governor of Bosnia, who was in the car behind them, called out to the driver of the lead car to stop and turn around. The driver stopped the car and prepared to back up. Just feet away, another Serbian from the same fanatical group, a nineteen-year-old boy, was stunned to see the royal couple stopped just a few feet away from him. He drew his pistol and raced forward. Leaping up onto the car, he fired two shots at point-blank range. The first hit the archduke in the jugular vein. The second bullet caught Princess Sophie in the abdomen. Both were dead before they could reach a safe haven.

The outrage swept across Europe like wildfire. Anti-Serbian riots broke out in Sarajevo. Accusations and denials flew back and forth. With war clouds darkening all across the continent, the world powers began to line up on one side or the other. One month later to the day, Emperor Franz Josef of Austria-Hungary declared war on Serbia. Three days later, Russia, a formal ally of Serbia, began marshalling its armed forces. The following day, August 1st, Germany began mobilizing and declared war on Russia. On the 3rd, Germany declared war on France. In the days that followed, so many nations were declaring war on one another that it was hard to keep up.

Only much later would people remember that Otto von Bismarck, the great German statesman, and the person most responsible for the unification of Germany, had once said, "One day the great European War will come out of some damned foolish thing in the Balkans."

August 4, 1914—Menzing, Munich, Germany

"Elder Reissner?"

The missionary from Idaho was in the tiny bathroom, brushing his teeth. The water was running. He didn't respond.

Elder Ronald Brighton from St. George, Utah, banged his fist on the door. "ELDER REISSNER!"

Turning off the water, he stuck his head out. "You calling me?"

"No." Elder Brighton held up the phone. "The mission office in Zurich is calling you."

"Zurich?" He grabbed a towel to wipe his hands and then tossed it on a chair before taking the phone. "Hello?"

"Elder Reissner, this is Elder Franklin in the mission office."

"Great, Elder. Thanks for returning my call. I—"

"Wait! You called me?"

"Yes, about half an hour ago."

"Oh. Elder, it's crazy here. I didn't get the message. I'm calling all of the district leaders on another matter."

"Oh?" He grabbed a chair, dragged it over, and sat down.
"Go ahead then. But I've got a question for President Valentine."

"President Valentine isn't here. He's doing a mission tour
with that elder from Salt Lake City."

"You mean Elder Hyrum M. Smith? He's an Apostle, you
know."

"Yes, I know." The missionary on the phone drew in a quick
breath. "Sorry, I'm a little rattled right now. But Elder Smith and
President Valentine are doing a mission tour. Didn't you get the
letter?"

"Of course we got the letter. But it said they're not coming
for another week."

"That's to Munich. They're starting the tour in the north and
working their way south. Then they'll return to Zurich."

"All right, all right. Take it easy, Elder. You're doing fine. So
what's your question?"

The voice on the other end lowered to a hush. "Have you
been listening to the news?"

"We don't have a radio, but we've been buying a newspaper
every morning. Haven't seen one yet today, though."

"Germany just declared war on France."

He leaned in. "You mean Russia, right? Yeah, we heard that."

"No. Russia was two days ago. Today it was France. And on
the news they're saying England's going to come in with France,
so Germany will declare war against them, too." His voice
was tinged with fear and awe. "Germany's going to war, Elder
Reissner. And the phones are ringing off the hook. Elders everywhere are in a panic. Banks have stopped cashing any foreigners'
checks. Post offices are refusing to cash their money orders. Some

153

have no money at all. Others will be out of money by tomorrow or the next day. They don't know what to do. The members are calling too. They want to know what's going to happen to the Church if the missionaries have to go."

"Okay, Elder. Slow down a little." He waved at Elder Brighton, lowering the telephone. "Get a paper. Write down everything you're hearing. Come close so you can hear what Elder Franklin's saying." Then he spoke into the phone again. "Tell the missionaries to stay put for right now. They'll have to do the best they can. If they're out of food, have them talk to the members. Then try to contact President Valentine."

"I did. Nothing. Can't reach him. No one knows where they are. They were supposed to have arrived in Berlin yesterday, but no one has seen them yet."

"No surprise there. Germany's mobilizing for war. I'll bet the railroads are a nightmare right now. Have you tried a telegram?"

A long pause, then, "Uh . . . no, I don't know how to do that. But they got a telegram from Salt Lake two days ago."

"Who did? President Valentine?"

"And Elder Smith too."

"What did it say?"

There was a sudden touch of huffiness in voice. "We don't open the president's mail. Especially stuff from Salt Lake. Elder Becker sent it on to Berlin, hoping it would get there before they arrive. He left a note to forward it on to Leipzig if it misses them."

"Where is Elder Becker?" Elder Becker and his companion were the most senior missionaries in the office.

"They're out trying to get some money for the office. Fortunately, Switzerland is neutral, and we're not having any problems yet."

"And you're there alone? Where's your companion?"

"He went with Elder Becker."

Elder Reissner rolled his eyes and covered the phone again and whispered, "Elder Franklin's only been out about three months. Not the best one to be left to deal with a crisis. You getting all this?"

"I'm writing as fast as I can," Elder Brighton replied.

When Reissner spoke into the phone again, he talked slowly and kept his voice as calm and soothing as possible. "It's all right, Elder Franklin. You're doing great. Tell Elder Becker to call me this afternoon. We're going out to check on our missionaries and the branch members here in Munich. Many of them don't have phones yet. We'll be gone for three or four hours."

"Right. Call you this afternoon. If he doesn't, you call back, okay?"

"I will, Elder. *Auf Wiedersehen*." He hung up and looked at Elder Brighton. "Get your coat on. We've got work to do."

Schwabing, Munich

As Elders Reissner and Brighton came out of their flat and reached the sidewalk, Elder Reissner stopped. It had rained the night before, but now the sky was crystal clear and the sun was filtering through the leaves of sycamore trees above them. It was going to be a beautiful day. But Elder Reissner's mind was not on the weather. He looked both ways, his mind working at full speed.

"What do you think, Elder?" Elder Brighton said. "Aren't the biggest banks down around Marienplatz?"

"*Ja*, that's what I was thinking. But they'll probably be the most crowded too. I'll bet half of Germany's trying to get money out of their accounts right now."

Elder Brighton was visibly nervous. He had been out for just over six months. It had taken Elder Reissner almost a year before he started to feel really comfortable here, and that was with his ability to speak German.

"Maybe we should wait until we hear from President Valentine. I'm guessing that telegram from Salt Lake City contains instructions about what we're going to do. Maybe we're better off to stay in our flat today in case they call."

"If we do, the banks may be closed by the time the call comes. If there's too big of a run on them for cash, they'll just close their doors."

"But . . ."

"Look, Elder. We don't know where President Valentine and Elder Hyrum Smith are. But when we do hear from them, there's a ninety-five percent chance that they're going to say, 'Get out of Germany now.'"

He blanched a little. "Do you really think so?"

"There is going to be a war here, Elder. A big war. And Germany is going to demand that all Americans and other foreign nationals leave the country immediately. Especially those who stand with the Allies."

"But America's not involved. They say they're staying out of the war."

"America is sympathetic to France and England. Germany is not going to let us stay. We have to make sure our elders have sufficient money for train tickets to Switzerland. No one is going to leave before we hear from the president, but we have to be ready."

That seemed to satisfy the younger missionary, but Elder Reissner decided it was good for him to understand exactly what they were about to do. "We can't go to the bank where we normally get our funds. Everyone there knows we're Americans. And right now, Elder Brighton, we are going to try to keep that fact hidden as much as we can."

Then a thought came. He turned right, motioning for Elder Brighton to follow. "Come on. Let's catch a trolley."

"Where to?" his companion asked, hurrying to catch up.

"To Marienplatz."

"But you just said . . ."

"That's just our trolley destination. A short walk from there is a district called Schwabing. It's where the Ludwig Maximilian University is. It's much quieter and there are always a lot of students about our age around there. And there's a branch of the Deutsche Bank just a few blocks away."

"Good thinking."

Elder Reissner reached out and touched his companion's arm. "Your German is improving rapidly, Elder, but you still speak with a noticeable American accent. So no talking if anyone's close by."

"Got it."

• • •

Elder Reissner was disappointed, but not surprised, to see that the line for the Deutsche Bank in Schwabing came out the door and snaked about half a block down the sidewalk. That was still significantly shorter than the lines in Marienplatz, which stretched two or three hundred yards at every bank they passed. He was also gratified to see that about half the line consisted of young men and women like themselves.

"*Das ist gut*," he murmured. "Now remember, Elder. No talking. Not even in German. With war breaking out, I'm hoping no one is going to be looking for light conversation this morning.

But if they do, let me do the talking. But remember: under no circumstances are you to say anything in English. *Nicht ein Wort.*"

"*Ja.* I understand. Not a word."

• • •

It took them an hour to actually get inside the bank. As they drew nearer, Elder Reissner watched the people coming out of the bank closely. No one seemed upset, and he saw a few putting cash into their purses or wallets as they walked away. That was good. His plan was to withdraw enough cash to give each companionship fifty marks, enough to get them into Switzerland if the order to evacuate came. That meant he needed at least six hundred marks. His greatest fear was that this little branch would run out of cash before he reached the tellers.

But when the bank guard opened the door with a sober but pleasant "*Guten Morgen,*" he felt a huge relief. There were fewer than a dozen people inside the bank now, and he assumed that if they were getting close to running out of cash, they would have stopped letting people in.

He had been right about conversation. People who knew each other talked in low voices about the war and what it would mean, but everyone else wasn't saying much. His hopes began to rise.

Elder Brighton stepped to one side when they reached the teller's cage. Elder Reissner withdrew the bank draft from his jacket pocket and slid it under the steel bars that covered each teller's station. He smiled at the woman, who was in her mid-forties. "*Guten Morgen.* Could I receive this all in fifty-mark notes?"

She glanced at him, then at the check, and then nodded. "*Papiere bitte.*"

Elder Reissner felt his heart drop. He had hoped that she wouldn't ask to see his papers. But there was nothing to be done for it now. He reached in his pocket and brought out his identity card, hoping against hope that she wouldn't ask to see his passport too.

She didn't, but the moment she read his identity card, she started shaking her head and her mouth pinched into a tight line. "*Nein*," she said emphatically.

"Why not? There are sufficient funds in the account to cover it." Out of the corner of his eye, he saw two things. Elder Brighton had a look of pure panic on his face, and others behind them in the line were leaning forward to catch what was going on. Neither of those were good.

"The government forbids any foreign national from withdrawing money from a bank or post office."

Instantly there was a murmur of sound behind him. He leaned in closer, lowering his voice, as he read her name tag. "But Frau Baartz, the government has also asked that we leave the country. That is what we are doing. I am responsible for myself and twelve others. We are leaving for Zurich today. But we cannot do that without money for tickets."

That took her aback, and for a moment she looked confused. "*Einen Moment.*" She backed away from the window and walked to a man in a suit. Behind him Elder Reissner heard something that sent a shiver down his back. It was a man's voice, and he uttered one word. "*Englisch?*" Angry mutters instantly followed.

Elder Reissner didn't turn around. He didn't dare. His eyes were fixed on the man and the teller. The supervisor started shaking his head even before she finished. "*Nein!*" he said emphatically. His head lifted and he looked directly at Elder Reissner. "*Nein!*" he barked. "*Geh weg!* Go away! Get out of here."

The muttering behind them was rapidly swelling in volume. "*Englisch? Englisch?*" people were crying out.

At that moment, Elder Brighton stepped up beside Elder Reissner and made a serious blunder. He grabbed him by the elbow, and in what he thought was a hushed whisper, said in English, "Elder, we've got to get out of here. They think we're English."

"Shut up!" Elder Reissner hissed. Then jamming his identity card back in his pocket, he grabbed Brighton's elbow. "Let's get out of here," he said in German. "Don't look at them."

As they turned and started for the door, the muttering was quickly becoming a chorus of shouts. Staring at the floor and gripping Elder Brighton tightly, Elder Reissner pushed through the people, keeping his eyes down, dragging his companion with him. He felt something strike his face and realized someone had just spit on him. Seeing them coming, the elderly bank guard opened the door for them, but just as they reached it, Elder Reissner saw a flash of movement. The fist caught him on his right temple and knocked him to his knees. Somewhere he heard Elder Brighton cry out, but it barely registered. In an instant he was swarmed under. Two thoughts suddenly came to him: "Roll into a ball and cover your head," and "Don't fight back! Don't fight back!"

#16 Herrenstrasse, Menzing

Paula Groll was seated at the table peeling potatoes for the *Bratkartoffeln*, a stew of fried potatoes, diced bacon, and onions that would be their supper that night. The radio was on, but at the moment there was no news, only classical music. Finishing another potato, she set the knife down, leaned over, and clapped her hands in delight. "Bravo, Bruno."

The baby, who had pulled himself up to a chair, turned and flashed her that smile that she so loved about him. She held out her hands. "Come, to Mama, Bruno. You can do it. Come to Mama."

He let go with one hand but immediately started to wobble and grabbed for the chair again. She got up and went to him, holding out two fingers for him to hold. "Come on, Bruno. You can do this. You are a year old now, son. Let's show Papa that he's wrong about you."

Eager to launch himself free, the baby clasped each finger and let his mother lead him away from the chair. She laughed when she saw the fierceness of his concentration. It was like he had understood all the jokes his father had made about him being so chubby that he wouldn't walk until he was three.

As Paula was leading her son across the floor toward the table, a movement out the window caught her eye. She glanced up. Two figures were coming slowly up Herrenstrasse toward their home. "*Ah, gut!*" she exclaimed, delighted to see who it was. Then she gasped in great shock and surprise. She swept Bruno up in her arms and leaped to the window, pulling back the curtain.

In three strides she reached the playpen and thrust the baby into it. She grabbed a rattle and shoved it at him and then raced to the entryway and flung open the front door. She went down the steps in great leaps, her hair flying.

"It's all right, *Schwester* Groll. I'm okay." It came through clenched teeth, and the pain on Elder Reissner's battered face told a different story.

"He's not all right," Elder Brighton said. "He's hurt bad." He had his arm around his companion and was half holding him up.

"What happened?" she cried as she reached them. Then,

before they could answer, she waved them off. "It doesn't matter. Let's get you inside."

It took Paula almost fifteen minutes to get the blood off and the wounds cleaned up enough to determine just how seriously he was hurt. She was greatly relieved to see that while he had been badly battered, most of the cuts and abrasions were superficial. Gretl watched in horror. Paula had sent her upstairs when the elders arrived, but Bruno had started to fuss and so she called Gretl down. Now the young girl looked on in horrified fascination as she walked Bruno back and forth and watched her mother work on her beloved Elder Reissner. On the table beside Paula was a small cardboard box that she used as a makeshift first aid kit. She reached in it now and took out several adhesive bandages. One by one, she removed the backing and carefully placed a bandage over each of the more serious wounds.

Gretl began to weep silently as she watched.

"It's all right, Gretl," Elder Reissner said. "Your mama is fixing me up. I'll be fine."

"Promise?" she sniffed.

"Promise."

"Hold still, Elder. I need to look at this cut over your eye."

"Yes, *Mama*," he said, managing a teasing smile.

Gretl took instant offense at that. "She's not *your* mama. She's *my* mama."

He laughed. "You're right, Gretl. Sorry."

Paula leaned in closer, gently probing the ugly cut over the elder's left eyebrow. "This one is pretty deep," she said. "It will need stitching. You're going to have to see a doctor."

"You know that's not going to happen right now, *Schwester* Groll. Just do the best you can, please."

Knowing he was right, she reached for one of the largest of

the bandages. Then she retrieved a small set of scissors and began to cut away parts of it.

"What are you doing?" Elder Brighton asked.

"Watch and see."

He leaned in closer as Paula cut the bandage into the shape of an H. Upon finishing, she held up and examined it. Satisfied, she carefully peeled the backing off and looked at Elder Reissner. "This is going to hurt, because I have to hold the cut closed while I put the bandage on."

"I'm ready."

Holding the bandage carefully so it didn't touch anything, she pinched the wound shut with one finger and her thumb.

Elder Reissner moaned and jerked once, but then he gritted his teeth and closed his eyes.

Very carefully she turned the bandage sideways and attached it to his forehead. The crossbar of the H went directly across the cut. When she removed her fingers, the wound stayed closed.

"Wow," Elder Brighton said. "That's neat. Where did you learn to do that?"

"I am a mother, that's how." She put everything back in the box and then sat back. "All right, Elders. Tell me what happened."

They exchanged glances, but Elder Brighton shook his head. "Your German is better than mine," he said in English. "You tell her."

Elder Reissner started with the phone call from Zurich and described the confusion and chaos that was going on in the mission office, his decision not to wait for their mission president to call, and their ensuing efforts to get funds.

"And have you heard from him yet?" she asked.

"No," Elder Brighton answered. "And we won't go until we do. Until then we are to be ready to leave on a moment's notice."

"How can you leave with no money?"

"President Jahn will take our check and cash it for us. He works at the post office."

Paula frowned. "He could get in trouble with the government for that."

"That's what we told him too," Elder Reissner said. "He said that if he didn't, he would be in trouble with the Lord."

To Paula's surprise, Elder Brighton was suddenly crying. "It was all my fault. I did something really stupid," he whispered. "I didn't want those in line right behind us to know what I was saying, so I told Elder Reissner that we needed to leave—in English." He turned to his companion and began to sob. "I'm so sorry, Elder."

Reaching out, Reissner laid a hand on his companion's shoulder. "It's all right, Elder. It's all right." Then he looked at Paula. "There were three guys just behind us in the line—the kind of guys you see coming out of the beer halls on a Friday night."

"Hooligans."

"Yes." He took a quick breath. "They went berserk. They thought we were British."

He looked up at her and gave her a strange look. "I'm a pretty strong guy, and for a moment I was tempted to fight back. But as quickly as the thought came, there came another. *Don't resist. It will only make it worse.* So I curled up in a ball and dropped to the floor."

Brighton spoke up. "He thinks they cracked one of his ribs."

"That was God's hand protecting you, Elder," Paula said gently. "If you had fought back, they would have killed you."

"God helped us in another way," Elder Brighton said, still tearful. "The bank guard shoved the men away and helped us out the door."

"You are very fortunate young men," Paula said, crying now too.

"I know."

They were all silent for a time, each lost in his or her own thoughts. Finally, Paula spoke. "I want you to go upstairs and lie down for a while. I'm going to call Wolfie and tell him what's happened. As soon as he can get home, we'll take you back to your flat."

Elder Reissner was shaking his head before she finished. "We've got to go now. There are two companionships we haven't reached yet."

For a moment he thought she was going to fight him on it, but she didn't.

"I can't tell you how grateful we are for your help," he went on, his voice heavy with emotion.

"I'm glad I was here." Paula got to her feet. "All right, then. You go, but get off of Herrenstrasse as quickly as you can. Take the back streets and alleys. Can you find your way?"

"Yes."

"I'm still going to call Wolfie and tell him what happened. Tonight we shall bring you supper and some other things you may need. I'll also start spreading the word through the branch."

"We're asking companionships without telephones to come to our flat. There will be more than just Elder Brighton and me there tonight."

She chuckled softly. "How do you say it in English? 'The merrier the more'?"

"The more the merrier."

"*Ja.* 'The more the merrier.' Go. We will see you tonight."

• • •

165

Paula and Gretl watched the two elders move away, Elder Reissner limping badly. She had made Gretl say good-bye to them inside so as not to call the attention of the neighbors to two young Americans—one of them injured—coming out of her house. But she came out on the porch and stood there silently. If they turned around one last time, she didn't want them to see a closed door. But they kept moving, slowly but steadily.

Just as Paula was about to step back inside, Elder Reissner suddenly stopped. The two of them exchanged a few words, and then they both turned around. When they saw her they waved. She waved back. But when they started back toward her, she ran lightly down the steps and went to meet them.

"I'm sorry," Elder Reissner said, "but I forgot one thing."

"What? I can bring it to you tonight."

"No, it's not that. It's Hans."

"Hans?"

"Yes, Hans Otto. I've been trying all summer to reach him. I know he graduated in June, but I thought he was going to be around until he went to university in the fall. I would like very much to say good-bye. This may be my only chance. Did he graduate?"

"Yes. And he was valedictorian, just like he said he would be."

Reissner laughed. "I knew he would be. Once he set his mind to something, there was no stopping him. So is he back home with his parents?" Then his face darkened. "Is he going to get called up in the army?"

"No. He didn't go home. He's in Nuremberg."

"Nuremberg. No wonder I can't find him." Then the light dawned. "Did he go to work for that guy who owns that big truck factory again?"

"*Ja.* He worked there for a few weeks last year, and Herr

Junker was so impressed that he brought him back as soon as school was out."

"That's wonderful. And what about the army? I'm sure they'll be calling up a lot of young men."

"That's the best thing. Inga is elated. The factory makes trucks, and now with the war coming, they will be making trucks for the army. They are doubling their output. Hans Otto is working on the diesel engines for the trucks."

Reissner was smiling broadly. "And because he's in a war industry, he will not have to go."

"*Ja*. They call it an 'essential industries deferment.' Then in the fall, when he starts university, they won't call him up either until he graduates."

"Thank the Lord," Elder Brighton said. "No wonder his parents are pleased."

"If you get a chance," Reissner broke in, "will you tell him what's happened? Tell him that we tried to see him to say good-bye."

"I will. Once you find out where you will be, send me a letter, and I'll send it on to him." She glanced around quickly. "Now go. Before someone sees you and starts asking questions."

Chapter Notes

In the latter half of the nineteenth century and the first part of the twentieth, the European missions were under the direction of what at first was known as the British Mission and then later was called the European Mission. Individual missions in France, Holland, Scandinavia, Germany, and Switzerland had their own mission presidents and considerable priesthood autonomy, but oversight from Salt Lake City came through the European Mission.

Because of its leading role, the European Mission was often led by members of the Quorum of the Twelve Apostles. That was true at the outbreak of World War I. Elder Hyrum M. Smith was held in high esteem not only because of his apostleship but also because he was the son of President Joseph F. Smith, who had become President of the Church upon the death of Lorenzo Snow in 1901. He was also the grandson of Hyrum Smith and a grandnephew of Joseph Smith, who were martyred in Carthage Jail. He had been called to preside over the European Mission in 1913 (*Mormonism in Germany*, 54).

Hyrum Valentine, a native of Brigham City, Utah, was called as the president of the Swiss-German Mission in 1912. He had served a mission in Germany starting in 1900. Both Elder Smith and President Valentine were in their early forties at the time these events occurred.

Even though people all over Europe were predicting war after the assassination of Archduke Ferdinand, no mention was made of the possible danger in the official records of the Swiss-German mission until a full month later, when it was noted that there were "rumors of war in Germany."

The mission records do not state exactly what day President Valentine and Elder Smith set out on their joint mission tour. What is known is that on August 2nd, the day after Germany declared war on Russia, a telegram came from Salt Lake City telling President Valentine to quickly move all of his missionaries out of danger areas. By that time, the two men had already left. As chaos spread rapidly, the pair seemed to have dropped off the map.

In reality, amidst all of the confusion of the declarations of war and the mobilization of Germany, the presidents of the two missions were arrested, along with an elder traveling with them, and were charged with being British spies. They were held for seven days while the American consulate worked to have them freed. When they were finally released, they took passage on an overcrowded train and went straight back to Switzerland. Elder Smith continued on to Liverpool, where the telegram finally caught up with him on August 22nd (*Mormons and Germany*, 40; and Gilbert Scharffs, *Mormonism in Germany*, 40–60).

In that volatile time, there are records of foreign nationals being mobbed and beaten severely. This was especially true of those who spoke English. There is no definitive record that missionaries were part of that, but it is included here to convey the tensions present in Germany at that time.

CHAPTER 12

September 3, 1914—Graswang Village, Bavaria, Germany

Inga Eckhardt sat at the kitchen table and looked out her window at the first ridges of the Bavarian Alps. They were still that deep, forest green that was so restful to the eyes, but she knew that very soon they would be splashed with brilliant fall colors, and soon after that they would wear a cloak of snow.

That didn't make her sad. She loved all of the seasons in their little valley. It was without question one of the most beautiful places on earth, and she was always grateful that it had been her privilege to be raised in such splendor of nature.

"Grandmama, Kristen is kicking me."

"Kristen, stop kicking your sister."

"She kicked me first."

She sighed. "Am I going to have to send Grandpapa up there when he gets home?"

"No, Grandmama." Both voices answered in unison and with the same weary surrender. Good thing. Hans and their parents had taken a wagon full of cheese wheels to

Garmisch-Partenkirchen and probably wouldn't be back until after midnight.

Inga thought about going up and making sure they quieted down, but she chose not to. The sun was now behind the hills, and very soon darkness would steal over the land and a hush would descend on their little hamlet. It was her favorite time of the day, and she decided to go out on the porch to enjoy it. She stood, took a scarf down from the rack for the chill, and slipped out the door, careful not to let it bang when it shut.

• • •

Inga came awake with a start, a spurt of panic sending her heart pounding. She looked around wildly before realizing where she was. She must have fallen asleep in her chair. Shivering, she pulled the wrap around her shoulders more tightly. Then she jumped as she heard the noise again. The moon had come up since she had come outside. It was full, and the night sky was clear. Everything was bathed in a velvety silver. She looked out toward the lane that led past their house. It was too far away to be sure, but she thought she could make out some dark figures coming toward her. Then she heard the murmur of voices. Some of the young people passing by? The Krauthammer boys coming back from a night at the beer halls?

She shook her head. No. If it were them, she would have heard them long before now, singing their ribald songs and belching out their beer breath. She stood up anyway. Whoever it was, she didn't feel like talking.

But just as she reached the door, a voice sang out. "*Hallo*, is there someone there?"

Inga hesitated but then shrugged. "*Ja*, this is Frau Eckhardt. And who is calling?"

The answer came joyously. "Frau Eckhardt? This is *Kirchen-ältester* Reissner. Do you remember me? I was friends with your son, Hans Otto."

For a moment, she was too dumbfounded to answer. She just stared at the two figures in suits and ties and Homburg hats standing at her gate, scarcely daring to believe what she was seeing.

"Frau Eckhardt?"

"*Ja, ja*, I am here. Of course I remember you. Come, come."

After ushering them in, Inga stepped back out and looked around to see if any of the neighbors were out of their houses or if anyone else might be passing along the lane. Then she shut the door quietly and went inside. Elder Reissner swept off his hat. In the full light she recognized him immediately, but she remembered the other one as not being quite so skinny.

"Frau Eckhardt, let me introduce my companion, Elder Ronald Brighton from Utah. Elder Jackson was transferred to Hamburg."

She inclined her head. "How do you do, Elder Brighton?"

He remembered to take his hat off too. "Very well, *danke*. It is a great pleasure to meet you after all I have heard about you."

She wasn't exactly sure what that meant, or who he had heard it from, but he seemed like a nice boy, so she nodded and thanked him. Then she peered more closely at Elder Reissner. "You look much better than I expected."

"Ah, yes. So *Schwester* Groll—Paula—told you about our little mugging at the bank? The bruises and bumps are all but gone now."

She lifted a finger and tapped her forehead above her left eye.

"Except for that one. You will have a nice scar to remind you of Germany, no?"

He laughed, but there was a tinge of sadness to it. "I will." He still had his hat in his hand, and he donned it again, pulling it down low over his eyes. "I can almost cover it with my hat if I pull it down low enough, but then I look like an American gangster."

"I do not know what an American gangster looks like, but it does make you look sinister. But I am forgetting my manners." She motioned to the chairs. "Please sit down. Can I take your coats?"

"No, but thank you. We can only stay for a few minutes. We have to catch the midnight train to Zurich."

"So you are leaving Germany now?"

"*Ja.* Finally."

"Paula thought that you were leaving three weeks ago."

"We thought we were too, but there was a mix-up with a telegram from Salt Lake and—"

"*Ja, ja.* She told me all about that. So they didn't order you out?"

"That first telegram just asked President Valentine to move us out of danger. That was sent just as the war was beginning. Then just three days ago he got another telegram. It told him to release all missionaries and to do whatever was necessary to get us to Liverpool by the 16th of this month. They'll have tickets for us on a steamer home."

"Ah," she said, understanding now. "Paula called me yesterday and told me that she had heard the missionaries were heading to England. She tried to call you, but your phone was disconnected."

"Yes, we were gathering up our missionaries."

"But she said you were going north, up to Holland and then across the Channel."

"That's true of some, but for those of us in the south of Germany, traveling all the way across the country would be dangerous. So we are going out by way of Switzerland and France and then coming back in just before we get to Holland."

"I'm glad for you but sorry for Paula. She says the members in the branch there are very sad that you are no longer their branch president."

Elder Reissner lowered his head and stared at his hands. "That is very hard for me. The hardest of all, actually." But then he straightened. "But enough of that. Paula told us that Hans Otto doesn't have to worry about going into the army."

Her face lit up with smiles. "It is an answer to my prayers."

"And mine. I am going to miss him very much."

"And he you. He called last week and asked if I had heard from you. He really wanted to say good-bye. I'll write and tell him that you came."

He leaned forward. "And give him my best wishes. He is a fine boy."

"I know," she murmured, her eyes suddenly glistening.

They were silent for a moment, and then Reissner straightened. "I am very glad we found you, Frau Eckhardt. I thought I would never see you again. Then the president decided it was safer for our missionaries to gather in Oberammergau rather than Munich, where there are so many soldiers in the train station. When I realized that we had an eight-hour time window, we decided to come and find you. Is there anything we can do for you before we leave?"

"*Ja.*"

"Name it."

"Call me *Schwester* Eckhardt instead of Frau Eckhardt."

His eyebrows shot up as he stared at her. "Is that all?"

"*Ja.*"

"All right . . ." He hesitated for a moment and then added, "*Schwester* Eckhardt."

"No," she shot right back. "You can't call me that."

Bewildered, he glanced at Elder Brighton and then back at her. "I . . . I guess I don't understand."

She smiled, and for a moment she looked like an impish little girl. "You can't call me *Schwester* yet because I'm not your sister yet."

He stared at her, still not comprehending.

She continued, "But if you were to baptize me, then I would be your *Schwester* in the gospel, no?"

Her laughter at their expressions was like the tinkling of a bell, and her eyes were dancing with delight. "Will you baptize me, Elder Reissner?"

"But . . ."

"I know, I know," she chuckled. "I haven't had any of the lessons. But Paula has told me all about Joseph Smith."

"And you accept him as a prophet?" Brighton said, looking almost as stunned as Reissner.

"I do. Without question. And Paula also gave me the Book of Mormon you gave her for me."

"Have you read it?" Elder Reissner asked.

"Four times."

"Really?" he blurted.

Tears came to her eyes. "I know that book is from God. So, can I be baptized?"

Reissner shook his head, but in amazement rather than denial. "But we're leaving tonight. Uh . . ." His mind was racing. "I suppose you could ask someone in the branch to baptize you the next time you are in Munich."

"I want *you* to baptize me, Elder. So that means you have to do it tonight."

"But we don't have any of the forms or—"

She smiled sweetly as she interrupted him. "Did Jesus bring forms to John the Baptist?"

Reissner shook his head ruefully. "Good point."

"What about your husband?" Brighton asked.

That startled her. "What about him?"

"You have to have his permission. Is he here?"

She shook her head. "He's in Garmisch-Partenkirchen, and he won't be back until after midnight."

"And we'll be gone by then," Elder Brighton said, sorrow twisting his face.

"If he were here, would he give his permission?" Reissner asked.

She considered that for a few moments before nodding. "I think so. I have not hidden any of this from him. He won't like it, but I don't think he would forbid it."

The two elders exchanged glances. Finally, Elder Brighton started shaking his head. "I don't see how we can."

Reissner got to his feet. "Look, Elder. Here's how it is. We don't have the proper forms. We don't have permission from her husband. We don't have our president here to okay it. And we're leaving because Germany's at war. Who knows how long it will be before missionaries can come back to Germany? I think all of that warrants an exception, don't you?"

Inga held her breath as Brighton debated it in his mind. Then a slow grin stole across his face. "Yes, I think an exception is warranted."

Inga wanted to leap up and throw her arms around them, but she sat quietly, almost primly. "So what do I need to do?"

"Is there some water nearby, enough to immerse you in?"

"We have a pond out behind our barn."

"Then get something warm to put over you afterward until you can come get dressed in something dry again."

• • •

Inga came back downstairs, freshly changed into dry clothes after her baptism. Elder Reissner had pulled a chair out and motioned for her to sit in it. Both missionaries then came around behind her, laid their hands on her head, and confirmed her a member of the Church. When Elder Reissner said, "Receive the Holy Ghost," she started to cry. After closing the prayer, he came around and pulled her to her feet. He opened his arms. "Now can I call you *Schwester* Eckhardt?"

Her eyes were radiant. "*Ja*," she whispered. "Now you can call me *Schwester* Eckhardt."

He did.

Her smile broadened. "Say it again."

He did.

She turned to Brighton. "You say it too."

He did, laughing and crying at the same time.

Her shoulders lifted and fell. "*Danke schön, meine Brüder. Danke schön.*"

• • •

Ten minutes later, as the elders put on their hats, the mood was much more somber. "I feel awful. I know we have to leave, but I hate the thought of leaving you alone."

"I am not alone."

"Of course not, and I didn't mean that God won't be with you. We all know that. But you'll be the only member within fifty miles. There is no branch of the Church anywhere near here. No missionaries. No one to give you the sacrament. No one to come and see how you're doing. That's what I meant by being alone."

Her head cocked to one side for a moment, and then she held up a finger. "*Einen Moment.*" She turned and went back into the kitchen. A moment later she came back. She was holding up her Book of Mormon. "I also have this," she said. "I am not alone."

Elder Reissner tried to speak, but he couldn't get the words out. He could barely see through the tears. Then came a sudden thought. He held up his finger. "*Und noch ein Moment.*" He dropped to one knee and opened his briefcase. He fumbled around for a moment and then came up with another book. He stood up and handed it to her.

A little confused, she took it and looked at the cover. "*Lehre und Bündnisse?*"

"Yes. We call it the 'Doctrine and Covenants.'"

Her eyes widened. "Is it a book like the Book of Mormon?"

"Yes. It is different in many ways, but what matters is that it will make you feel the same way you do when you read the Book of Mormon."

She laid it on top of her Book of Mormon and then pressed them both to her chest. "Then I really am not alone."

September 7, 1914—Graswang Village

"Mama?"

Inga jerked up from her sewing, instantly recognizing her son's voice, even though it was strangely muffled. She tossed the skirt she was working on aside and leaped to her feet. "Hans! Is that you? I'm in here, son."

She heard his footsteps start down the hall but didn't wait for him to come into the bedroom. She stepped into the hall, almost running. Ahead of her, a figure approached in a lumbering gait. It was not her Hans. She screamed, falling backwards. It was some kind of horrible monster, and it was coming straight at her. She ducked back into the doorway and slammed the door behind her. Looking around wildly, she saw the scissors on the chair. She dove for them and came up with them in her hand. She tore to the window and shouted at the children. "Annalisa! Kristen! Run! Run!"

She whirled back and froze as the footsteps clunked up to her bedroom door and stopped. "Stay back!" she shouted. "I've got a weapon!"

To her stunned amazement, she heard laughter. Wild, almost maniacal laughter. Then the door jerked open. The sight almost made her faint. The body was that of a man, but it was clothed in a long greatcoat, with amulets on the shoulders and brass buttons. The feet were covered by highly polished black boots that came to the knees. But it was the face that chilled her blood. A dark green, metal helmet framed a round face. A horrible, round face. The skin was glossy and black; the eyes large and vacant and covered with a glassy material. But the nose was the worst. It was huge and tubular. It hung down at least six inches, forming an enormous snout. Instead of nostrils there was a single hole, and it was covered with a metallic-looking mesh.

She couldn't move. She couldn't breathe. Her heart was hammering so hard in her chest she thought she might faint.

There was more laughter and then a muffled voice. "Mama, it's just me." One hand came up and ripped the hideous face away. Waves of relief shot through Inga. It was Hans, and he was laughing. He was laughing so hard that he bent over and held his stomach.

"It's a gas mask, Mama." He held it up by the straps and waved it at her. "It's just my gas mask. It's not going to bite you." He strode to the window and stuck his head out. "It's all right, children," he called. "It's just me."

Still numb, Inga stared at him for several seconds. Then her eyes narrowed. Her jaw clenched. Her head lowered, and she went after him with the scissors. "That's not funny!" she bellowed. "Not one bit."

He tore off the greatcoat as he danced around the bed, keeping it between him and her. "I'm sorry, but . . ." He had to stop and catch his breath. She stopped too, her breath heaving in and out of her. Finally she tossed the scissors on the bed and pushed past him. She slapped him hard on the rump as she passed. "I don't know you. Get out of my house."

This only sent him into more peals of laughter.

It took almost fifteen minutes for her to let him come back into her presence, and it was another five before she was laughing too. The grandchildren were trying on the gas mask now, trying to scare one another. She looked away. She still found the thing horrible. Eventually she reached the point where her mind started to focus again. "Why didn't you tell me you were coming?" she asked.

"I didn't know until this morning."

"I thought you were supposed to start university this week."

"I was."

"But . . ." She looked more closely at him. "And what are you wearing?"

For a moment, there was panic in his eyes, but he quickly

pushed it back. He came forward and gathered her into his arms, pulling her close. "Mama. I joined the army yesterday."

Her jaw fell open. She tried to get words out, but nothing came. He rushed on. "I am off for training, and then I shall be sent to France. Like Grandfather Eckhardt did in the Franco-Prussian War, I am going to fight for the Fatherland."

She froze in place again, and this time the horror twisting at her stomach was worse than before. "Oh, Hans. Oh, my son. What have you done?"

He stepped back, stricken. "Mama. You have to help me. Please, Mama."

"Help you?"

"Yes. Father is going to be livid. You have to help me tell him. You have to make him understand."

Her hands came up and she buried her face in them. A very different kind of horror was sweeping through her, turning her heart to stone. "Oh, Hans," she cried. "You foolish, foolish boy. What have you done? Oh, what have you done?"

Chapter Notes

Elder Hyrum M. Smith returned to Liverpool, England, on August 22nd, 1914. By that time, war was no longer imminent, it was a reality. But communication with the continent was still difficult. Not until August 30th was he able to get a telegram through to President Valentine in Zurich. The telegram came in both German and French. It read: "*Release all missionaries and take immediate steps to get them here for September 16th and 30th sailings. Wire acknowledgement of this message.*"

Valentine immediately withdrew 20,000 German marks from the mission account. He wired a nine-word telegram to all of his missionaries: "MISSIONARIES CALLED HOME. MAKE PREPARATIONS. I AM COMING. VALENTINE." He left immediately on a ten-day tour of the mission. He went through the mission distributing cash to the missionaries so they could pay off their obligations and make the necessary travel arrangements to Liverpool. Many of those missionaries were aided on their way by the mission president of Holland, Elder LeGrand Richards, who would later become an Apostle.

By September 28th, exactly three months after the assassination of Archduke Ferdinand, President Valentine was able to send a telegram to President Joseph F. Smith in Salt Lake City. "EVERY ELDER, SWISS-GERMAN MISSION, POSITIVELY SAFE, WELL AND SECURED. VALENTINE" (see *Mormons and Germany*, 45–46; *Mormonism in Germany*, 55).

We know that not all missionaries went directly through Holland. Some went through Switzerland first and back into Germany and Holland without problems (*Mormons and Germany*, 44). But it was the author's assumption that those would likely have been missionaries in the south of Germany, who were closest to Switzerland.

Though the exact number of missionaries evacuated is not known, there were about 200 missionaries in the Swiss-German Mission at that time. Probably about 150 of those were in Germany (ibid., 41). One missionary did not leave: Elder Wilhelm Kessler, who was a native-born German who had emigrated with his family to America and returned as a missionary, decided that he had an obligation to stay and serve the Fatherland. He became an officer and fought valiantly in the war. He was killed in the line of duty on July 1, 1916 (ibid., 49).

CHAPTER 13

September 11, 1914—Camp Otto Von Bismarck
Near Piesenkofen, Germany

S ir?"

The sergeant with massive shoulders and a face like a rhinoceros, whose name was Jessel, jerked around as if Hans had slugged him in the back. "What did you call me, soldier?" he barked.

Hans fell back a step. "I . . . uh . . . Sir, there's been a terrible mistake here and I—"

Suddenly fingers were pinching deep into both of Hans's upper arms. He screamed in pain as the sergeant lifted him a foot off the ground and shook him like a rag doll. "Don't call me sir," he roared. Little drops of spittle sprayed onto Hans's cheeks. "I am not an officer. I am a noncommissioned officer. Which means that I work for my pay." He slammed Hans back down so hard that he almost lost his footing and went down.

The other forty-seven men stared in openmouthed horror.

"Do you understand me, soldier?"

"Yes, sir . . . I mean, yes, sergeant. But I have a problem and was wondering if—"

Jessel leaned in again, his face turning purple. "Do I look like your mother, soldier?" He jabbed Hans in the chest with both hands, sending him sprawling. Instantly the sergeant was towering over him. "You don't want to start your service like this, boy!" he growled. "You don't ever want to get on my bad side"—he glanced down at his name tag—"Private Eckhardt." Then he let loose a stream of profanity that shocked Hans almost as much as the physical manhandling had. Breathing hard, the sergeant finally stopped. "So you'd best keep your mouth shut, your eyes open, and your ears tuned to my every word. Is that clear, *Schweinkopf?*"

Afraid to move, afraid to do anything more to incur his wrath, Hans nodded quickly. "Yes, Sergeant Jessel." His face was burning. The sergeant had just called him a pig head.

"Pick up your bags, *Schweinkopf!*" he bellowed at the top of his lungs. "Fall into two columns and follow me. Double time."

Hans scrambled to his feet and grabbed his bag. As they started out at a trot, calling cadence, Hans found one tiny glimmer of hope. The sergeant had called *all* of them pig heads. So it wasn't just him. It wasn't much, but after the humiliating pummeling he had just taken, it was something.

They stopped outside a long, low hut with a Red Cross sign on it. "Leave your bags here, maggots," Sergeant Jessel cried. "The army wants to inoculate you against measles and smallpox and who knows what else. The doctors will also examine you to make sure you're healthy enough to die for the Fatherland." He smirked at his little joke. "Finally, you will go to the barbershop, where you will be given regulation haircuts. Any questions?" He glared at them, daring them to so much as open their mouths. No one moved. No heads turned to look at him.

"Good. All right, you sorry excuses for soldiers," he barked.

"Line up at that door there. When you're finished, come back here and stand in formation until I return." He started to turn away but then swung back. A wicked grin was playing at the corner of his mouth. "By the way, those shots may make some of you nauseous. You may even feel faint. But you will not break formation to sit down. Is that clear?"

"Yes, Sergeant Jessel!" they shouted in chorus.

The smile broadened. "If you do faint, then you have my permission to lie down. Otherwise, you will stand at ease until I return."

"Yes, Sergeant Jessel!"

Hans had thought he had a pretty good idea of what army life would be like. He knew it wasn't going to be all roses and sunshine, but he was excited for what was ahead for him: learning how to shoot a rifle, hand-to-hand combat, bayonet training—maybe even being trained to fire a machine gun or throw a hand grenade. But more than all of that, he looked forward to the manly association with his fellow soldiers. His grandfather had talked about that—"the brotherhood of arms," he called it. Even after all the years, he had still treasured his military experience.

Hans's first encounter with Sergeant Jessel had seriously dented that perception. But in the next hour, he discovered that any illusion he'd had about the warm nature of army life was the greatest delusion of all.

As they went through the front door of the building they entered an alcove large enough to accommodate about five men. A sign on the door said WAIT HERE UNTIL CALLED. Hans was in the front half of the line, so he entered about five minutes after they started. Each time the door opened, an attractive young nurse with a shapely figure invited the next man to come in. "Not bad," he thought. "I can handle a shot from someone like that."

But when his turn came to step through the door, two things caught his attention. The lovely girl was not giving shots. She was simply the escort. Two older nurses with faces that somewhat resembled the sergeant's were standing on either side of him. Both had needles in each hand. "Face forward," one growled. As he did so, Hans was stunned to find himself staring at a life-sized black-and-white photograph tacked to the wall directly in front of him. It was of a scantily clad woman seated on a blanket, smiling seductively at him. It was so totally unexpected, so out of context in this sterile place, that he just gaped at it. And that's when the two nurses hit him. POP! POP! POP! POP! Four needles, four inoculations—two in each arm—in under three seconds. "Next!" the larger one barked.

The examination room was a long, narrow room with two stations where two doctors sat behind small tables filled with jars of tongue depressors, cotton, and other medical supplies. The doctors didn't look up as all forty-eight men filed in. As the door closed behind them, the older doctor looked up. "Everyone strip," he called. "There are hooks on the wall behind you. Hang your clothes there, and then get in two lines. Everything comes off, including your socks." Hans stared at him for a moment; then, as he turned toward the benches against the wall and began to unbutton his shirt, he leaned in close to the man next to him. He was a dark-haired boy who looked about his own age. "This is going to take forever," Hans whispered. "And it's cold in here. Why don't they let us keep our clothes on until it's our turn?"

His companion laughed. "You have to stop assuming that the army is a logical, rational system. You think that and it's going to

185

drive you mad. Just remember: nothing makes sense in the army. Nothing. Trust me on that."

It took almost an hour to examine all four dozen men, and they wouldn't let anyone get dressed until the last man was done. Hans guessed there might be a reason for that: total humiliation. And if that was their goal, they had achieved it.

• • •

The barbershop was at the far end of the building. The men were told it was too small for all to get inside, so they were to wait out in the hallway until their time came. Hans was near the door and so was one of the first four to go in. There were four barbers. They wore white aprons and stood ankle-deep in hair of every color. Under their aprons, they were all in their fatigues and combat boots, the everyday uniform of the soldier.

As Hans sat down in the third chair, the barber gave him a pleasant smile and put a cape around his shoulders. "How would you like it cut, soldier?"

Pleased to be asked, Hans settled back. He had his father's hair, thick, wavy, and very light brown. He was very particular about how he wore it because he had learned that it was one of his most favorable features—with girls especially. "It's getting a little long," he said, turning to the barber. "Take a little off the top, but not too close around the ears."

"Right," the man said, grinning. He picked up a set of barber shears from the table. Hans started to suggest that scissors might be better, but he didn't have a chance. The barber came around to the front of him, straddled Hans's legs, and leaned in and touched the shears to his forehead right in the center. With great dexterity, he started working the shears back and forth and plowed into Hans's hairline.

"Ow!" Hans yelped. "That hurts." Then, horrified at the large tufts floating downward past his eyes, he jerked his head away. "What are you doing?"

"Sit still, soldier," the man snarled, "or I'll take your ears off with it."

Wincing as the shears cut into his scalp again and again, Hans clamped his mouth shut and dug his fingers into the handles of the chair to stop from jerking his head.

No more than sixty seconds later, the barber stepped back. He reached around to his little table and lifted up a hand mirror. When he saw himself, Hans had to bite his lip to stop from crying. He barely recognized the man staring back at him. He was all but bald, and there were several places where the cutters had nicked the skin and he was bleeding.

"What have you done?" he whispered.

The barber laughed as he put away the mirror. Then he plucked at the shoulder of Hans's shirt. "Why do you think they call these uniforms, soldier?"

"What?" Hans was still half in shock at his denuding.

"They call them uniforms because they're all the same. It's the same with your hair. You're not a person anymore. There is no individual in this man's army. You are a soldier now, and we're all the same. Haircut and all."

The final humiliation of the day came as they stood in formation waiting for the rest of the men to come out of the barbershop. The afternoon sun was hot. Hans could feel the cuts on his head scabbing up, and the itch from the hair on the back of his neck was driving him crazy. But Sergeant Jessel had returned.

He sat in the shade of the building smoking a cigarette, watching them with those hawklike eyes.

At first, Hans thought his light-headedness was from heat, but as his vision began to shimmer in front of him and the nausea started rolling in waves, he realized that something was wrong.

"It's the shots." His companion from the examination room was right beside him. "Take deep breaths," he whispered. "Don't lock your knees. That cuts off the blood to your head."

"Need to sit down," he mumbled.

"No!" came the urgent whisper. "You're already on Jessel's list, and he's watching."

"Right. Thanks." He slightly bent his knees and took three deep breaths. As he let the third one out, his eyes rolled up in his head and he collapsed to the ground. The last thing he remembered was, "If you faint, it's all right to lie down."

September 24, 1914

The company commander stuck his head out from the door to his room, which was on the far end of the barracks. "Eckhardt?"

Hans was lying on his bed studying the manual on assembling and disassembling their rifles. He jumped down immediately. "Here, sir."

The officer jerked his head toward his own room and then stepped back inside.

Franck Zolger, who bunked directly below Hans, grinned up at him as he straightened his uniform. "What did you do now, Hans?"

He shrugged, looking worried. "I don't know, Franck."

"Well," he said, smiling even more broadly, "be polite. That always helps."

"You're the career soldier boy," Hans growled. "Not me."

Hans saluted Lieutenant Moeller as he stepped inside. "Private Eckhardt reporting as requested, sir!"

"At ease, Eckhardt," the lieutenant said. He was seated behind his desk and flipped him a casual salute in return.

Hans spread his feet apart and clasped his hands behind his back in the traditional at-ease stance. The lieutenant had a folder spread out before him. He examined it for another minute and then looked up. "Sergeant Jessel tells me that you have a grievance."

"Not against him, sir, but yes."

"Good. The sergeant is a good man. A good soldier."

Hans agreed with the second comment. He wasn't sure about the first, but, of course, he said nothing. "Sir, I recently graduated from the Von Kruger Academy in Munich. I suppose you've not heard of that school, sir."

"That's right. I'm from Hanover. That's a long ways from Munich."

"Well, sir, it's a premier private school. I graduated with an emphasis in science and engineering. In fact, I graduated *summa cum laude*." The officer was reading the file again—his file, Hans assumed—so Hans paused. The lieutenant waved his hand.

"Go on, Eckhardt."

"I was accepted at the University of Berlin in engineering for this fall, sir."

Maybe the lieutenant didn't know about the academy but he certainly recognized that name. Hans was pleased to see a glint of respect in his eyes. "Go on," he said again, listening now.

"When war was declared, I immediately enlisted, sir. I wanted to fight for the Fatherland."

"*Gut, gut.*"

"When I got my letter of induction it said that after basic training, I am to report to a truck driver's school in Stuttgart."

Moeller tapped the letter in the file. "*Ja*, I see that here."

"But, sir. The sergeant at the recruiting station told me that if I volunteered instead of waiting to be conscripted, I could choose whatever army job I wanted. I told him I wanted to be in an engineering battalion because of my training, and he said that was an excellent idea and enrolled me."

The lieutenant stared incredulously at Hans's face for a long moment and then burst out laughing. "And you believed him?"

October 20, 1914—Graswang Village, Bavaria, Germany

Inga Eckhardt watched anxiously as her husband grew more and more agitated. Whatever it was that Fritzie Heinkel, their postman, was telling him, it was not good news. When they finally parted, Hans whirled around and stormed toward the house. Inga met him as he came in. "What is it, Hans? What's wrong?"

"It's Hans Otto."

One hand flew to her mouth. "Has something happened to him?"

"*Nein*." He was already moving for the stairs.

She rushed to him and grabbed his arm. "Then what is it?"

He turned, his face flushed and his mouth pinched. "He's in Oberammergau."

"*What?* But—"

"He's actually hiding in the men's toilet at the train station. He sent a note to Fritzie and asked him to bring it to us. He wants to see us."

"Hiding? I don't understand. Why would he be hiding?"

"I can only think of one reason," Hans said grimly.

Inga shook her head, not understanding. "What?"

"He's AWOL from the army."

"AWOL? What does that mean?"

"Away without leave. He's run away."

"No, Hans. No. That can't be."

"Well, I'm going to go and find out."

"Get my coat too. I'm going with you."

"No, Inga. You will stay here."

Her eyes flashed in anger. "I will either go with you or I will walk there myself. He is my son, too."

For a moment, she thought he was going to turn his anger on her, but then he nodded. "All right. But I am leaving in two minutes."

• • •

Hans Otto whirled around in disbelief. "You thought I had deserted? Thank you so much," he said bitterly. "Thank you for trusting in me. I have a three-day pass." He reached in the pocket of his uniform and withdrew a folded piece of paper and waved it at them. "I am not that big of a *dummkopf.*"

"Then why were you hiding in the toilet?" Inga asked. They were no longer in the train station but in a grove of trees about a block away. Hans Otto had made them wait until the train station was empty, and then they had come here—or rather, sneaked here.

He threw up his hands. "Because I didn't want anyone to know I'm here. The last thing I want is a bunch of stupid questions."

"Because you're thinking about not going back," his father shot right back. It wasn't a question.

For a moment, Hans Otto looked like a trapped animal, and

191

then he looked away. That was when Inga saw the bruise on his neck. She went over to him. He shrank back a little when she raised one hand and pulled down his collar. "What happened to you?"

"It doesn't matter." He turned away from her.

"Hans Otto Eckhardt," she snapped. "I asked you a question and I expect an answer."

"All right then," he burst out. "I'll show you what happened." He took off his coat, wincing sharply as he pulled it off his shoulders and laid it across a nearby bush. He quickly unbuttoned his shirt and removed that as well.

Inga gave a low cry. Hans Senior jerked forward, staring. His son's whole upper body was covered in bruises. They ranged in size from as large as a melon to several fist-sized ones. There was also a three-inch abrasion on his shoulder. The largest bruise, centered on his right rib cage, was a sickly yellow-brown. Hans Otto slowly turned to reveal a similar sight across his back.

"What happened to you?" Inga cried, her voice filled with horror.

He picked up his shirt and gingerly slipped it back on. "We had this big inspection of our barracks. The battalion commander was there, as well as our platoon sergeant and our company commander. Sergeant Jessel had screamed at us for a week that there couldn't be one thing out of order or we would all end up cleaning every toilet on the base. So we really went after it. We even stayed up all night to make sure everything was perfect."

His father was nodding. "My papa used to tell me about those inspections."

"So we were all lined up, standing at attention when they came in. The lieutenant and the sergeant just followed behind while the colonel went through our barracks. I couldn't believe it. He had a pair of white gloves with him. He would climb up on a chair and actually wipe his gloves along the top of the window frames. He checked the floors, the toilets, the sinks, the showers. He even made us pick up the rifle racks—" he looked at his mother. "Each rack holds twenty rifles, so they weigh two hundred pounds or more. He made us lift them off the ground while he swiped the floor underneath with his gloves. But we had been told to expect all of that, and so he found nothing."

He stopped as he retrieved his jacket and put that on as well. "After that, he inspected our rifles." He closed his eyes for a moment as the memory came back. "I don't know how it happened, but my rifle was not completely clean."

Again he looked at his mother, hoping to win her to his side. "I had cleaned my rifle. Or at least what I thought was my rifle. I don't know if someone switched it on me, or what, but—"

"Hans Otto?" his father said, giving him an accusing look. "Don't lie to us."

"I swear, Papa." He sighed, which caused him to wince in pain and hold his side with his elbow.

"So *he* did this to you?" Inga asked incredulously.

"The battalion commander?" Hans Otto exclaimed in surprise. "Oh, heavens no. He just assigned our platoon to clean toilets for a week." He shook his head. "Not just me. He punished the whole platoon."

"And they punished you," his father said, seeing it instantly.

"Exactly. The night after we finished our last day of latrine duty, I was sound asleep. We were all exhausted. Suddenly I woke up with a blanket over my head. Hands were grabbing at me. They lifted me up and took me out behind the barracks. And then everyone either took a punch at me or kicked me." He touched his side. "The doctor thinks I've got a cracked rib. They kept yelling at me and calling me a pig, a maggot, a filthy dog, and every other horrible name they could think of. Fortunately, they also kept yelling at each other not to hurt my face." His voice was filled with bitterness. "They didn't want anyone to see what they had done to me."

"That's horrible," Inga cried. "Did you tell your sergeant?"

Hans Otto laughed bitterly. "I didn't have to. He knew. The next morning when he saw me hobbling down to the latrine, he sneered at me and asked how I had slept."

"He probably put them up to it," his father said. "It's the army way. Deal with your own problems."

"That's not the only thing, Mama. There are so many other things I could tell you. But . . ." He looked at his father. "But I'm not going back. I've come to say good-bye. I'm going to catch the next train to Austria and—"

His father exploded. "*You will not!*"

"Papa." He was pleading now. "Remember how they promised they would assign me to an engineering battalion? Well, guess what. When I finish basic training I get to be a truck driver."

"Then be a truck driver," his father roared. "There's no shame in that. But don't you quit. Don't you turn tail and run like some back alley cat slinking away in the night."

"You can't make me stay, Papa," Hans Otto cried. "I don't need your permission."

"Hans," Inga snapped. "You will not talk to your father like that."

"I don't, Mama. I'm eighteen now. I don't need his permission for anything."

His father took a step closer, raised a finger, and shook it in his face. "If you do this, if you make that choice, then we will never—"

Inga quickly stepped between father and son, but she was looking up at her husband. "Before you say that, Hans, may I speak to our son for a moment?"

His eyes were spitting fire. "No, Inga. You've spoiled him enough. It's time he faced up to his responsibility and—"

"*I've* spoiled him?" she cried in disbelief. "Am I the one who gave him lavish birthday presents his whole life? Was I the one who sent him to Oberammergau to a special school? Was I the one who decided he needed private tutoring? Was I the one who refused to punish him when he did wrong, saying that he was cute, or he was adorable, or he was just being a boy? No, Hans. That wasn't me. That was you."

She caught her breath, glad to see that she had shocked him into silence. "Oh, I'm part of it too. I went along. Cooked his favorite foods. Made his bed for him until he went off to the academy. But now our chickens have come home to roost. Now we reap the consequences. And therefore, I have a right to speak as much as you do."

His chest was rising and falling and his face was livid. "Don't you stand against me on this, Inga," he hissed. "I'm warning you."

She reached out and took both of his hands. He tried to jerk them away, but she refused to let go. "Perhaps if you will let me speak, you might learn that I don't stand against you on this, Hans. Perhaps you will see that I stand firmly with you."

He searched her eyes for a long moment, not convinced. But he was swayed by her intensity. "All right," he finally said. "You may speak."

She turned to her son, who had watched this exchange with

195

growing dismay. "Mama," he said, "I am so sorry that it's come to this."

"No, Hans. Sorry is a word that means nothing coming from you right now. It is the same word you used when we caught you lying about that girl. It is the same word you used when you came home and told us you had joined the army. You refused to seek our counsel then, because you knew what we would say. Have you learned nothing from that? Oh, no. You come having already decided to become a deserter. You're not here for counsel, you are here to seek our blessing."

Her voice went very quiet. "But I cannot give you my blessing, and neither can your father. You cannot escape the consequences of your foolishness. You want us to say that it's all right for you to become a deserter? An outcast? A runaway?"

"But, Mama, I—"

"No," she cried. "How could you ask our blessing—my blessing—when you dishonor our family, our name, and yourself?" She turned away, fighting to keep her voice steady. "I am so ashamed of you at this moment. I'm not even sure I can call you my son any longer."

His head dropped and he started to cry. "No, Mama. Please. Don't say that."

She stepped back and looked up at her husband. He was staring at her in astonishment. Then he reached out and took her hand and kissed it softly. "Thank you, my dearest wife. I am sorry that I doubted you."

Then he turned to Hans Otto. "Here is what you are going to do. You are going to get on the train and go back to the base. You will tell everyone that you had a wonderful visit with your family on your three-day pass but that you are anxious to finish your training."

"Papa, I . . ." One look from his father and he dropped his head again.

"And you will become a truck driver, the best truck driver in your unit. And if necessary, you will drive all over France, or Belgium, or Holland. You will serve in the Imperial Army. You will do your duty to the Fatherland, and you will make us proud."

Inga looked up. "Actually, I thank God that you will be driving trucks, Hans. For that means you will not be on the front lines. You will not have to face the actual horrors of war."

He didn't look at his mother. His eyes were fixed on his father. "And if I don't do as you ask?"

For a long moment, his father stared at the ground. When he looked up, tears had filled his eyes. "Then," he said, very slowly and very softly, "we shall take down your picture from the fireplace. We shall box up the things in your room and give them away. Then we shall go to the land office in Garmisch-Partenkirchen and have your name removed from the deed as our heir. And when we die, the farm will go to another, for you will no longer be our son."

He lifted his finger and shook it under Hans Otto's nose. "But none of that will matter, because deserting in wartime is treason. And the penalty for treason is death. You are not clever enough to escape them, Hans Otto. They will find you, and they will shoot you down like a dog."

Hans looked at his mother. Her eyes held his, but she said nothing more. He spun away, angry that the tears were coming fast now and that his voice was so choked up that he couldn't speak.

After a moment, Inga went to him and gently turned him around to face her. She laid a hand on his cheek. Then she went up on tiptoes and held him tightly. "The boy that hid in the men's toilet is no more," she whispered. "Go back, Hans. Become a man. Then come see us. Your room will be waiting and your picture will still be on the mantle."

He looked up at his father. To young Hans's astonishment, he came over and stood beside his wife. There was no anger in him now, just an infinite sadness. He laid a hand on his son's shoulder. "Come home again, son. And we will never speak of this again. You have my word."

"Our word," Inga murmured.

Chapter Notes

Camp Otto Von Bismarck and its location are not based on any actual military camp in Germany at that time.

Life in the German army as depicted here is based on personal military experience and research about military life in general. Regardless of what country it is, the experience in basic training is very similar. It is deliberately designed to be demoralizing and dehumanizing in many ways. Its purpose is to crush the independent spirit so that in combat, soldiers obey without hesitation. Most nations expect and demand absolute loyalty to the army during this process, and until the acceptance of their authority becomes automatic, they are not satisfied.

Some of the experiences that Hans undergoes here reflect the author's basic training experience. One young man there who had failed to clean his rifle and caused his whole platoon to be punished was stuffed into a footlocker and rolled down three flights of stairs. He was in the infirmary for two days but never again failed an inspection.

CHAPTER
14

April 28, 1916—Somewhere in Occupied France

Dearest Mama, Papa and family,

I am so sorry that I haven't been able to write for almost two months now. There is a major offensive going on and we have been part of that as we drive our trucks day and night to keep our division supplied with food, clothing, and ammunition. It is quite a sight to see a convoy of trucks five or six miles long all going to the front and then returning empty to our rear base.

Let me tell you what our trucks are like. Ours have high sides and are covered with canvas so we can keep the loads we carry dry. As for the cab, this is a big drawback. There is a light framework over the cab that has canvas stretched across. It is open on three sides. The cover supposedly keeps the rain and snow off of us as we drive. This works wonderfully IF (1) the truck is not moving and (2) there is no wind of any kind. Yes, in the winter it is terribly cold and we wear heavy coats, caps, scarves, and gloves and wrap our legs in blankets.

I have decided that this is how I am going to make my fortune after I become an engineer. I will design a truck that is fully enclosed, with glass windows and perhaps even a heater that utilizes the heat from the engine to warm the cab. Fortunately, spring is coming and things will be warmer.

By the way, I am delighted to tell you that the friend I made in basic training, Franck Zolger, was also assigned to be a truck driver. We came here together and are again in the same platoon. We share a tent, and we persuaded our sergeant to let us be a driving team. This is an enormous boost to my morale. We have grown as close as brothers, which is wonderful for me because I never had a brother.

We are now in France. I cannot say where because the censors will only strike it out. Our army is temporarily stopped due to fierce resistance from the French, though I am sure we will soon be on the move again. Once we destroy the French armies, they will have to surrender and the war will be over. Our officers are saying we will be home by fall. But for now, our forces and the French have entrenched themselves, and there is no more movement either forward or backward.

I wish you could see the trenches. On one run, we took ammunition up near the front lines. It was hard to take in once we got down into the trenches. What was once green forest is now a denuded landscape of death and suffering. The earth has been rent by the constant shelling, and large shell holes filled with rainwater are everywhere. The trees are gone, and only burned and blackened stumps remain. Fences made of barbed wire run all across no-man's-land. You can see dead horses and burned-out tanks. And the smell is unbelievable.

In some ways, the trenches are a marvel. They snake for miles across the desolate landscape. Some are four and five feet wide and the walls are reinforced with wood slats and planking. Those closer to the front are often barely wide enough for two men to pass. In the more established ones, men will make dugouts in the sides to provide places to eat and sleep out of the rain. Command posts are larger rooms with beams overhead and pillars to hold up tin roofs covered with dirt. We heard a report that one of those roofs collapsed and several of our men were buried alive.

Mostly the trenches are a nightmare. With all of the rain, side walls collapse all the time, and the mud can be a foot deep. It rains almost every day now, sometimes in torrents. Everything is wet, and almost every man has some kind of fungus infection on his feet or in his crotch or armpits.

There is a joke the men in the trenches tell. The company commander gathers all of his men together and says, "Men, I have some good news and some bad news. The good news is, you all get a change of socks. The bad news is, Georg, you change with Heinz. Fritz, you change with Manfred."

Franck and I are very fortunate. Sometimes we have to sleep in our trucks when we are on the road, but usually we are back to our tents each night. Our tents have wooden slats for floors, so our feet stay mostly dry.

After seeing the front lines, I went back to our base grateful to be a truck driver and not a combat infantry man. Thank you, Mama. Thank you, Papa. I am so ashamed when I think back on that day in Oberammergau. How close I came to making the biggest mistake of my life. Well, the second biggest mistake. The biggest was joining the army instead of going to university.

One more thing, and then I must close. About a week ago, we saw our first gas attack. We had heard that the German Imperial Army had used poison gas against Russian soldiers on the Eastern Front back in January. Now both sides are using it more and more. This is a horrible thing. There are different kinds of gasses—tear gas, chlorine, and phosphine—which are delivered by opening large canisters on the battlefield when the wind is blowing in the right direction or by putting it in artillery shells.

The worst is the mustard gas. Normally it is not fatal, but it is heavier than air and so when a shell explodes, the gas sinks to the ground and drifts downhill into the trenches. And once in the soil, it can remain active for several days. If it gets on your skin, it creates great mustard-colored blisters. If it gets in your eyes, your eyelids stick together and it can cause permanent blindness. The worst is when you breathe it. It sears the throat and the lungs, and they say the pain is excruciating. It can also cause brain damage. Very nasty stuff.

Fortunately, we have been trained what to look for and what to do the instant a gas attack comes. And we always have our gas masks with us, even if we are not on duty. So I don't want you to worry about this, Mama. We are very careful.

One of the horrible things of war is that when a gas attack occurs, the wind can blow it into nearby villages or towns. The civilians there have no training, and only a very few have gas masks. A few days ago, as we were returning from the front, our trucks were stopped because there had been a gas attack up ahead of us. We were not in danger, so we sat around for a couple of hours playing cards and grabbing a quick nap. When we were finally given the go-ahead, we started again, all wearing our gas masks. About two miles later, we passed through a French village. It was horrible. The village was directly downwind of the attack, so the gas had drifted there. Most of the young men of the village are off to war, so it was mostly old men, women, and children there.

I will not try to describe what we saw, for I do not want you to have these images in your mind. I will only say that it was ghastly beyond anything you can imagine. For some reason, I always thought of war only in terms of the combatants. Now, as I see whole villages turned to rubble, or rich fields of wheat churned into mud by the tracks of the great tanks, or dead bodies lying in the streets, I realize that war affects everyone.

How grateful I am that thus far Germany has not seen war in the Fatherland. I pray that it will always be so until we are victorious.

Well, I must close. Thank you, Mama, for the knitted mittens and scarf. The weather is finally turning warmer, but for weeks I was the envy of my whole outfit. When I saw the box with three dozen cookies in it, I was sorely tempted to keep it hidden and share it only with Franck. But knowing what you would say, especially since you have become a Mormon, I finally shared it with all of my squad. You now have twelve soldiers in northern France who are madly in love with you and beg you for more cookies whenever you can send them.

My love to all. I miss you more fiercely than I could ever say. I am well. I am safe. And I am where I need to be. Thanks to both of you.

With all my love, your son,
Hans Otto

December 16, 1916—Verdun, France

Hans shifted down, and the engine growled as the truck began to slow. Franck came awake with a start, his arms flailing. His eyes were wild and he looked at Hans as if he were a stranger.

Hans braked to a stop and then pulled up the lever that set the parking brake. He set his cigarette on the floor, careful not to touch the burning end with his gloves, and then reached over and shook his friend hard. "Franck! Wake up."

Recognition finally dawned. "Hans?"

"Yes. It's me. You're all right. You were having a bad dream."

Franck looked around them. It was bitterly cold, and Hans stuck his hands beneath his armpits to warm them. "Where are we?" Franck asked.

Hans reached down, picked up his cigarette, and drew deeply on it. Then, as he exhaled the smoke through his nose, he handed it to Franck and grinned. "Actually, I have no idea other than I think we are still in France."

Franck puffed on the cigarette and the end glowed bright red for a moment. "What time is it?"

Hans shrugged. "I'm guessing we've got about half an hour until dawn, but with the rain, can't tell for sure."

Taking another deep draw, Franck blew smoke out of his nostrils and then flipped the butt away. "I'm serious, Hans. Where are we?" He opened the door, stepped out on the running board, and looked behind them. He gasped and stiffened. "Where is everybody?"

"Somewhere in the night, I got us lost, Franck."

"You what?" he exploded. "How could you lose a whole convoy?"

Hans shut off the truck's engine. "It was pouring rain all night. And with the blackout, none of us had our headlights on." He blew out a long breath. "And I got so cold and tired, I pulled off the road to grab some quick shut-eye." He glanced at his friend. "I tried to wake you up, but you were like the dead."

Disgusted, Franck turned and looked forward. "We are still headed west, so the front has got to be straight ahead of us."

Hans nodded. "I'm guessing that we're still about ten miles away."

"Is the reserve division we're supposed to be supplying ahead of us or behind us?"

"Don't be a *dummkopf*," Hans said. "The division left before we did. I would know it if we passed a whole division. So, what do we do?"

Franck slid back in and shut the door. "I guess we keep going forward until we either find the front lines or start getting artillery down our exhaust pipe."

• • •

About forty-five minutes later, Franck sat up straight in the seat and pointed forward. "What's that?"

"What's what?" Hans leaned forward, straining to see in the half light of morning. The rain was now just a drizzle, but the overcast sky still kept things pretty dark.

"In the road. Left side. About seventy-five yards ahead of us." Franck was squinting to see better. "It looks like . . ." He fell back and then barked, "Stop!"

Hans had seen it too. Movement. He stomped on the brake and the truck slid to a stop in the heavy mud. He reached over the back of the seat and groped for his rifle. Franck was ahead of him. He turned around in his seat and in a moment had both of their rifles beside them. Franck checked to make sure each had a round in the chamber and then looked at Hans. "What do we do?"

Hans said nothing. He was totally focused on the movement up ahead of them. It was men; there was no question about that. And they were in two rough columns, so they were soldiers. His heart was pounding and his mouth was suddenly dry. Then Franck cried aloud, "They're ours."

Hans saw it at the same moment. The helmets confirmed it. He let out his breath in a long sigh of relief. Those were definitely German helmets.

"Ach, du liebe!" Franck breathed, leaning forward, peering

out at the approaching columns. "Just look at them." His voice reflected both surprise and pity at what they saw before them.

Hans shut off the truck's engine. He took his rifle, and together he and Franck got out of the truck and started forward.

The first thing that hit them was the smell. With an open cab, the smell was not new to them, but the diesel fumes usually helped cover some of the stench of death. Now it was like a physical blow to the nose. Hans swallowed hard, feeling like he was going to retch, and raised his arm and put it across his face. Franck clamped a hand over his nose and mouth, nearly gagging. "How can those on the front stand it?"

As they moved forward, what they saw coming toward them made them forget the smell. It was a formation of soldiers, who—no, not a formation. A formation suggested some kind of order. Here there was none. It was a line of men, sometimes two abreast, sometimes three. Some men were right behind someone else; in other cases there were gaps in the line as long as twenty or thirty feet. And they came not like soldiers on the march, but like a line of skeletons—the walking dead. Their heads were down, their arms dangled at their sides, their feet shuffled along as if they were men in their nineties. Hans saw only one or two rifles in the whole group. Their uniforms were black with mud. Half were without helmets. The second man in line was barefoot. A man behind him wore only his socks and puttees.[*]

Hans felt a growing horror as he surveyed the oncoming men. One man had a bandage wrapped around the stump of his arm. The end of it was bright red. Another had a cloth bandage around his head that covered one eye. They walked as if they were

---

[*] A puttee is a long piece of fabric or soft leather that is wrapped around the legs from the ankle to the knee to provide support and warmth.

drunk. And then Hans realized that they were drunk—drunk with exhaustion, drunk with shock, drunk with horror.

"He's an *Offizier*," Franck said in a low voice.

Hans nodded. He too had just seen the captain's bars on the leading man's shoulders, nearly obscured by the mud that caked his uniform. "But where's the rest of his company? Surely this can't be all . . ." He counted swiftly. A company was over a hundred men. With the captain, he counted eighteen.

Hans straightened and stepped forward. Franck fell in beside him. Seeing that, the officer raised a hand and shuffled to a stop. The men did the same. One or two were peering up ahead to see what it was. Most didn't even lift their heads.

"Captain," Hans said, snapping off a salute. "Lance Corporal Hans Otto Eckhardt, sir." He half turned. "And this is Corporal Franck Zolger."

The hand at the man's side lifted slightly and then dropped again. It was as if he couldn't remember what he was supposed to do with it. His eyes were glassy and had a faraway look in them. But finally he did manage, "Captain Detman Adenaur." Then he looked past them. "Is that your truck?"

"Yes, sir."

"Would you have room to give us a ride back to our unit?"

"Uh . . . no, sir. I'm sorry, sir. We have a load of supplies for the Third Division, who are coming out of reserves to help counter the French attack. You didn't happen to see them, did you?"

Again a long pause as he tried to process that. "Yes. They came in last night. Relieved us of duty."

"Ah, that's good news, sir." Then he had a thought. "We have rations on board, sir. And barrels of coffee. It's cold, sir, but you and your men would be welcome to what you need."

Tears sprang to the captain's eyes. His hands trembled. And then he dropped to his knees and threw his arms around Hans's legs and began to sob uncontrollably.

• • •

By the time Hans and Franck got the rations out and passed their own tin cups filled with coffee around from man to man, the rain had begun to turn to snow. The men didn't seem to notice. They sat in a ragged half circle around the back of the truck and began to eat. Though Hans and Franck had not eaten since the night before, they stood back. Hans knew that with the smell in the air, the moment he opened his mouth to eat, he would lose everything.

Finally, after watching them for several minutes, Hans sat down beside Captain Adenaur. He had an open can of salted pork beside him, but at the moment he was eating his biscuit in prim, small bites. It reminded Hans of how his grandmother ate. Hans had a dozen questions he wanted to ask, but he held his tongue. He could see that the food was already having a positive effect on them.

"What unit are you from, corporal?"

Hans was surprised. Adenaur was watching him now. His eyes were clearer, but still haunted.

"Fourth Transport Brigade, Third Division, Fifth Army, sir," Franck answered for them.

"And you, sir?" Hans asked. "Did you command a company?"

His eyes held Hans's for a moment and then jerked away. Tears shone brightly as he choked back a sob.

"It's all right, sir. We understand."

He shook his head. "When I saw you two boys in your neat

uniforms and your heads held high, I thought of my company. Seven days ago, I walked down this road with a hundred and twenty men." The tears spilled over and trickled down his cheeks. "Now—" He turned and looked at the shells around him. "Now I have only twenty left. And half of those are insane."

Eighteen, actually, counting yourself. But Hans didn't say that aloud. "What happened?"

"The hell that is called Verdun," he whispered. "That is what happened. Four days and four nights of continuous bombardment. Ninety-six hours. With no protection except for a narrow trench filled with mud and ice and rats. The night became as day as the shells exploded almost continuously. The earth shook like jelly. You cannot hear anything but the explosions, which seem to be inside your own head. Hour after hour. Day after day. Night after night.

"And always the mud. The interminable mud."

Hans and Franck turned. The man who wore only muddy socks and leather puttees caked with mud had stopped eating to chime in. He raised one foot and shook it at them. "I saw you looking at my feet. You are wondering what happened to my boots, *ja?*"

After a moment, Hans nodded. "Yes, I guess we were."

"When the French attacked, they marched their artillery bombardment up the hill about a hundred and fifty yards ahead of the infantry. It was like the jaws of hell itself were opening before us. We could see it coming closer and closer, with the French troops following right behind it. So we ran. We ran for our lives."

He looked at his feet for a moment and then back to them. "As I ran, I jumped into a shell hole filled with water. The mud on the bottom was so thick and so miry that when I jerked my feet up, my boots came off." He shook his head grimly. "I determined that I could do without them at the moment." He turned and looked at Hans. "You wouldn't happen to have a pair of boots in that load of supplies, would you?"

Hans looked at him and slowly shook his head. "If we did, they would be yours."

Suddenly the captain spoke again. "Can you smell it? The stench of death?"

"Of course we can smell it," Franck said.

"I can't. Not anymore. None of us can, because it's part of us now. Not just on our clothes, but in the pores of our skin. It was in the mud we crawled in, in the water we drank, in the air we breathed. There are hundreds of unburied dead scattered across no-man's-land. Maybe thousands. No one dares go out to retrieve their bodies."

Suddenly he was fishing in the pockets of his uniform. He withdrew two small items, placed them on his palm, and held them out to Hans and Franck. "Here."

"Garlic cloves?" Franck asked in astonishment as he took them from the officer.

"Yes. Put one in your nostrils. It helps you cope with the smell. I don't need them anymore."

Chapter Notes

A letter written from combat zones in wartime would never have been allowed to contain the kind of detailed information found in Hans Otto's letter to his parents. Censors went through all mail and blacked out any references to locations, battles, or other aspects of the war that might be useful to the enemy. However, those details are included so that the reader might get a small glimpse of what war meant for those who were immersed in it.

The use of poison gas in the Great War, also called the World War (it wasn't called World War I until the outbreak of World War II), is estimated to have inflicted 1.32 million casualties. The estimates of civilian casualties from gas attacks range from 100,000 to 260,000. Commanders on both sides were aware of the danger to civilians, but nevertheless continued to use gas attacks throughout the war. One British commander wrote in his dairy: "My officers and I were aware that such [a] weapon would cause harm to women and children living in nearby towns, as strong winds were common in the battlefront. However, because the weapon was to be directed against the enemy, none of us were overly concerned at all" (L. F. Haber, *The Poisonous Cloud: Chemical Warfare in the First World War* [Clarendon Press], 106–108; as cited in http://en.wikipedia.org/wiki /World_War_I#Chemical_weapons_in_warfare).

Much of the description given here by the captain and the man with no boots comes from eyewitness accounts of the battle, both French and German (see http://wereldoorlog1418.nl/battleverdun/index.htm).

The Battle of Verdun, in northeast France, is the longest single battle in the history of warfare, and the costliest in terms of casualties. The Germans launched an attack on February 21, 1916. The battle raged back and forth until December 18, 1916, when the French launched a major counterattack. In preparation for the attack, the French bombarded the German lines for six days. They fired 1,169,000 shells from over 800 artillery pieces. Estimates of casualties (dead, wounded, and missing) are 714,000, with about the same number coming from both sides. That is about 70,000 casualties per month (see http://en.wikipedia.org/wiki/Battle_of_Verdun#15 .E2.80.9317_December_1916).

CHAPTER 15

December 17, 1916—Verdun, France

C orporal?"

Hans turned around, lowering his razor. A tall man in an officer's uniform with major's emblems on the shoulders was coming toward him. Hans snapped to attention and saluted him. He saluted back.

"This your truck, Eckhardt?" he asked, glancing at Hans's name sewn over his right breast pocket.

"Yes, sir. My codriver and I are with the Fourth Transport Brigade, Third Division, sir. We just got in yesterday."

He watched the man carefully. Something about the officer suggested that he came from a family of some influence. You could see it in his bearing, and Hans noticed that his uniform was tailor-made. He wore a mustache that covered his upper lip. It had obviously once been carefully trimmed and shaped, but now the mustache was ragged and unkempt. He had three days' worth of whiskers that were almost blond, like his hair. His blue eyes were wide set and intelligent, but now darted back and forth, as if he were searching for the enemy even here in the rear echelon.

The flap to the tent opened and Franck stuck his head out. When he saw the major, he practically leaped out and saluted smartly. "Corporal Zolger, sir."

The major came up to them, looking around. "Where are your rifles, soldiers?"

"In the tent, sir," Hans answered.

"This is the front line, Corporal," he snapped. "You are to have your rifles within reach at all times. Do you understand me?"

"Yes, sir." Hans jerked his head at Franck, who darted back into the tent and came out with their rifles.

"Where are the keys to your truck, Eckhardt?"

Puzzled, Hans fished in his pocket and held them up.

"Good. Leave them on the seat. Get your gear and be ready to leave in ten minutes."

"Sir?" Hans asked, stunned.

The major, who hadn't given his name, stepped up and stuck his face right next to Hans. "We have four French divisions attacking on all three of our flanks," he hissed. "You two are no longer truck drivers. You are now in the infantry."

He walked over to where Hans had been shaving and picked up the razor. He looked in the sliver of mirror that Hans had saved from a shattered farmhouse. Leaning in closer, he rubbed his hands across the stubble on his chin. "Leave your razor and shaving gear, Eckhardt. Where you're going, you're not going to need it."

January 6, 1917

Hans nudged Franck's shoulder. "I don't like the look of that," he muttered under his breath.

"The look of what?" Franck turned his head toward where Hans was looking. They were sitting in the mess tent, which was barely above freezing. They were eating a breakfast of scrambled eggs that were as tasteless as putty, dark brown pumpernickel bread that tasted of mold, and cold coffee that was so bitter one could hardly gag it down. But then, there was nothing else to gag down in its place, so they kept spooning the food into their mouths and then washing it down with coffee.

Hans was looking at the far end of the mess tent, where the officers sat.

"So?" Franck said. "They have hot coffee and we don't? Does that surprise you? Rank hath its privileges."

"No, *dummkopf*," Hans hissed. "Look at the guy sitting with his back to us. Next to *Oberleutnant* Habbes. Isn't that the major that dragged us into all of this?"

Franck squinted at them. As he did so, the man turned around and waved his cup at one of the cooks. "Yeah," he said, "and it looks like he's still using your razor."

"I don't like the look of it," Hans growled. "*Oberleutnant* Habbes has looked over in our direction three times now. I think they're talking about us."

"No!" Franck exclaimed softly. "Not another patrol. That will be our third one this week."

They dropped their eyes as the major stood up and the three lieutenants with him got to their feet too. The major said something about the morning and walked out. The other two lieutenants followed him out, but First Lieutenant Habbes came straight toward Hans and Franck. They both stared into their coffee, pretending not to see him. It didn't slow him down even a fraction.

"Lance Corporal Eckhardt."

Hans looked up, feigned surprise, and then shot to his feet and saluted. "Yes, sir!"

"We've just learned that our forward outposts reported movement during the night. They think French troops are moving up, possibly preparing for an assault. You will take your squad on a scouting patrol and probe their positions."

Hans wanted to scream out at the way the army cloaked the ugliest of concepts in the most pleasant of terms. "Probe their positions" meant expose yourself to their fire and see if you can figure out how many there are. But instead he barked out, "Yes, sir, Lieutenant, sir."

"Report at battalion headquarters for briefing at oh-nine hundred."

"Yes, sir. How long do you expect we'll be out, sir?" he asked, dreading the answer.

"Until you get the intelligence the major needs. Take a bedroll and enough rations for overnight."

"Yes, sir." He saluted again, but the lieutenant had already turned away and was headed for the door.

"A bedroll?" Franck exclaimed. "In this kind of weather? That's insane."

"No, that's the army."

January 7, 1917

Ignoring the cold that was seeping through his overcoat and uniform and turning his belly to ice, Hans slowly swept the stark landscape below them with the binoculars. Nothing. Even the birds had better sense than to be down in no-man's-land. There was no movement. No sound. Just the eerie silence of the battlefield. He rolled on his side and handed the field glasses to Franck. "Nothing. You take a look."

Frank sat up, pulled his knees up, and propped his elbows on them as he put the glasses to his eyes. "Stupid forward observers," he muttered. "Seeing ghosts in the night. Too scared to go down and take a look themselves, so they call on us grunts." He made a wide sweep and then lowered the glasses. "I say we pack it in and head back. We're freezing our tails off out here."

"You know that those same observers are watching us right now, Franck. And if we go back without going down there, they'll report that, and that major will cut our tails off."

There were murmurs of agreement from the ten men spread out in the snow behind them.

"Then I say we go up and shoot the forward observers."

Laughter. Hans sighed. That was Franck, always griping even though he knew full well that it never got him any—CRACK!

The sound of the rifle shot broke the silence. Hans felt the snap of the bullet just above his head and jerked away. "Sniper! Sniper! Get down! Get down!" He jerked up his rifle and blasted off a shot, though he had no idea where the rifleman was.

CRACK! Another round zipped over his head. Behind him, the other men opened up, blasting away at nothing. "Hold your fire! Wait until you see him." Then he turned his head. "Franck, give me the glasses."

No answer. Hans slid backward, getting off the ridgeline, and then lifted his head to see where Franck had disappeared to. A cry of anguish was ripped from his throat. Franck was three feet away from him, sprawled on his back, his eyes wide open and staring at the sky. Leaping to his knees, Hans was to him in a second. "Franck! Franck." There was a small black hole in his chest, just above the heart. Clawing at him, Hans ripped Franck's greatcoat open and then gasped as he saw the red stain that covered the whole left side of his chest. "No!" he screamed as he put his fingers to his friend's throat, feeling for a pulse.

Suddenly the world erupted. A machine gun opened fire from down below. Then another. Rifles were cracking almost continuously. Not waiting for his command, his squad opened return fire.

Hans didn't have time to wait to see if there was a pulse. He scuttled forward, peering over the ridge. What he saw was so shocking that for a moment he couldn't take it in. The snow-covered field below him was now a mass of movement. At least a hundred French infantry in white greatcoats and with white coverings on their helmets were on their feet or just getting up from the snow. He could see the flashes of their rifle muzzles winking at him as the deafening fire increased every moment. Others sprang out of the snow even as he watched.

Behind him his men were pouring their own fire downward. Their position gave them the advantage, and Hans exulted as one Frenchman after another was slammed back or stumbled and went down.

As he watched, a machine gunner walked his fire up the hill, kicking up geysers of snow with every round, but it was off to his left. Hans took another quick look. Now he saw that the enemy wasn't just directly in front of their position. They had hidden in the snow in a long, U-shaped formation, hoping to trap the Germans within their perimeter. Hans guessed that the sniper had fired too soon, giving away their position. Now they were coming up the hill in the same formation, screaming like banshees and firing as they ran. Hans understood instantly what they were doing. They were going to try to encircle his squad.

"Run!" he screamed. "Get back to our lines. Go! Go!"

He leaped to his feet, shouldering his rifle. In two steps he reached Franck. Dropping to one knee, he lifted Franck to a sitting position and then hoisted him up onto his shoulder. "I've got you, buddy. Hold on." Shocked by the dead weight, he staggered for a moment and almost slipped.

"He's dead, Eckhardt!" someone screamed. "Leave him."

"No!" He lumbered forward toward his retreating men, staggering under the weight. Hans had always kidded Franck about how someday, if he lived right, he would grow up to be a real man like Hans. Hans outweighed him by forty pounds or more and had three inches of height on him. But now it felt as if Hans were carrying a horse on his shoulder.

"Here they come!" someone shouted. Hans didn't turn around. Bullets were flying all around now. He felt a little thrill of hope when he saw that his men had stopped and formed a skirmish line and were firing as fast as they could pump shells into their chambers. Though he felt as though his legs were on fire and his lungs were going to burst, he increased his speed and rushed past them.

"He's dead," someone cried again. "You have to leave him."

"You don't know that," Hans half-yelled, half-sobbed. "You don't know that."

The next half an hour would forever be a blur in his memory. His ears were ringing from the constant rifles being fired off all around him. His lungs were on fire. His feet were like great clogs of iron. A man walking half-backward alongside him, providing covering fire, cried out. He went to his knees and then fell face-first into the snow. Another man off to his left took a round in the back of his helmet. There was a sharp ricochet and he went sprawling. Hans couldn't tell if the bullet had pierced his helmet or if the force of the blow had knocked him down.

They reached the first trench, which was abandoned, and dove into it. Suddenly a shell whistled overhead and exploded fifty yards away, knocking three Frenchmen flying. Another, then another exploded.

A shout went up from his men. It was *their* artillery firing. And the forward observers were calling it down just ahead of them with deadly accuracy. The line of oncoming men faltered as the roar intensified and shells began to decimate the advancing line. He heard an officer shouting something in French. Hans turned his head enough to see that those in the attacking line had stopped and were beginning to fall back. They were still firing, but sporadically now, and without taking aim. Hans slumped down in the mud and let Franck slip off his shoulder. He immediately felt for a pulse. Nothing. He felt again. There was nothing.

"He's dead, Hans," the man next to him said softly. "He's gone."

"I don't care," he sobbed. "Help me get him up." When he stood, taking a moment to steady himself, he looked at the men around him, counting swiftly. Seven now, counting himself. He wouldn't let himself think about that. "All right. This trench goes almost to our lines. Stay low. We've got to get out of here before the French regroup. Go! Go! I'll bring up the rear."

CHAPTER 16

April 15, 1917—Graswang Village, Bavaria, Germany

My dearest Hans,

It has been two months since we last heard from you, and that was only a brief note. I am sure you do not often have time to write, so we understand. I also know how devastating it was for you to lose your closest friend in such a tragic way. Even now I find myself weeping when I think of Franck and the positive influence he had on you. I pray for his family every night that they might find peace.

There is a bit of worrisome news. I hesitate to share it with you because of all the pressure you face, but I feel I must. Your father has been complaining about stomach pains for a month or so. It is probably just too much schnitzel and strudel, but it's not going away. I'm sure you can imagine what he said when I suggested he see a doctor. "Doctors are a bunch of quacks just trying to get our money."

Paula and Wolfie were down to visit a couple of weeks ago. When they saw Papa wincing, Wolfie called a doctor in Munich who specializes in stomach ailments and asked if he would be willing to come down and examine your father if Wolfie paid him. The doctor agreed to come and, to my surprise, your father agreed to see him—which tells you that this is more serious than he is letting on. I will let you know what the doctor says after he comes.

Now, Hans, as your mother, I must chide you for not sharing your good news with us. Yesterday, Fritzie Heinkel brought us a letter from the War Department. It gave us quite a start because we feared the worse. So imagine our delight and surprise when we opened it and found a copy of a letter to you informing us that you had been awarded the Iron Cross, Second Class, for conspicuous bravery in battle.

Why didn't you tell us about the Iron Cross? What a great honor. We are so proud of you. I hope it is not a secret, because I'm afraid that your father has already told everyone in the village and probably half of Oberammergau. The letter gave no details as to why you were awarded this honor, so please, don't be modest. Tell us what you did to earn such a prestigious honor.

Well, I must close. I see that the United States of America has entered the war on the side of the Allies. Oh how I pray that this does not mean the war will be prolonged. Everyone said the war would be over in a year. We are now into our fourth year with no end in sight.

I pray for you morning and night, as do your sisters and their families. As you know, Papa is not a praying man. But the other night, he came in as I was saying my prayers. He knelt down beside me and held my hand. "Say a prayer for me, too," he said. "Pray for my Hans Otto."

We know you are in constant danger and under continual stress. May God keep you in the hollow of his hand.

All my love,
Mama

June 13, 1917—Verdun, France

My dearest Mother,

Thank you for your letter. It did not arrive until just a few days ago. My time is short, so I shall be brief.

I wish Papa had not told everyone about the Iron Cross. I did not write to you about it because I am not proud of it. Just the opposite is true. I will say only this. I was in command of the patrol that day. I was responsible for the safety of my men. I knew the French had long-range snipers, but I didn't think of that until it was too late. Now Franck, the best friend I ever had, is dead. There was no honor in bringing out his body. The only honor would have been to bring him out alive. Please tell Papa not to speak of it further. Also I would appreciate it if you would tell people not to ask me about it when I come home. *If* I come home. The one good thing I will say about it is perhaps now you and Papa can be proud of me again.

On another matter: I do not wish to hurt you, Mama, for I know what you believe, and I know of your faith. But please do not write anything more in your letters about prayers or God. If you and Papa want to pray, that's your right. But I don't want to know about it. After all that I have seen and been through, I can no longer accept the idea that there is a benevolent deity out there watching over his children. How can any God look down on the blood and the stench and the death and the horror that I have seen and not intervene?

One last thing. A few days ago we got a new captain in our battalion. He will be our new company commander. He is about thirty-five, I would guess, but he graduated several years ago from the University of Berlin. Care to guess what his field was? That's right. Engineering. That's why he entered the army as a commissioned officer rather than as a grunt like me. If there is a god, he has a perverse sense of humor. I now have a company commander who every day reminds me of what I could have had, of what I could have been.

Remember what you said when I joined the army? "What have you done, you foolish, foolish boy?"

Hans

P.S. I am sorry that this letter will make you cry. But that too seems to be my lot in life.

July 6, 1917—Graswang Village

Dear Hans,

Once again I feel as if I am standing outside the men's toilet in the Oberammergau train station, trying to coax a young boy to come out and become a man. Your father has told me not to say anything to you, that you have enough to cope with as it is.

I'm sorry, but I do not agree. But I shall say only three things to you.

I have inquired further into the actions that led to you receiving the Iron Cross. There is no shame in what you did. If Franck were alive, he would tell you that and rebuke you for thinking otherwise. In dishonoring yourself, you dishonor him as well. You say you were a fool for not considering the possibility of snipers, and that may be so. But then wasn't Franck also a fool when he sat up? And all of your men? Or was it just a natural oversight considering the fact that you were in a very dangerous and stressful situation? Grief for one whom you loved as a brother is a noble thing. Punishing yourself for something that is the natural result of your circumstances is not. I have never been prouder of you than I am at this moment, nor have I ever loved you more. Please don't make me feel otherwise by being ashamed of it.

As for God? I don't remember asking you to believe in Him or to pray to Him. I simply expressed my own faith and my own trust in Him. I'm sorry if that offended you somehow. That is easily fixed. Either you can skip over those parts of my letters, or I can stop writing to you altogether. But do not ask me to turn away from that which is as central to my existence as is the air I breathe.

Now, it deeply saddens me to say one more thing to you. Your burdens are beyond what most are called upon to bear, but I must add one more. The doctor examined your father two weeks ago. At first he thought it might be kidney stones or gallstones, but after an examination and talking to your father, he suspected it might be something else. He asked us to bring Papa to Munich for further examination at the hospital there. There is a recent development in medicine that they call an x-ray machine. I don't understand how this is possible, but he said that with that machine they could take a picture inside Papa's stomach, and that would help him decide what was wrong.

I took Papa up by train last Monday and we just returned this afternoon. The picture showed a mass inside Papa's stomach about the size of a small loaf of bread. The doctor said it is almost certainly cancer. He also said that if it is not treated, your father has no more than six months to a year to live. When I asked him how cancer is treated, he said there is only one way. Surgery.

So on August 1st, we will take Papa back to Ludwig Maximilian University Hospital, where this doctor is on the staff. There he will undergo a five-hour operation.

I ask two things of you as you contemplate this terrible news. First, I know that in times of war, it is highly unlikely that they will give you leave, but will you please ask? Beg them if you must. This may be your last chance to see your father alive.

Second, I am praying for your father night and morning. Can you find it in your heart to put aside your pain and your anger against God and pray with me for your father? It may mean nothing to you, but I believe that God will hear our prayers and that it could make a difference in the outcome.

Forgive me for hurting you further.

Mama

August 1, 1917—Ludwig Maximilian Hospital Munich, Germany

Inga woke with a start as someone gently shook her shoulder. She opened her eyes and sat up and then gave a low cry. "Hans?" She leaped to her feet and threw her arms around him.

"Hello, dearest Mama." He pulled her close and held her fast as tears instantly overflowed in both of their eyes. "I'm here, Mama. I'm here."

"Oh, Hans," she said with a cry. "Is it really you?" She stepped back and held him at arm's length. He was in his dark green dress uniform with his cap placed jauntily on his head. He looked more handsome than she could ever remember. "I can't believe it's you. It's a miracle."

"I'm sorry, Mama. I was supposed to get here last night, but with the war, train schedules are not dependable. We had to wait on a side track while several troop trains went by."

"You're here. That's all that matters."

"Any word on Papa yet? They said at the front desk that he was still in surgery."

She glanced up at the clock. "They started about three hours ago, but I have heard nothing. The doctor said it would be four to five hours."

He took his mother by the arm and gently helped her sit down again. Then he sat beside her. "I never dreamed they would let me off, but I decided that all they could do was to say no. So I talked to *Hauptmann* Bergdorf. He's the new company commander that I wrote you about, the one that graduated from the University of Berlin."

"*Ja*, I remember. And he said yes?"

"Not at first. He said that the Fifth Army is going to be part of a major offensive against the British and Americans in a few weeks and that there was no possible way he could let a platoon sergeant take leave."

"Did you tell him about Papa's operation?"

"Yes. He sympathized but said that there were many other soldiers whose parents had serious health problems. But, I could tell he was wavering due to the Iron Cross. I could tell he wanted to do it. I started to turn and walk out when a thought came to me. I told him that I was your only son—that I had three older sisters but that I was the youngest, and the heir of our dairy farm. I couldn't believe what happened next. He told me that this was exactly his family situation—he'd had three girls and then a boy. You could see his eyes shine with pride as he spoke of his boy, who is just six. And that did it. He wrote me out a four-day pass and then wrote me out a chit as well."

"A chit?"

"Yes, a voucher for a train ticket. He wrote on there that I was on official army business, which helped me get a ticket, even when the trains were full."

Inga's lower lip was trembling. She bowed her head and momentarily closed her eyes.

He laughed. "Are you praying, Mama?"

"I am thanking the Lord for giving me this miracle. I didn't think there was a chance in a thousand that we would see you."

"It's not a miracle, Mama, it's just very good luck."

"You call it what you will, I will call it what I will."

Just then, they heard a voice calling, "Inga. Inga."

They looked up. Down at the far end of the hall two figures were coming toward them at a rapid walk. Hans jumped up. "It's Paula and Wolfie," he cried, then dashed away. Inga got up and followed after him.

Paula stopped dead when she saw who was coming. Then she squealed aloud and ran to him, arms extended. "It's so good to see you, Aunt Paula," he said, hugging her tightly. Then, as Wolfie joined them, the two shook hands vigorously.

Paula stepped back as Inga also joined them. She looked at her sister. "He's here. This is a miracle."

Inga reached out and poked her son in the ribs. "What did I tell you?"

He just chuckled.

"Come," Paula said. "Catch us up. When did you get here? How long can you stay? Did you get to see your father before he went in?"

Laughing aloud now, and suddenly filled with an overwhelming sense of joy to be here with his family, Hans waved toward the bench. "Come. Let us sit down and talk."

• • •

The doctor came out shortly after noon. Instantly they were all on their feet. The doctor broke stride for a moment when he saw a man in uniform, but then his face was wreathed in smiles. "Ah," he said. "Sergeant Eckhardt. Welcome, welcome. Your mother was afraid you would not be allowed to come."

"I was given a four-day pass, sir, for which I am most grateful. How is my father?"

Motioning toward the bench, he said, "Sit down."

As they did so, he walked over to the nurses' station and

retrieved a chair. He brought it back and set it down in front of them. As he sat down and faced them, Inga saw the deep lines of exhaustion on his face. But she was relieved to see no pain in his eyes.

"The operation went well," he began. "Everything went as planned, with the exception that the tumor was slightly larger than we expected. However, the good news is that it seemed to be pretty well contained in one place. We could find no sign that it had spread to other organs."

Inga's head dropped and tears came. "*Danke schön*," she whispered.

"However, Frau Eckhardt, I must warn you that sometimes the cancerous cells spread unseen to other places in the body. We're not sure how that happens, but it does. But I am very optimistic that we got it all. And that is very good news."

Hans reached out and took his mother's hand and then tipped his head down to rest against hers. "Oh, Mama. That *is* wonderful." Then he looked up at the doctor. "How soon can we see him?"

The doctor shook his head. "Not for several more hours. He is still heavily sedated, and he will be in a lot of pain." He held up his index fingers, holding them apart to demonstrate. "The incision we made to get in and take out the tumor is about six inches long." He smiled briefly. "And, sadly, as we grow older, we do not heal as fast. But perhaps by this evening he will be awake enough for you to visit for a few moments."

He stood, and they all stood as well. "When do you have to return, Sergeant?"

"I can stay through tomorrow afternoon and then I must start back."

"You will be able to talk to him by then," he said.

They thanked the doctor profusely, and then he excused himself and walked away. After a moment, Hans turned to his mother. "We can do nothing here for now. I didn't get much food on the train. Let's go find somewhere to eat. Do you know how good it sounds to have something other than army chow?"

Wolfie laid a hand on his shoulder. "It shall be my treat. I know just the place. But I warn you, we are on food rationing due to the war. It won't be much."

Hans slapped his uncle on the arm. "It won't take much to beat army food."

Smiling, Inga touched her son's arm. "You go. I will stay here just in case something comes up."

Paula was immediately nodding. "I'll stay with Inga. Bring us back something."

As they sat down again, Paula laid a hand on her sister's arm. "Before I forget, Inga. I did talk to President Hoffman. He is happy to come and give Hans a priesthood blessing. Would you like him tonight or tomorrow?"

"The sooner the better."

"Good, I'll have him come tonight. Hopefully, Hans will be awake by then." She gave her sister a questioning look. "How will young Hans feel about that?"

Inga's head came up slowly. "It doesn't matter what he thinks. It is not his decision."

"Good."

But Inga was clearly irritated by the question—not at Paula, but at her son. "I talked to my Hans about it. I explained what it was and what it was for. I told him that we would only do it if it was something that he wished to have done."

"And what did he say?"

"He said he would be glad for any prayers in his behalf

—Mormon, Lutheran, or Catholic." She sighed. "So if young Hans doesn't like it, he can step out of the room."

August 2, 1917

Hans put his arms around his mother. "Mama, it's all right. Come in with me. Papa will want to see you again, too."

She shook her head. "I have plenty of time to be with him. This is your last chance."

Hans Otto glanced up at the clock on the wall. It was 1:10 in the afternoon. Finally, he nodded. "I would like that. Thank you, Mama."

When he went in, it took a moment for his eyes to adjust to the dim room. As he approached the bed, he couldn't tell whether his father was asleep or not. But then he saw a hand rise and wave weakly before dropping back again. He moved to the bed and took that hand in his. "Hello, Papa."

He felt a squeeze in response. Still holding onto his hand, he pulled a chair closer and sat down beside the bed. "How are you feeling today, Papa? You're looking much better."

Hans Senior turned his head back and forth and pulled a face. Hans smiled. "You're looking much better than you did last night, anyway."

There was a slight tug on his hand. Hans scooted his chair closer and leaned in so his face was just a few inches from his father's. It was hard to look at him this closely, even with the curtains drawn. He was shocked to see the toll the disease had taken on him. His skin was a sickly gray and sagging around the cheekbones. The luster was gone from his eyes. One corner of his mouth sagged a little, but the doctor said that was probably from the anesthetic. What hurt the most was that there was so little left of the robust, energetic man who had been his father, his mentor, his model, his advocate, and his best friend during his childhood years.

"How soon?" It came out as a barely audible croak.

"How soon? Oh, do you mean how soon do I leave?" His father nodded. "I have to be back to my unit by tomorrow night. My train leaves at 3:15 this afternoon. Wolfie will drive me to the train station. I have about half an hour before I have to leave."

Another barely perceptible nod.

"Did you know that Wolfie bought a motorcar?"

To his surprise, his father rolled his eyes. Hans laughed. That was more like the father he knew. With the war on, Wolfie had progressed rapidly in his civil service job and was now making a comfortable salary. Everyone liked Wolfie, but his father had always groused about how he liked to put on a show.

Another tug. Hans leaned down again. "Yes, Papa?"

"Tell me."

"Tell you what, Papa?"

"About war."

"Ah," he whispered.

"War is hell," he croaked.

Hans was surprised by the vehemence in his father's voice. He reached in with his other hand and clasped his father's hand in both of his. "How long was Grandpapa on the front lines, Papa?"

His other hand came up and he held up one finger.

"A year?"

He nodded.

"He never talked about it, Papa. Remember how I would pepper him with questions? But all he would talk about was being a soldier, never about combat itself. Now I understand why."

"Tell me."

231

And so, Hans leaned in and began to talk, softly and calmly, as though he were describing someone else's life. He talked about basic training, about the injustices and hardships. He talked about driving trucks and the interminable boredom. Then he recounted how the major had come to him when he was shaving and ripped him and Franck from boredom to battle.

He talked for several minutes, almost forgetting that he was speaking to his father. Suddenly, he stopped, thinking his father had gone to sleep again. But his eyes were opened, and filled with understanding.

"Don't tell Mama, Papa, but after I won the Iron Cross, they asked me if I wanted to go back to the Transportation Brigade." He shook his head in wonder. "I told them no. Part of that was because I thought that it would be a betrayal of Franck. And by then, I was a platoon sergeant and I thought, 'How can I go back to driving trucks when the others in my platoon don't have that choice?' So I told them no."

"More though."

He looked up in surprise. "More? You want me to tell you more?"

Hans Senior shook his head. "No. More than honor. In the blood."

For a moment, Hans wasn't sure what his father meant, but then he understood. "Yes, that too. It was unbelievably awful—the mud, the rats, the rancid food, the mold, the latrines that smell so bad you have to wear your gas mask when you go, the never-ending stench of death. But soon I began to dread the down times, the endless waiting, more than combat itself. When you're on patrol, or in a firefight, you feel alive in no other way I've ever experienced. I hated it. I dreaded it. And yet . . ." He rubbed his eyes. "I longed for it. Hoped for it. Volunteered for it." Almost in awe, he continued. "Even loved it, in a way. And they keep giving me medals for that. How's that for irony?"

"I know. I know."

"Papa, I have to go soon, but I want to talk to you about something. You don't need to respond. But I need to say it, okay?"

Another wan nod.

"I . . ." He shook his head. "I can't say this to anyone else, Papa, but I think we are going to lose the war."

"Yes!"

"With the Americans in now, the tide is turning against us. We were told that they are coming in at a rate of ten thousand per day. And we have lost so many men. Many of our units are at half strength or less, with virtually no reserves." He shook his head. "It is bad luck to think about the future, because I may not have a future, but sometimes at night, I cannot help myself."

"I understand, son."

"I made a huge mistake when I turned my back on the University of Berlin. You and Mama saw that immediately. Now, at last, I see it too."

"Good."

"I want to make something of myself, Papa. But . . . I can't do that on the farm. I can't do that milking cows. If I go to university, you know that I'll never come back, don't you?"

"Yes. I've known that for many years."

"I'm sorry, Papa. But you have good sons-in-law who will help you. They love it like you do, Papa. It is only right that it should go to them."

He nodded, obviously tiring rapidly now.

"The war has robbed my generation of our lives. On both sides. As I see the dead bodies strewn across no-man's-land, I want to weep. Where is their happiness? Where is their opportunity? Where are their wives and children? So if I am spared, if I come out of this alive, I must seize life while I can. I must make something of myself. And when I do, I will take care of you and Mama in your old age. And Grandmama and Grandpapa, too."

As he looked down, he saw that his father's eyes were glistening, and he stifled a sob as he stood up. "I have to go, Papa. I love you so much. I am so glad I got to see you."

His father squeezed his hand but couldn't speak for his emotions.

"You're going to get better, Papa. I feel it."

"Yes. Many prayers."

"Including mine."

As he bent down and kissed his father's forehead, a sudden dread swept over him. Would he ever see this man again? The thought was more than he could bear. The sobs began to shake his body. *"Auf Wiedersehen*, Papa. I love you."

CHAPTER

17

October 28, 1918—The Siegfried Line—Northern France

Sergeant Hans Otto Eckhardt's first sight of the Siegfried Line stunned him into awed silence. He had heard about it, of course. Anyone fighting in France or Belgium knew about the massive defensive line erected by the Germans after their defeat at Verdun.

With serious losses at places like Ypres, the Somme, and Verdun, the German High Command knew that they could no longer throw an endless stream of men, equipment, and supplies against the growing power of the Allied Forces. They were a long ways from being defeated as 1917 began, but they needed a place where they could more easily defend themselves while they consolidated their forces and resupplied their armories.

So they chose a line that started near the northern coast of France and ran all the way south past Verdun. Under General Ludendorf's direction, 500,000 contract workers from Germany, along with thousands of Russian prisoners of war, were brought in. In five months' time, they had destroyed the infrastructure and demolished all civilian bridges and roads, leaving a "desert" behind for any invading armies.

Thousands of small concrete bunkers called *stollens* provided secure firing positions for the German machine guns. Each of these was fenced in by thousands of rolls of the dreaded concertina wire. The whole area was crisscrossed with trenches and tank traps. To the far west, along the line that the Allied forces would have to cross first, no-man's-land was strewn with tens of thousands of mines. When finished, the Germans had a swath of defendable ground that was a hundred miles long and 6,000 yards wide.

As far as Hans could see, it looked more like a scene from Dante's depiction of hell than a piece of earth where people had once lived and worked and laughed. Here and there he could see stands of trees, but most of these had been shredded by shelling. Sunlight glinted off thousands of pools of standing water, mostly shell holes filled in by the rain.

Hans felt a strange melancholy come over him as he contemplated what war had brought and what men were willing to do to prolong it.

And now, with the Germans still entrenched behind the Siegfried Line, the Allied Forces were massing, bolstered by a huge infusion of American troops. Things were looking more and more grim for the German Empire.

"You seen enough, Sergeant?" the corporal, who looked like he might be all of fourteen years old, asked. "They are going to start the meeting in five minutes, sir."

"Don't call me sir," he barked. "I am a noncommissioned officer. I work for a living."

"Uh . . . yes, Sergeant. Sorry, sir. Uh . . . I mean, Sergeant."

Face flaming, he turned and hurried down the steps of the observation tower.

Hans actually smiled for a moment, remembering his first day in the army and Sergeant Jessel. He wondered if Jessel was somewhere in France screaming his lungs out at anyone who wore a uniform and was of lower rank than he was.

• • •

The colonel, whose name Hans could not recall, came to the front and stood behind the small table. He took a moment to survey the fifty or more men in the room. As usual, the officers were in the chairs while the noncoms—all platoon sergeants like Hans—stood in the back.

"Men," he began without preamble. "I don't need to tell you that our situation is grave. I have come from army headquarters, where General Ludendorf had called in all corps, division, regiment, battalion, and brigade commanders. He did so because, to put it bluntly, we have reached a position where we can no longer *win* this war."

He stopped as the shock rippled through the group. Hans guessed that the shock was not from hearing that they were not going to win, but that the high command was acknowledging that fact publicly. That spoke reams about where the situation stood right now.

"But," he roared, stabbing a finger into the air, "neither can we afford to *lose* it."

That brought a smattering of applause and a few cheers. He went on without acknowledging it. "General Ludendorf is now in negotiation with the Allied commanders for a cease-fire and eventual peace." More murmurs, mostly of approval now.

"But," he went on grimly, "so far, the Allies are not responding. They believe that the stag is down and they have the scent of blood in their nostrils. They are pressing for an unconditional surrender and an armistice to follow."

No surprise. If the situation were reversed, the Fatherland would do the same thing.

"The purpose of this meeting is to help the Allied commanders change their minds. We need something to bring them to the bargaining table. As you know, the British First, Fourth, and Fifth Armies, joined by the French First Army and the American expeditionary forces, supported by as many as eight hundred tanks, are currently attacking up and down the full length of the Siegfried Line. Our troops are putting up a fierce resistance, but they are advancing."

Hans was staring at the man. So the rumors were true. For a week now, word on the front line was that since August their losses had been staggering. Some were saying that the Allies had captured over a hundred thousand German troops—roughly ten divisions. No one spoke of how many dead, wounded, and missing had also been lost. The stag was not just down. It was being devoured by the hounds.

"Therefore, our orders are to make them pay dearly for every inch, every foot, every yard of terrain. You all know that we do not have the tanks to stop eight hundred of theirs, but we can slow them down, make them pay."

His eyes lifted to the back of the room. "This is why you platoon sergeants have been invited to this staff meeting. It will be on the platoon and company level that this occurs. It will be your men fighting in the trenches and enduring the artillery barrages. General Ludendorf asked me to have you tell your men that he

has never been more proud of them than he is on this day. It will
be in the trenches that we will save the Fatherland."

And it will be in the trenches that we will die.

Hans shook it off. Or tried to. That day when he had said
farewell to his father in the hospital, Hans had experienced a momentary premonition of death. He thought it was because his
father had cancer and he might never see him again. Now . . . ?

•   •   •

He filed out after the others, not joining in their hushed conversations. The melancholy he had felt earlier was back. Worse,
the feeling of dread that he had felt at his father's beside was also
back. And he now knew why. It wasn't because his father was
going to die. According to his mother's latest letter, though his
father's recovery was slow, he was steadily progressing.

Angrily, Hans reached in his pocket for his cigarettes. As he
stopped and lit one up, he realized something else. That familiar
tingle that preceded a coming battle was not there today—only
an overwhelming sense of dread and a profound sorrow.

November 1, 1918

They felt them even before they heard them.

At first it was barely perceptible. Then the earth began to
visibly tremble. Inside the dugout that served as their platoon
armory and supply shed, the ground was dry. Pebbles started to
dance along the ground. The puddles outside, whose surfaces
only moments before had been as smooth as glass, were now covered with concentric rings of ripples.

Instantly, everyone went very still. As the tremors increased, they heard the first low rumble of powerful engines. Dozens of them. Maybe more.

Hans was looking through a handheld periscope that allowed him to see over the top of the trench without exposing himself. Not that he could discern much in the near total darkness.

"Can you see them?" one of his men called to him.

He shook his head. "But they're coming. And they sound like the heavies." Which was what they feared the most.

The Allied Forces had created both "light" and "heavy" armored battalions. Each light battalion had about seventy of the French-made Renault FT tanks. These were only slightly taller than a man and not much bigger than an automobile. They carried only one operator. They were faster and more maneuverable but easier for the opposition to stop. Even a hand grenade, if placed right, could blow off the tracks and immobilize them.

The heavy tank battalions had about fifty of the British-made Mark VI tanks, or MK 6, as the armored cavalry men called them. The MK 6 was a massive and ponderous behemoth, with tracks as tall as a man. It carried 57-mm cannons and two machine guns, one on each side. It could go right over the top of an artillery piece, push over a truck, or knock down full-grown trees. It was virtually unstoppable unless it took a direct hit from an artillery shell or someone ran up behind it and shoved an explosive charge into the tracks.

Hans's platoon supposedly had artillery support three or four miles behind them, but with the army's usual efficiency, his platoon had been given a radio whose batteries were so weak that it had gone dead after only four calls. So now they were totally dependent on the forward observers, who were at least half a mile away, to call in their artillery report.

They had been given two cases of explosive charges specifically designed to stop a tank, twelve in each case, but after a full day of fighting yesterday, they were down to ten charges. And judging from the growing roar of the engines, Hans guessed that a full battalion of heavies was approaching their position.

Again he looked in the periscope. Against the black earth and the black sky he could see no silhouettes, but now he could make out dozens of tiny slits of light. There was no question what they were. The night was so dark the tanks had to turn on their headlamps, which were completely blacked out except for one horizontal slit across the width of the light.

"You ready for a flare, Sarge?" someone called.

"Not yet. Our orders are to stop as many of the forward tanks as possible so the others can't get around them. Then they'll be sitting ducks for the artillery."

"Got it."

He lowered the periscope and turned back to his men. "They'll probably have a bulldozer or two leading so they can fill in the tank traps. Harnack and Veizey, you two use the trench to get past those tank traps. As soon as they're close enough, place the charges on the dozers. Be sure you jam them into the tracks so they don't fall out. Then get out of there."

"Right, Sarge." Both men were staring at the ground. Neither of them had looked up.

"Schulze and Streiker, you're coming with me. We're going to go after the first three heavies. We've got to disable them. Langer and Udke, your job is to take anything we don't stop. You'll have five charges. Let's hope you don't have to use them."

"Okay."

"The rest of you will give us covering fire. But be sure of your targets. We don't need you maggots putting holes in our backsides."

They nodded, so relieved that they weren't going out on point that they actually smiled.

Hans stood up and stepped inside the dugout. He bent down over the case that held the explosives. But just as he reached to open the box, they heard a sound that was one of the most dreaded on the battlefield—the scream of an incoming artillery round. "Down!" he shouted.

Twelve men threw themselves facedown in the mud. KABOOM! The shell hit about thirty yards behind their trench. Instantly a spray of mud and shrapnel rained down on them.

"Here comes another!" Hans threw his arms over his head and opened his mouth so that the concussion wouldn't blow out his eardrums. The explosion was deafening. He shook his head, his ears ringing.

The next one was even closer and caused one of the poles holding up the canvas awning over the dugout to collapse. A gush of water spilled down on them. The fourth shell hit so close that it slammed Hans back against the wall of the trench. He bounced off and knocked two of his men down.

"They're ours," someone screamed. "That's our artillery."

He leaped up, swearing bitterly. He was right. The shells were arcing in from behind them. And they had no radio.

"It's those idiot forward observers," someone said, cursing. "They're calling it in before they know where the tanks are."

Hans knew immediately that he was right. "Find cover!" he yelled. "I've got to get to company headquarters and have them call it off." He didn't wait to see if they obeyed. He sprinted down the trench. As he ran, he could feel the rain on his head and face and realized that he no longer had a helmet. It must have blown off in that last hit.

Running as fast as he could, he raced down the trench line

242

that led to the positions behind them. The shells were whistling overhead and exploding every three or four seconds now. The gunners had started a major bombardment, and hell itself was raining down from heaven.

When he reached a point where he was a good fifty yards from his platoon, he scrambled up a ladder and sprinted across the open field for the headquarters bunker. He was screaming at them before he ever reached them.

A sergeant stuck his head out the door. "What?" he called, putting one hand up to his ear.

"They're too low. Your gunners are too low. They're shelling my platoon's position," he shouted.

The man swore and stuck his head inside, shouting at someone. Then he looked up at Hans again. "We'll call them off, Sergeant. Thanks."

"There's a battalion of heavies about a hundred and fifty yards directly west of our position. Tell them to raise their fire and give us some help with them."

The guy waved and disappeared into the bunker. Spinning around, Hans took off again, zigzagging between the barbed wire and the shell holes. He felt a surge of hope a moment later when the screaming started to noticeably diminish. He cupped his hands and shouted at the top of his lungs, "Hang on, guys! Almost over."

• • •

Four miles behind where Hans was racing through the darkness, the first lieutenant in charge of the battery of 155 howitzers slammed the phone down. He turned, waving his arms and screaming, "Cease fire! Cease fire!"

He raced to the left, running hard, shouting his message. As soon as he saw the last gunner shutting down, he spun around and started back toward the right side of the line. The closest ones, seeing the others backing off, were shutting down even though they hadn't heard the lieutenant. But on the far end of the line, the gunners were still firing. Then one by one they turned, saw their commander running toward them, and hesitated.

Except for one. The gunner on the next-to-last gun had his back turned away from the line and was watching as his crew slammed another the shell into the breach. "Clear!" they shouted and jumped back. He turned, opened his mouth, and pulled the lanyard. The cannon bucked and roared and rolled back, smoke shooting out of its barrel. Then, and only then, did he hear the shouts of "Cease fire! Cease fire!"

Chapter Notes

The Siegfried Line was the German name for the massive defensive fortifications they built in the five months following their defeat at Verdun. The Allies called it the Hindenburg Line, after Germany's commanding general. Some of the Allied generals said that the Siegfried Line was a desperate, last-gasp attempt by the Germans to avoid defeat, but in actuality it was a brilliant strategic move. Not only did it give them a place that was easily defended, but it protected the German border. It also consolidated the Western Front into a much straighter line that needed far fewer troops to defend it. When it was finished, it actually freed up about thirty-eight divisions to be utilized elsewhere. It was finally overrun by the British, French, and American forces late in the war as described in this chapter.

Tanks were first used as a major battlefield weapon in World War I, but not until about 1917. The famed World War II tank commander General George S. Patton commanded one of the American armored battalions that fought in France in World War I.

CHAPTER
18

November 7, 1918—Pasewalk Military Hospital
Berlin, Germany

Hans recognized her footsteps the moment she entered the ward. Strange, in a way. He couldn't do that with any of the other nurses or staff. Just Nurse Fromme.

As expected, the footsteps stopped after a moment. *That would be bed number one*, he thought. He guessed that she checked to make sure the patient was asleep, maybe glanced at his chart to see if there was anything new on it. After a moment, the footsteps moved to his right a few steps. *Bed number two, across the aisle*. Ten seconds exactly. She was always very precise. About ten seconds at each bedside, unless there was a problem. He liked that.

He lay perfectly still, listening to her back-and-forth pattern, counting each bed off. Finally, she finished bed number eight, directly across from him, and came over to the foot of his bed. There was a soft scrape as she picked up his chart and read it. He assumed that there must be night-lights that allowed her to read, but with his eyes bandaged so tightly, he couldn't tell.

Another scrape as she replaced it. That was the signal he was waiting for. "Nurse Fromme?"

There was a soft exclamation of surprise. Then her footsteps moved up beside him. "Sergeant Eckhardt," she whispered. "You're awake?"

"Yes."

"Is something the matter?"

"No. I . . . I just always wake up about now."

He heard the rustling of her starched uniform and then was surprised when she laid the palm of her hand on his cheek. It was cool and very soft. And he caught a faint wisp of flowers.

"Really, I'm all right."

"How did you know it was me?"

He shrugged and smiled. "I just did."

"Can I get you something?"

He hesitated and then plunged. "I have a question for you."

"Yes?"

"I know you do your rounds of the wards every two hours. What do you do in between?"

Her hand pulled away, and a moment later the chair beside his bed scraped on the tile floor. He heard more rustling of her uniform as she sat down beside him. The floral scent was immediately stronger and he breathed it in, trying not to be too obvious.

"I do various things. I have to do my charting, or paperwork, as you would call it. Some patients need medication in the night. Sometimes we have a new patient arrive during our shift and we check him in. If it's slow, we'll sometimes just sit around and talk. Why do you ask?"

"I . . ."

"What?"

"Do you ever read to patients?"

Somehow he could sense that he had surprised her again. "Not as much at night as on the day shift, because most of the patients are sleeping now. But yes, occasionally." There was a moment's hesitation, then, "Would you like me to read to you, Sergeant?"

"Well . . . I don't want to put you out."

"It is not an imposition. That's what I'm here for."

"Then, yes, I would like that."

"I can only do it if you are already awake. I'm not allowed to wake a patient up for that."

"I'm almost always awake about this time."

Her voice softened with concern. "Are you having nightmares, Sergeant?"

That took him aback. "Why do you ask that?"

"Many do," she responded. "And . . . And last night about this time, as I passed your bed, you were thrashing around and moaning, as if you were in pain. You actually even sat up and cried out. You were very distraught."

"What did I say?" he asked, shocked by her words.

"Nothing intelligible. I pushed you back down and held your hand for a few minutes, and you quieted down again."

"You held my hand?"

She laughed softly. "Yes. Do you not remember that?"

"No. None of it."

"So, do you have nightmares every night?"

He let out a long breath, not sure if he wanted her to know this, but then finally nodded.

"And you can't go back to sleep afterward?"

"No. Not for an hour or more."

"Then I shall come and read to you. We have a small library here. What would you like?"

"What do you have?"

Again there was that soft chuckle. "Our hospital director is a former schoolmaster. I'm afraid he's quite cerebral."

"Cerebral?"

"Yes, sorry. The cerebrum is part of the brain. Cerebral means he's kind of an intellectual thinker. So we have the biography of Sigmund Freud and also his *The Psychopathology of Everyday Life*. We have a book called *Collected Writings of Preeminent German Philosophers*. That includes writings by Kant and Nietzsche."

"No thanks. Any novels?"

"Oh, good," she said merrily. "I was hoping you wouldn't choose philosophy."

He felt himself relaxing. He loved the sound of her laughter and wanted to say something that would bring it forth again.

"Do you speak English?"

Surprised, he nodded. "Actually, yes I do."

"So do I. So we could do James Fenimore Cooper's *The Last of the Mohicans*. We also have *The Swiss Family Robinson*, in German, of course, and . . . let's see. What else? Oh, yes. I must not forget Jane Austen's *Pride and Prejudice*. And that would be in English as well. That's my personal favorite." She sounded a little embarrassed as she added that last sentence.

"Let's do *Pride and Prejudice*," he said without hesitation.

"Really?" she exclaimed. She reached out and touched his arm. "Or are you just saying that because you think that's what I would choose?"

"Does anyone go to war in it?" he asked.

"No. It's a very happy book."

"Actually, that sounds quite wonderful."

She was back about twenty minutes later. As she drew closer, he could tell she had gone up on tiptoes when approaching his bed. When she stopped, he heard a very soft whisper. "Sergeant Eckhardt? Are you still awake?"

"I am," he said. "Very much so."

"Oh, good." She came around and sat down beside him. As she opened the book, he turned his head toward her. "Before we start, can I ask you a couple of questions?"

"Of course."

He rose up on one elbow. "Am I blind?"

He heard her quick intake of breath.

"Please be honest with me, Nurse Fromme. The nurses tell me that they can't say and the doctors are pretty vague. They say I have to wait until the bandages come off to know for sure."

She was silent for a long moment, and he realized he had probably put her in an awkward position. "If you can't say, that's all right."

"Nurses are not allowed to talk to patients about their condition. Only doctors can do that."

He fell back, not surprised.

"But . . ." She lowered her voice. "But I can tell you what happened to you, if you promise not to tell anyone. Nurses are not supposed to read patient files, either, but I . . ." He could almost feel her blushing as her words died away.

"Good for you," he exclaimed. "You have my word. I won't say anything to anyone. All they've told me is that I was caught in an artillery bombardment."

"You don't remember anything?"

"I remember going to a briefing about a major Allied offensive in the morning. The next thing I remember is waking up here in the hospital two days ago."

Her hand came out and touched his arm briefly. "Four days, actually," she whispered. "They kept you heavily sedated the first two days you were here."

He didn't say anything as he took that in, so she went on. "Your platoon was on the front lines somewhere in France with an assignment to stop an attack from tanks. Suddenly, you started receiving friendly artillery fire."

He jerked up. "Friendly? You mean our own guns?"

"Yes, that's what your patient history said. I guess 'friendly fire' is not the best of terms, is it?" She withdrew her hand. "You left your men in the trench and went back to try to stop the firing, which you did. But just as you were returning to your men, one last round came in. It exploded just behind you."

He could hear the emotion in her voice now. "Evidently, you heard it coming and started to turn around, because the blast caught you sideways. You were peppered with shrapnel, nearly a hundred wounds."

He swore softly, astonished to be hearing this for the first time. Then he remembered where he was. "Sorry," he murmured. "Go on."

"Most of the wounds were superficial or required only a few stitches. But you took a bad hit in your right hip, one in the right side of your chest that broke a rib, and one in your right arm."

"Yeah," he said, "I can feel every one of them."

She stopped, and he wondered if she had started to cry. But her voice was steady when she continued. "And one piece about the size of your thumb hit you in the right temple. It penetrated the skull and lodged against what we call the cranial nerve II. That's the nerve that transmits visual information from the eye to the brain. We also call it the optic nerve."

He lay back, his face registering shock. "What about my platoon?"

She hesitated and then very softly answered him. "Six of them were killed in the shelling. Three, in addition to yourself, were critically wounded. One of those died in the field hospital."

A groan of tremendous pain came from somewhere deep inside him as she finished. "Two came out of it with only minor injuries." She was silent for a moment. "I am so sorry," she went on, "but you should know that you are a very lucky man, Sergeant. Another—"

"Just Hans, okay?"

"Okay. But if that piece of metal had gone a fraction of an inch farther, there would be no question. You would be blind. The surgeons were able to remove it successfully."

"Did it damage the nerve at all?"

"The doctors don't think so, but they won't know until they take off the bandages. They wanted the wound to heal some before they look at it."

He threw up his hands. "So it's not hopeless?" he cried. "Why didn't they tell me that?"

She poked his arm. "Shhh. Don't wake up the others." Then she answered his question. "Because they weren't sure. They didn't want to give you hope if there is none."

"What about my left eye?"

"It's fine."

He swore again. "Couldn't they have at least told me that? I thought I was blind for life."

"They did tell you, Hans. But you were so drugged, I'm not surprised you can't remember."

"Oh." He felt really stupid and didn't know what to say.

"It's all right. You've been through a lot."

"One more question?"

"If I can answer it."

"When do they plan to remove the bandages?"

"Nine o'clock this morning."

Now he clutched for her hand. "Really?"

"Yes, really. They told you that, too, but . . ."

He sighed, but it was filled with hope. "How about reading something happy to me?"

"I would be pleased to do so." She picked up the book, and he heard her open it and ruffle a couple of pages. Then she began:

"*It is a truth universally acknowledged, that a single man in possession of a good fortune, must be in want of a wife.*"

• • •

Hans could sense that there were several other people in the surgery room, but no one spoke except Colonel Peter Wobbe, the chief surgeon in the hospital. "Anyone else coming, Nurse Rhinehart?"

"No, Doctor."

"Would you see to the drapes?" he asked.

Footsteps moved across the floor, and then Hans heard drapes being pulled shut.

"Sergeant Eckhardt?"

"Yes, sir?"

"Your eyes have been bandaged for a full week now. That means they are going to be sensitive to light. So I want you to keep your eyes shut until I tell you to open them."

"I understand."

"Are you ready?"

"More than ready, sir."

"All right."

Suddenly Hans felt cold metal against his skin just below the bandages. Then he heard the snip of scissors and felt the bandage begin to loosen. He felt his heart start to race a little. Two more snips and he felt hands come up. One hand steadied his head, while the other began to unwrap the bandage. "Keep them closed," the doctor warned.

"Yes, sir."

As the last of the bandage was pulled away, Hans could see light through his eyelids. He felt a surge of hope. He thought it was so in both of his eyes, but he couldn't be sure. Before he could figure it out, he felt the doctor's hand on his shoulder. "All right, cover your right eye, and then very slowly open your left eye."

He did so, wincing a little at the sudden brightness. Then things began to come in focus. The doctor was directly in front of him, no more than a foot away. He was watching him intently. Behind the doctor were three other men, all wearing white coats over their uniforms. He turned to the right. Two more men in white were there. Slightly behind them was a nurse who was smiling at him warmly. He turned to the left and reared back a little. He was looking into the face of a beautiful woman standing right next to him, who was giving him a brilliant smile.

He was taken aback. No, *stunned* was a better word. For a moment, he thought someone had invited Lady Magdalena von Kruger to be here for this moment. She had huge dark eyes, jet-black hair, and translucent skin. She was incredibly beautiful. And she was smiling at him like she knew him.

"Sergeant, this is Nurse Rhinehart."

"Hello, Sergeant Eckhardt." There was a momentary stab of disappointment, but then he remembered that his mother had sent him a clipping announcing the marriage of Magdalena to some duke from Spanish royalty. "Hello."

"Please cover your left eye now. Keep the right eye closed for a moment longer."

He did so, holding his breath.

"Okay, slowly, slowly now. Open your other eye."

He did so. No one in the room moved. He could feel everyone's eyes upon him. Then his mouth relaxed into a slow grin. "Good morning, Colonel Wobbe," he said.

Instantly, the room erupted into applause and cheers.

It took another half an hour of testing before Colonel Wobbe was satisfied and pronounced that Hans's right eye was as healthy and normal as his left one. By that time, the other doctors had excused themselves and gone back to work, and Nurse Rhinehart had started her rounds on the burn ward.

The colonel shook his hand one last time and warned Hans to keep his eyes covered at least half the time until that afternoon. Then he began to gather up his things. As he did so, Hans was surprised to see that one nurse was left. It was the one who had smiled at him when he first took the bandage off. She had stayed in the corner through the whole examination, smiling shyly at him when he looked in her direction, but never saying anything.

He had wondered about her, thinking that maybe she would be his nurse on the day shift. Now, as she watched the colonel putting his things into his bag, Hans studied her more closely. She was a little taller than average height, maybe five foot three or four. She had brown hair pulled back in a knot below her nurse's cap. Her eyes, placed over a pug nose that was slightly turned up on one end, were a light blue. At the moment, they seemed to be smiling at him too, as if there was some secret amusement behind them. She was somewhat plump but had a pleasing demeanor and a cheerful air about her. Hardly in a class with Nurse Rhinehart, but pleasant enough.

Colonel Wobbe snapped his bag shut, congratulated Hans, and exited. Hans waved and then turned back as the nurse came forward. He stuck out his hand. "*Guten morgen*. I am Sergeant Eckhardt."

She laughed softly. "May I call you Hans?"

He did a double take. "Nurse Fromme?"

"In person."

"But . . ." He was stammering now, surprised at the disappointment he was feeling. He had pictured her as blonde, statuesque, and amazingly beautiful. "I thought you . . . uh . . . were . . ." He stopped.

She tipped her head to one side and looked up at him, the amusement literally dancing in her eyes now. "You thought I was what?"

He was scrambling. "My . . . uh . . . My day shift nurse. Wait! You shouldn't be here."

"I shouldn't? Why is that?"

"Because you're night shift. You should be home in bed."

"That's where I am going now."

"But . . ."

"I wanted to be here, Hans," she murmured. "And besides, I had to ask Dr. Wobbe an important question."

"What question?"

"I asked him if you had to be careful with how you use your eyes for a while. And he said yes."

"I do? What can't I do?"

Her smile became impish. "You can't read books yet."

For a moment he didn't understand, but then he laughed right out loud. "You don't say."

"*Ja,*" she said, with that lilting laugh that delighted him. "Good thing you have someone to read to you, right?"

He stuck out his hand again. "Right, Nurse Fromme. Right you are."

"You can call me Emilee," she said as she shook it solemnly.

That was not expected. "Emilee. Isn't that French?"

"No," she shot right back. "Amélie is French. Emilee is very German."

"I beg your pardon," he said, bowing low. "I am very pleased to meet you, Emilee Fromme."

"And I you, Sergeant Hans Otto Eckhardt."

November 10, 1918—Pasewalk Military Hospital
Berlin, Germany

H ans." Emilee bent down and laid a hand on his shoulder. "Hans, wake up!"

His eyes flew open and his arms began to flail as he cried out, looking around wildly. She grabbed his hands and hung on. "It's me, Hans. It's Emilee. It's all right."

Gradually recognition dawned, and he flopped back against his pillow. "Don't do that, Emilee." He swore softly. "You can't sneak up on a soldier like that."

Then, four things registered at once. The recovery ward was flooded with sunlight. All the other beds were empty and unmade. The clock on the wall read 9:37. And Emilee had a dress on beneath her winter coat, not her uniform.

After years on the front line, Hans had the ability to come alert instantly. He smiled up at her. "Look, Emilee, I like *Pride and Prejudice* as much as you do, but . . . you can't start coming in during the day to read too. You . . ." He stopped, suddenly realizing that they were alone. "Where is everybody?"

She removed her coat and tossed it on the bed next to his.

Then she reached down to the small chair beside his bed and picked up a folded newspaper.

Seeing that, he chuckled. "Really, I love to have you read to me, but don't you think—"

She stopped his words mid-sentence when she unfolded the newspaper and held it up for him to see. It was the *Berliner Morgenpost.* But it was the headlines in one-inch tall letters that seized his attention:

KAISER WILHELM DEPOSED, FLEES TO HOLLAND. EBERT NEW CHANCELLOR. END OF GERMAN EMPIRE, NEW GERMAN REPUBLIC DECLARED. GOVERNMENT EMISSARIES NEGOTIATING SURRENDER TERMS IN FRANCE.

BERLIN SEIZED BY REVOLUTIONARIES. CHANCELLOR BEGS CITIZENS TO MAINTAIN ORDER. RIOTS SPREAD ACROSS COUNTRY. BOLSHEVIKS SEEK TO OVERTHROW THE GOVERNMENT.

For several seconds he just stared at it, his mind unable to process it into something rational. Emilee thrust it at him. "Read it."

He picked it up and then handed it right back to her. "I still can't make my eyes focus on something that small."

"Sorry," she said, taking it back. Sitting down, she leaned forward and began to read.

"'Under tremendous pressure from military leaders and the heads of the Christian Democratic Party and the Catholic Centre Party, Kaiser Friedrich Wilhelm Viktor Albrecht von Preussen, Emperor of the Second German Reich and King of

Prussia, renounced his right to the throne last night shortly after 9:00 p.m. Earlier in the day, Prince Max von Baden also resigned the office of Chancellor and appointed Friedrich Ebert, a prominent leader in the Christian Democratic Party, Germany's leading political party, as the new Chancellor.'"

Hans gave a low whistle. "Did you know this was coming?"

She shook her head. "There's been tremendous unrest since the Sailors' Revolt that occurred about two weeks ago, and that—"

"Wait!" he cried. "Sailors' Revolt? You mean like the Imperial Navy?"

She apologized again. "I forget how much you have missed. So much has been happening all over the country. But yes. About ten days ago, even though the navy admirals knew that the war was coming to an end, they started to plan for one last sea battle against the British Royal Navy in the North Sea. This was done without the knowledge of the German High Command. As they issued the orders and prepared to sail, the sailors mutinied. They had no desire to risk their lives when the war was already over in all but name. They also knew that democratic winds were blowing in the *Reichstag* and that powerful leaders were seeking to end the war as soon as possible. The sailors, who were as sick of war as you are, knew that an attack on the Royal Navy would ruin everything."

"Wow!" he breathed. "I knew that thousands of soldiers were deserting all along the Western Front, but mutiny?"

"Oh, Hans. It's been awful. People all over the Fatherland have been rioting against the war. Millions of workers have gone on strike. With all the unrest, the Communists have seen this as a chance to overthrow our government and tried to seize power."

"Why shouldn't they?" he said bitterly. "That's what they did in Russia last year. Three hundred years of Romanov monarchy came to an end in the October Revolution."

"And did you hear what happened to Czar Nicholas and his family?"

"No. Only that were deposed."

"Four months ago, the Supreme Soviet asked Czar Nicholas and his family to get ready to be transported to a safe house. When they were gathered, armed men rushed in and shot them dead." Her voice was taut with horror. "Nicholas, his wife, and all five of their children."

"And they'll do the same thing here," he said. He swung his legs out of bed and faced her. "They've got to be stopped."

"That's why there's battle in the streets of Berlin right now, Hans. The people are rising up to stop the Bolsheviks."

He leaned back on his hands, dazed. As he considered all that she had said, he noticed again that they were the only ones in the ward. "Where has everybody gone?"

"They're all down in the dining room. Someone has rigged up a wireless set and they're monitoring military radio traffic."

"I want to hear it too." He got to his feet and then clutched wildly for her as the room began to spin. She was up in an instant, gripping his shoulders. "No, Hans. Doctor Wobbe says you have to stay in bed for another day or two. You are not well yet."

He allowed her to sit him back down again and even allowed her to push him back so he was lying flat. "That's why I'm here, Hans. I knew you'd want to know about all of this."

He covered his eyes with one hand to stop the room from whirling around him. "So," he said after a moment. "Is the war over, then?"

"Not officially, but it's close." She picked up the paper, found her place, and continued to read.

"'Even before Kaiser Wilhelm abdicated, Chancellor Max von Baden, with the encouragement of Generals von Ludendorf and Hindenburg, sent a delegation to France to negotiate peace with the Allied Forces. Matthias Erzberger, leader of the Catholic Centre Party, was appointed to lead the German delegation. On the afternoon of the 7th of this month—'" she looked up. "That's three days ago now." Then she read on. "'—the delegation boarded five railway cars and was transported across the front lines and into northern France to meet with Marshal Ferdinand Foch, commander-in-chief of the Allied Armies.'"

She looked up. "Is that how you say it? Fotch? It's spelled F-O-C-H."

"The French pronunciation is Fuhsh."

She nodded and went on. "'In Paris they were transferred to Marshal Foch's private train car, an Imperial leftover from Napoleon the Third, and they were then taken to a secret location in the Com–Compignee Forest.'"

He took her hand, smiling. "Compiègne. They pronounce it Coh-PYEN-yeh." He pronounced it again more slowly. "Coh-PYEN-yeh. The m is almost completely silent."

She waved a hand. "Whatever. Anyway, they went to that forest. They say the location was kept a secret so they wouldn't be bothered by all the war correspondents."

She summarized the rest of the article. "Marshal Foch stayed only long enough to ask our delegation what they wanted and then turned the negotiations over to French, British, and American officers. No press representatives have yet been allowed on site, but it seems the Allied officers showed no interest in Germany's wishes. Instead they arrogantly presented our delegation with a list of Allied demands and said we had seventy-two hours to accept them or face the consequences of hostilities resuming. There is little hope that the Fatherland shall come out of this with much that we can rejoice in. We have lost the war. We know it, and our enemies know that we know it."

Lowering the paper, Emilee looked up. "That's it."

He was staring over her shoulder, seeing nothing. "The stag is down."

She gave him a questioning look, but he just shook his head and closed his eyes. "They are going to sell us out. After all the blood. After all the suffering."

"Who is?"

"The politicians." He nearly shouted it. "Those stupid, pig-headed, brainless imbeciles who run our government. And we are lost."

November 11, 1918—Near Compiègne, France

In two days of bitter negotiations, the German delegation received very little that they asked for. They were the vanquished. The victors always set the terms for peace.

When he was told on the afternoon of the second day that a consensus had been reached, Marshal Ferdinand Foch returned to Compiègne and called for all delegates to assemble at 5:00 a.m. the following morning to sign the official armistice agreement. A few hours before dawn, all delegates gathered in the railway car to sign the final document. There were thirty-five conditions listed.

With the formalities over, as supreme commander of the Allied forces, Foch sent a telegram to all of his commanders saying, "Hostilities will cease on the entire front November 11th at 11:00 a.m. French time." Matthias Erzberger, head of the German delegation, sent telegrams to Chancellor Ebert and the Imperial Army commanders. Word spread like wildfire all across

Europe. Hundreds of telegrams followed. The airwaves hummed with radio traffic. Couriers were dispatched. The press corps raced to telephone exchanges or telegraph offices.

And so it was that as they approached the eleventh hour of the eleventh day of the eleventh month of 1918, officers on both sides of the Western Front stood with watches in hand, their men standing in ranks, gravely waiting for the precise moment. As the final seconds ticked by, they raised their arms high. Then precisely at eleven o'clock, the hands dropped. "Cease fire!" came the command.

Journalists waiting far behind the front lines would later describe what happened next. "The expectant hush that had fallen upon all of us deepened. And then we heard a rippling sound, like a light wind stirring the leaves of the trees. At first, we didn't realize what it was, but as it increased in intensity, we began to weep, for we were hearing tens of thousands of voices on both sides of the line cheering the end of the war. That sound rolled across the fields of France and poured down from the mountains to the sea."

Celebrations erupted in the streets of national capitals. In cities, towns, villages, and hamlets across Europe, millions of non-combatants dropped to their knees and wept. Germans, Russians, Hungarians, Poles, French, Belgians, Dutch, and English—all were united in this moment of joy.

France and Germany had sent about eighty percent of their male populations between the ages of fifteen and forty-nine into battle. The Great War took the life of some nine million soldiers. Twenty-one million more were wounded. Civilian casualties numbered close to ten million. Loss and destruction of property was on so vast a scale as to be incalculable.

Precisely at eleven o'clock that morning, bells that had been silent since the summer of 1914 began to ring. In minutes, bells all across Europe were tolling out the good news. The war to end all wars had come to a close.

Pasewalk Military Hospital—Berlin

In the dining hall there was total silence for several seconds. Then the deep, sonorous sound of the massive bells of the great Berlin Cathedral pierced the silence. No one moved. No one spoke. These men in the room were the detritus of war, the rubbish left in the wake of it. They could think of nothing to do or say that would rise to this occasion. So they sat there and quietly wept.

Emilee Fromme also wept. She let her eyes move around the room to the men she had cared for and nursed back to health. *Here are the ones who made it possible for the bells to ring this day,* she thought. The corporal there in the corner with one leg missing. The sergeant who was paralyzed from the waist down. The lieutenant blinded by mustard gas and his captain, whose lungs were seared so badly in that same gas attack that he would not likely live to see Christmas. The fifteen-year-old boy in the corner who stared blankly at nothing, not knowing and not caring about what was going on around him.

And here, right beside her, was Hans. So strong and so handsome, with his light brown hair and dancing blue eyes and his teasing manner. He would carry several scars to his death, including some that couldn't be seen. She reached out and took his hand, not caring who was watching.

He didn't turn. As the sound of the bells swelled and spread across the city, he suddenly hunched over, burying his face in his hands. Great, racking sobs shook his body. Emilee turned and threw her arms around him, pulling him close. "It's all right, Hans," she cried. "It's over. It's over."

He clung to her in desperation and cried until Emilee thought that her heart would break.

Chapter Notes

The *Berliner Morgenpost* (*Berlin Morning Mail*) was a popular daily newspaper at this time. However, the headlines and the news story Emilee read from the newspaper were not taken from the actual newspaper. They are typical of headlines and articles written on that day.

We now call November 11th Veterans Day. Originally it was known as Armistice Day or Remembrance Day. It celebrated the end of World War I, though the war did not officially end until the Treaty of Versailles was signed on June 28, 1919, in the Palace of Versailles south of Paris. That day was chosen because that was the fifth anniversary of the assassination of Archduke Ferdinand and his wife.

On May 13, 1938, Congress declared Armistice Day to be an official federal holiday. But in 1954, after millions of other soldiers had died in World War II, Congress changed the name to Veterans Day to honor all who fought for the freedom of our country.

It is still traditional in many places in Europe for people to stop what they are doing at 11:00 a.m. on November 11th for a moment of silence. Often at the end of that silence, church bells toll as an additional remembrance of that moment.

In addition to the horrific war statistics given in this chapter, it is also worth noting that many credit World War I as being the initial cause of what came to be known as the Spanish flu pandemic of 1918, which killed about 100 million people worldwide.

Victors of war are rarely either generous or humble. America, through President Woodrow Wilson, tried to convince the Allies not to impose terms on Germany that were so harsh that they would not allow wounds to heal. But Germany and France had been bitter enemies for centuries, and the French, jubilant with victory, were not about to lose their opportunity to stick it to their longtime rivals.

Immediately after the war, the French government started work on a grand memorial at the site of the treaty's signing. It came to be known as the Glade of Compiègne. A statue of Marshal Foch was erected. A bronze sculpture of a huge sword striking down the Imperial Eagle of the German

Empire was made into a monument. In the clearing, on a large, stone slab, the following was inscribed in French:

> Here, 11 November 1918,
> succumbed the criminal pride of
> the German Empire. Vanquished
> by the free people it sought to enslave.

Just over twenty years later, on June 22, 1940, that decision would come back to haunt them. A new document would be signed at the Glade of Compiègne. Another delegation would gather at the site. Only this time it would be the German generals setting the terms, and those terms were the creation of "occupation zones" in northern and western France.

Three days after the signing, which erased the humiliation of the German people, the Fuehrer ordered the memorial site to be totally destroyed and any signs of its existence completely erased. The statue of the German eagle impaled by a sword was demolished. The plaque was broken up, and pieces of it were put on display in a museum in Berlin. The one thing left intact was the statue of Marshal Foch. Hitler ordered that it be left so that everyone could see that all the French general looked out upon was an empty wasteland.

After World War II, the French restored the memorial site as it had been at first, using German prisoners of war to do the labor (see http://en.wikipedia.org/wiki/Second_Armistice_at_Compi%C3%A8gne#Destruction_of_the_Armistice_site_in_Compi.C3.A8gne).

CHAPTER 20

November 12, 1918—Pasewalk Military Hospital
Berlin, Germany

Hans heard the footsteps as soon as they entered the ward. He didn't look up from the book that he was reading. He could tell the footsteps didn't belong to Emilee, and Emilee wouldn't be coming in until sometime after eleven tonight anyway.

To his surprise, the sound kept coming and stopped alongside his bed. "Sergeant Eckhardt?"

He looked up."

"I'm Nurse Weisemann. I will by your nurse for today."

He nodded and then went back to reading. She was pleasant-looking and had a nice smile, but she wasn't Emilee and he wasn't interested.

"Sergeant?"

"Yes?"

"Have you had your breakfast?"

"I'm not hungry."

"You need to eat."

He ignored her, turning back to his book.

Taken aback, she started away but then had another idea. "Did you hear about the pastor who's coming to speak to our men today?"

"I'm not looking for God, thank you."

He saw her flinch, and hurt filled her eyes. He felt a twinge of guilt but not enough to try to undo his gruffness.

She started away again and then whirled back around. "I don't think he's going to be talking about God," she said curtly. "They say he's going to talk about the November criminals."

That broke through. He laid the book aside. "What November criminals?"

"Chancellor Ebert. Matthias Erzberger. The others who sold us out at Compiègne."

"And he's a pastor?"

"Yes. I don't know him personally, but I've read about him. He's very political. Very outspoken about his beliefs. He thinks the Jews and the Communists are the ones behind this . . . this . . ." She couldn't find a strong enough word.

"Betrayal? Treason?"

"Yes!" she cried.

He threw back the covers and started to get up. She hurried back to him. "No, Sergeant. He's not coming until ten. You still have half an hour."

"Can you find my clothes?"

"I . . ."

"I know what it says on my orders. But I'm fine. Yesterday I was a little dizzy, but there's no problem. If this preacher is what you say he is, I would very much like to hear him."

She hesitated for another moment and then nodded. "I will ask the doctor and see what he thinks."

"No!" he blurted. Then his voice softened. "You know how doctors are, Nurse . . . uh . . ."

"Weisemann." Then she smiled. "Yes, I do."

Hans decided it was time for a little charm. "What if I sit in the back where the doctor can't see me? You could sit beside me, and if he does say anything, I'll tell him that I asked you to help me."

That did it. "I'll find your clothes and be back at about 9:45. In fact, perhaps I'll get you another pain pill now so it will be working by then."

"You are an angel," he said. "Thank you."

• • •

Pastor Luther Wunderlich was not what Hans had expected. He had expected a lean, maybe almost haggard-looking young man in his mid-twenties with fiery eyes, tousled hair, and a voice that crackled with passion. Instead, he was closer to fifty. He was short, no more than five foot six or seven, and probably weighed close to two hundred pounds. He had a few strands of wispy hair, which he brushed forward in an unsuccessful attempt to cover some liver spots on his head. His eyes were dark blue and seemed kindly, almost grandfatherly. And his name was Luther—Pastor Luther of the Lutheran Church. Hans wondered if his parents had named him that with the intent of steering him toward a career as a cleric or if it was just a happy coincidence.

As the hospital chaplain introduced him, Hans was tempted to slip out and go back to bed. This was going to be a disappointment. Nurse Weisemann's pain pill hadn't yet knocked back the throbbing in his head. But she had blocked him in, no doubt trying to keep him out of sight of the doctor, and so he sat back.

There was a smattering of applause as the chaplain sat down and the pastor stood up and came to the little pulpit that someone had placed on one of the dining tables. He stood there for a moment, his eyes sweeping slowly across his audience. Hans felt the first glimmer of hope. There wasn't much grandfatherly kindness in his eyes now. What he saw was a seething anger.

"My brethren," he began, ignoring the fact that there were eight or ten female nurses in the room, "I am humbled to be in your presence. I know who you are, and what you are, and what you have done."

Hans sat up a little. The man's voice was deep and resonant—a preacher's voice. But something in the way he was looking at them caught Hans's attention and held it.

"As I look into your faces, I think I see you more clearly than you see yourselves. I can see the anguish and horror of war written on your faces. I can see the wounds in your flesh, and I sense the scars on your souls. I know that your nostrils are still filled with the stench of the dead and that your eyes have seen things no human being should ever be forced to see."

His voice lowered in sorrow. "I see the loss of brothers in arms written in the lines of your faces. I see how you mourn for the loss of your innocence. And I weep for you and with you."

Suddenly he slammed his fist down against the pulpit with a crash that caused most of them to jump. He was suddenly breathing hard, his nostrils flaring in and out. "But it is not only sorrow that I feel this day," he thundered. "It is not only anguish for you who fought so bravely for the Fatherland." His fist came down again, and Hans thought for a moment he had broken the pulpit. "No, my brethren," he shouted, shaking his fist at the sky. "What I feel today is rage. I burn with indignation. I am consumed with anger." He waved an arm in a sweeping gesture toward the windows. "Why? Because out there, people are saying that it was *you* who lost the war. That it was *you* who were not brave enough, not strong enough, not powerful enough to vanquish our enemy."

A wave of anger started to rise in his audience. It started to well up in Hans as well.

"How dare they!" the pastor thundered. "How dare our leaders sit there in their jeweled robes and on their cushioned thrones and point the finger of shame at you? How dare they impugn the names of those thousands who still lie unburied in the muck and mud of France? You did not lose this war, my brothers. *They* lost this war!"

Several men leaped to their feet, shouting and pounding their hands together. Without realizing it, Hans was one of them. "Bravo!" he shouted. "You speak the truth!" someone else yelled.

Hans turned and saw that Nurse Weisemann had tears streaming down her face and that she too was applauding wildly.

Pastor Wunderlich stood there, his shoulders rising and falling, meeting their gaze and accepting their praise. He let it roll for almost thirty seconds and then raised his hands. Slowly the tumult died and the men returned to their seats.

"What happened yesterday was not inevitable," he began, his voice calmer now. "The chancellor and his fawning lackeys say that we had no choice but to surrender—that it was our noble generals who begged for the armistice." His voice shot up in pitch and volume. "But I say, shame on them! Shame on them for blackening the names of our courageous military leaders. Shame on them for placing the blame on others when it is their own yellow cowardice that has wrought the work of surrender."

Again, the passion on him was like a fire. "And I say," he

roared, "let us call our leaders what they really are. They are criminals who have stolen our honor, who have stabbed our generals in the back, and who have brought all of Germany to its knees and asked us to lick the boots of our enemies. These are the November criminals, and I say that we must bring them to justice or the shame becomes ours as well."

Now everyone in the room was shouting and clapping and stomping their feet. Suddenly, a man two rows ahead of Hans leaped up. He swung back and forth, his eyes wide and wild as they scanned the faces around him. "No!" he roared. "I can stand this no longer. Everything is going black before my eyes." He groped for the back of his chair, tottering as though he was going to faint.

Every eye in the room was on him. He was a slender man with dark hair and haunted eyes that looked almost black. He was about the same height as the pastor, maybe five eight or nine. Then, as he weaved back and forth, Hans saw that around his eyes the skin was red and puffy and his eyelids were swollen nearly shut. He knew instantly what this soldier was here for. He had been exposed to mustard gas. Was he blind? Hans couldn't tell for sure.

The man's head dropped and his eyes closed. The pain in his voice tore at Hans like a knife.

"So this has all been in vain?" he sobbed. "In vain, all our sacrifices and privations? In vain, the hours in which, with mortal fear clutching at our hearts, we endured hundreds upon hundreds of shells raining down on us from the sky while the earth shook all around us? Was it in vain that we did our duty? Was it in vain that two million of our brothers in arms have perished? Did they die for this? So that a gang of wretched criminals could lay their hands on our beloved Fatherland and wrest it from us?"

With that, he kicked his chair away and began groping his way through the crowd, sobbing uncontrollably. Instantly a nurse was on her feet and coming to him. She tried to take his hand to guide him, but he jerked away, shouting something at her. She followed quickly, moving up beside him to prevent him from crashing into anything.

Hans turned to Nurse Weisemann. "Who was that?" he asked, still shocked by what had just happened.

She shook her head, as dazed by it all as he was. "I don't know. He's on the ward next to ours, the one that treats burn victims."

"I saw that he has been gassed. Do you think he's blind?"

She considered that. "I'm not sure. It looked to me like he had some sight, but . . . Either way, his pain must be horrible."

• • •

Hans waited until nearly nine o'clock that night, when the ward was mostly quiet. Some of the men were still awake, writing letters or reading, but most were asleep or close to it. He slipped out of bed, slid his feet into his slippers, and then got up and started toward the main hallway. The air was a little chilly and he considered getting his robe for a moment, but then he brushed it aside.

Nurse Weisemann had said that the man who had been so racked with passion and grief was in the ward next to theirs, but Hans wasn't sure whether that was to the north or the south. He stopped at a bed near the door for a moment. The soldier there was awake, just finishing a letter. "Excuse me, but do you know which way it is to the burn ward?"

The soldier looked up in surprise but then nodded and pointed to the left.

"*Danke.*"

"*Bitte.*"

Hans moved away, hoping that he wouldn't run into any of the nurses. As he entered the next ward, to his surprise, quite a few of the beds were empty. On his ward nearly every bed was full. There were fewer lights on here, but there were enough that he could see. He moved along slowly, searching faces, occasionally having to stop if a man was lying down with his face turned away. Then, about halfway down the ward, he saw a man sitting up in bed, his head turned in Hans's direction. It was him.

Hans moved forward and then stopped at the foot of the man's bed. His head had turned to follow Hans's movements. Hans noticed that his eyes were bandaged. "*Guten Abend.*"

"Good evening," he replied, not seeming at all surprised that he should have a visitor.

"My name is Hans Otto Eckhardt. I wonder if I might have a word with you."

The man sat up straighter, his bandaged eyes looking directly at Hans. "Is this about what happened today in the dining hall?"

"*Ja.*"

"Are you a doctor or a patient?"

"A patient. I am in the ward next to yours."

He pointed to a chair. "Sit. Tell me about yourself."

Hans did so, pleased to see that he was happy for the company. "I am—I was a sergeant in a combat infantry unit."

"A platoon sergeant?"

"*Ja.* I started out as a truck driver but was conscripted into the infantry at the Battle of Verdun."

There was a soft exclamation of respect. "Ah, Verdun. Then you too served in hell."

"Were you at Verdun?" Hans asked in surprise.

"No." There was a touch of amusement in his voice. "I was in another corner of hell. I was a dispatch runner in the First Battle of Ypres in Belgium." He pronounced the French correctly as ee-PRAY.

"I was still in training then," Hans replied. "But we all heard about Ypres."

The soldier was quiet for a moment. "In four days of combat, my regiment was reduced from thirty-five hundred men to six hundred. After that I bounced around from battle to battle—the Somme, Arras, and eventually back to Ypres, where we tried to stop the British advance."

"Is that where you were gassed?"

"Yes. We were near the bottom of a hill when the British released hundreds of canisters. We could see it coming, the horrible river of yellow gas. It flowed right down on our position." He spoke as if it had happened to someone else.

"I'm told it is unbelievably painful," Hans said softly.

He sighed. "By the time I reached the hospital, my eyes felt like two red-hot coals stuck into my face."

Hans didn't know what to say to that, so he said nothing.

After a moment, the man went on. "But I am one of the fortunate ones. The doctor is confident that my eyes will heal. I already have some of my sight back. But you tell me. Why are you here? Were you gassed too?"

"No. We were trying to repel a column of American tanks when our own artillery opened fire on us. I was just a few feet away from one of our shells."

There was a soft sigh. "Wounded by friendly fire. How terribly ironic that must feel."

Hans shrugged and then remembered that the man couldn't see him do so. "I too was lucky to not be left blind," and he told him about his head wound.

"Then perhaps fate has spared us for some grander purpose," the man said wryly. "So we must get better so that we can meet our destiny."

Hans laughed. "I'll be happy just to go home again."

"And where do you live?"

"In a little village near Oberammergau called Graswang."

He jerked forward. "But I too am from Bavaria. My regiment was the 16th Bavarian Reserve Infantry. I am actually Austrian, having been born just across the border, but I have been through Oberammergau several times. A place of great beauty."

"As is all of Bavaria," Hans agreed. They were quiet for a moment, so Hans decided to get to his purpose for being there. "I was very moved by what you said today."

"I . . ." There was a self-deprecating laugh. "I am afraid that the good pastor stirred emotions in me that I didn't know I had."

"As he did in me," Hans said eagerly. "I was greatly impressed by what he said."

"As was I. What did he say after I left?"

"He talked about forces that are tearing our country apart."

"Such as?"

"The government, of course. But also the Bolsheviks, the Communists, the Jews, the greedy industrialists."

The man nodded but fell silent. When he began again, he was far away. "I was wounded in the leg in that first battle of Ypres. I was in another hospital here in Berlin, not far from here, but when I was released for convalescence, I returned to Munich, which is my home. I was shocked beyond belief at the scoundrels I found there."

"Scoundrels?"

"*Ja!* Everywhere I went, I found people cursing the war and wishing for a quick end to it. When I would try to tell them that we fought for the Reich and for the Fatherland, they wouldn't listen. There were slackers everywhere. People cheating the populace for profit. People who cared only for themselves."

"I know."

"And as I went around, I discovered something that I had not really seen before."

"What was that?"

"Everywhere I went, I found that these cheaters and scoundrels were Jews."

That took Hans by surprise. "Really?"

"Yes," he exclaimed. "The offices were filled with Jews. Nearly every clerk was a Jew and nearly every Jew was a clerk. They were running our country. In that year, which was 1916, the whole production in our land was under the control of Jews. I realized that they were robbing our nation and putting it under their own domination. Haven't you seen that?"

"I . . . I don't think we had any Jews in Graswang, or Oberammergau."

"Ah, not that you knew of. But turn over any prosperous business or enterprise and you will likely find a Jew beneath the rock." He sighed, and some of the pain that Hans had glimpsed in this man earlier was there again. He went on. "It was then that I realized with some horror the catastrophe that was approaching our beloved country." His voice choked up. "I could not bear what I saw and was grateful when I returned to the front to fight for the Fatherland."

"And now," Hans said, happy to change the subject back to what was on his mind, "the November criminals have betrayed us."

"Don't start me on that," he growled, "or I shall not sleep for the rest of the night."

Hans stood up. "Thank you for talking with me. What you did and said today affected me deeply. May we talk some more tomorrow?"

"I would like that very much. I am a little embarrassed at my outburst, but I feel it so strongly that I cannot contain myself sometimes." A fleeting smile came and went. "And so now the war is over. What do you plan to do with your life, Sergeant?"

"I'm not sure. I had a scholarship to the University of Berlin before the war started."

"Of a truth!" his friend cut in. "I am impressed."

"I'm thinking of pursuing that, but for a time, I may just go home to my father's dairy farm and milk cows."

The soldier nodded, his face quite somber. "The simplicity of that has a great attraction, doesn't it?"

"It does. And what are your plans?"

"I was lying here thinking about that very thing when you came to join me."

"And?"

Very thoughtful now, he leaned back on his pillow. "I have just decided that if I am to do anything to help save the Fatherland, which I love with all my heart, perhaps I must go into politics."

Hans laughed but then saw that he was deadly serious. "I wish you luck in that. You are right, of course, but I would rather go through another shelling than be a politician."

"A wise man, Sergeant," he chuckled. "A wise man, indeed. Tell me your name again."

"My name is Hans Otto Eckhardt. And yours?"

He stuck out his hand. "My name is Adolf. Corporal Adolf Hitler. Come back tomorrow. Let us talk again."

Chapter Notes

Hitler was caught in a British gas attack on October 13, 1918, and for a time feared that he would be blind. He was in the Pasewalk Military Hospital near Berlin when the war ended. There, a pastor came to the hospital to speak to the soldiers. No name is given for this man, nor does Hitler say that he was Lutheran, but since the Lutheran Church was the state-supported church in Germany, it is likely that he was. In his autobiography, *Mein Kampf* ("My Struggle"), Hitler described that day as a turning point for him.

Hitler wrote in *Mein Kampf* that "two million of his brothers in arms" had been lost. Other sources confirm that this was not an exaggeration. The Great War, as it was commonly called at the time, was one of the deadliest conflicts in history, with more than 10 million military and 7 million civilian deaths. The German Empire alone lost between 1.77 million and 2.04 million combatants. If you add in the countries allied with Germany, such as Austria, the numbers would be 3.38 to 4.39 million military deaths (see http://en.wikipedia.org/wiki/World_War_I_casualties). His rantings about the Jews that he found while he was in Munich also come primarily from his own words as found in *Mein Kampf* (ibid., 31).

BIBLIOGRAPHY

Anderson, Jeffrey L. "Mormons and Germany, 1914–1933: A History of The Church of Jesus Christ of Latter-day Saints in Germany and Its Relationship with the German Governments from World War I to the Rise of Hitler." Master's thesis, Brigham Young University, 1991.

Scharffs, Gilbert. *Mormonism in Germany: A History of The Church of Jesus Christ of Latter-day Saints in Germany Between 1840 and 1970.* Salt Lake City: Deseret Book, 1970.

Shirer, William L. *The Rise and Fall of the Third Reich: A History of Nazi Germany.* 30th Anniversary Edition. New York: Simon and Schuster, 1990.

Trager, James. *The People's Chronology: A Year-by-Year Record of Human Events from Prehistory to the Present.* Revised and Updated Edition. New York: Henry Holt, 1992.